Riccardo Galante
"The crimes of Summerville"

Novel

Dedicated to those who have always supported and listened to me.

PART ONE

A Quiet Town

PROLOGUE

Somewhere in Africa   10,000 B.C.

That night Izuma could not sleep, even though it became a habit. Never before then, the head of the nomadic Akkrasa tribe, the largest and most organized community in the present Niger Valley, would have liked to embrace his Khalima, talk to her and discuss how to solve the problems that plagued him and his people.

But the spirits decided to take her away from him two weeks earlier.

Izuma had asked shaman Dikur for help, to the gatherers of medical herbs and to the wise elders of the tribe, but despite their collaboration and attempts to heal his beloved, the spirits took her, in a spiral of suffering and agony that had started the worst period of his life.

Numerous sleepless nights and hidden cries seemed destined to last until the end of his days and the tribe suffered with him the lack of the good soul that accompanied his leader and managed to support him and give him advice in each of his decisions.

Right now Izuma remembered the episode of the thief who had been caught in their hut stealing their skin, six months before: where he would organize a trial with subsequent public execution, she had questioned and understood that the poor man had been moved only by the affection of his own children, who would have not survived that harsh winter with normal goat skin.

Since then the man had become one of the best skinners of the tribe and everyone had been granted the possibility of having heavier skins in view of that cold and long winter that they could not know to be the last for the men of their time.

Izuma got up , sweating and went out of the hut.

He looked at the sky that had been the same for months: devoid of stars and full of dense white snow, even though it was late summer.

Unfortunately for him, his companion hadn't been the only major loss in recent times and this time he couldn't blame the spirits. His only son Tasi, had been killed by an arrow during a hunt.

Osu, his friend and companion, had been the only one of that company of five young people, to be deliberately spared in order to return to the camp to recount of the incident to the rest of the tribe.

Izuma bit his lips as he remembered Osu's words, the description of the costumes of those men that Izuma knew very well, the way they cut off their victims ears.

In his heart he knew that the Tequisha, a tribe of murders and cannibals, had left one of the five alive as a warning of an imminent attack on their post.

The Tequisha were numerous and that endless winter did not help to appease their hunger for meat.

He put on his bear fur and walked towards Dikur's hut: it was now, only after two sun's that Izuma had in mind only one solution to end his pain, for the survival of his people and to find a safe place to spend the winter without having to live with the fear of attacks by animals or cannibals.

Assaulting the Tequisha caves, exterminating every single individual of that race of monsters and establishing once and for all safety within the village, was the only solution to solve all the problems.

He found Dikur in a trance state and as soon as he touched him to reveal his plan, the Akkrasa shaman already knew what he would have asked him later.

Nevertheless he tried to explain how Khalima would have disapproved and acted differently, of how that small community of shepherds, hunters and good people not used to fighting would have been massacred, Izuma reiterated his request: an unknown and cursed weapon created under the guidance of one of the three spirits, the Akkrasa believed and worshiped, the goddess of the abyss, darkness and the deceased.

Seven suns passed since Dikur had gone in search of the material to be used to manufacture the weapon.

Izuma had seen the frightened gaze of his shaman at the end of the vision and of the dialogue with the dark goddess under the effect of the concoction of herbs an potions.

It was enough to know that he would return with a lethal and indestructible weapon, with which he would cut off numerous heads of his enemies.

As soon as he saw Dikur return with the charge bag he had organised a ceremony in the village for the same evening. His son`s funeral would take place, the presentation of the new weapon and the planning of the attack.

All the Akkrasa members were gathered around a small square beside the river, under the natural protection of a huge protruding rock and warmed by a huge bomb-fire placed in the middle of the group.

After the lean dinner of mushrooms, acorns and walnuts that the harvesters had collected that day and the remains of two wild boars, hunted the day before by the men of the tribe, hymns and praises were sung to the two major deities as the body of the young Tasi approached, died in an unjust manner and in an age that was still too unripe.

Izuma stood up and asked Dikur to advance and present his creation, impatient to discover his form, precisely because the body of his beloved son was there to ask him.

Dikur began to describe to all the people, pausing several times before his king, the prestigious material he had found on the slopes of the volcano, light but at the same time resistant. He had then joined that strange clay of stone dust, two crystals of amber from a cave not very far away and requested the help of a craftsman of the tribe to be able to make changes to the shape of his weapon in order to facilitate its owner. He then asked Izuma the blood of the young Tasi and his tears, easily accumulated and collected in the waiting days of the sorcerer`s return.

After carrying out a sorcery under the guidance of the dark deity and having amalgamated it all, Dikur had placed the weapon in a wooden container and was now proudly handing it to his king.

Izuma got up abruptly, looked at the members of his tribe who could feel his agitation and never, as on that night, wanted to remain close and faithful to him, despite having seen him suffer, have excesses of anger, pray and change drastically in the last few months, a sign of deep respect they felt for him and his family.

Together, as a single and solid unity, they went with their eyes to discover the mysterious content that Dikur had given him.

Izuma`s expression of surprise also appeared on each of the Akkrasa present, when a horrible mask spotted with amber crystals appeared in his hands, a coarse lace that dangled from ear to ear and a patch of Tasi`s blood that, like a lightning bolt, covered its entire surface.

Izuma threw the mask on the ground and took Dikur by the neck, lifting him half a meter from the ground.

Just as the eyes of the poor sorcerer were splashing out of their sockets and his soul seemed to leave the body in order to join those of Khalima and Tasi, one of the Akkrasa sages succeeded in separating Izuma and helping Dikur.

As soon as he recovered, the shaman insisted on gestures to convince Izuma to wear the mask, sure that his leader, even for a few seconds had not killed him, would have been satisfied with his work.

Izuma driven by the conviction with which the shaman gave himself up to convince him, he approached the mask slowly, picked it up and with a quick movement placed it against his face, after securing it to his head.

Suddenly his heart found peace and for a few but endless seconds the people watched him on their knees with open hands, looking at something they couldn`t understand.

Then got up, approached Dikur, who began to tremble at seeing him ever closer, and with a light and cured movement knelt before him.

The Akkrasa people did not understand: never a sovereign had bowed to thank a simple member of the community for no reason, even of the utmost importance.

Izuma ran into his hut, picked up his own spear and after a loud and wild war cry began his march towards the Tequisha caves, followed by every member of his people who, like him, ran to get the sharpest weapon available and joined in that long line of spears, axes and torches under the incessant snow in the middle of the night that would forever change the Ankara's tribe and his descendants.

Dikur was one of the few to remain in that settlement and making his way through the few children and women left, approached the eldest member, said something in his ear and brandishing his knife, cut his throat with a single, quick movement.

That night the Akkrasa conquered the caves, survived the harshest and most enduring winter ever seen until then and the elder of the tribe coined a new word, suggested by Dikur before his suicide gesture, aware of having pruned a new feeling through the dark goddess.

A feeling unknown to those people of ancestors who would have written, however numerous and bloody pages of human history: Dikur had brought the *"mahal"* in the form of a mask for his king.

That night the evil had begun to spread everywhere.

CHAPTER 1

Los Angeles Suburbs   *January 10th, 2017*

Here it is. Surrounded by a large garden well cared for, protected by a thick green wall of hedges , stood the house of Alan Wilder, a quiet home for a normal man who loved his wife and his two children.

Everyone looked at that couple in harmony, with respect and admiration, especially after the adoption of their two Indian sons which took place three years before their marriage. Only in the mind of special agent, Katrine Steward, the house looked different: The shelter of the killer she had been working on for months which people had nicknamed *"The Ghost"* simply because he had never left any trace, no connection between his six victims and no witnesses who could recognize him. Not to mention the fact that the victims had always been killed with the same method, slaughtered and positioned as puppets with eyes full of terror, as if they had just seen a ghost.

All six had been laid in different places where the killer had struck, with their hands attached to their ears with super glue, the mouth and the eyes wide open in a macabre figure, which Katrine had compared to the famous painting of Edvard Munch.

Undecided about what to do, the police finally got up from the playground bench located a little higher up where she had been looking at the back of the house for an hour, undecided about leaving or following her instinct, but finally made her decision.

As she walked down the slope that led to the house, Kat was uncertain about her intuition about the element that could link the killing of four well-known actresses, a television conductor and a young debutante, as well as her friend , Melanie Andrews, during that winter in Los Angeles, was licked up or had taken a crazy mistake.

Kat turned at the intersection that led to the path to the driveway, the main entrance.

Yet while she was ringing the intercom of the Wilder house, the cameraman who had been working for a long time in those same studios from which the assassin had removed six important figures from the scene, she felt a slight sense of danger and a sort of déjà vu that helped to keep her focused and indifferent to the serene aspect of the house or his image of the perfect Alan Wilder that seemed to express to the people.

A little further away a window opened, from which appeared a man who corresponded to the description that her colleague Lucy had given her a long time ago: in his sixties, completely bald but with a thick red beard which he seemed to be proud of; now he was wearing glasses and was scrutinizing her with indecisive curiosity, whether or not to open the main gate.

"Agent Katrine Steward, Los Angeles police, we met about five months ago on the issue of the disappearance of Melanie Andrews, the first of the *Ghost* victims"

Alan seemed to mistake her for her colleague because within seconds he pressed the button to open the main gate.

Kat thought back to Lucy`s story still shocked and devastated by the loss of a common friend, that told her how Alan had seemed shocked and no help for the investigation: Was she right? Was Alan another blind alley in the *Ghost* case? Had Kat caught a glimpse of suspicion of this man so well seen? For the umpteenth time in her career she was confronted with the opinion of the press, most of the people and her colleagues: on the one hand she hoped she had been wrong.

Now, as she climbed the steps that led her to that man, she was less convinced that this beloved figure was responsible for the death of as many as six souls who had died after suffering sexual violence.

Kat clenched her fists and was glad to have come alone without notifying anyone of her move: she would have avoided demonstrating to her superior and her colleagues how little the investigation was beyond her starting point. She looked a little farther and saw only Alan`s car in the garage, a black Ford Mustang polished and perfectly maintained. She decided she had to fully convince herself in what she was doing otherwise her plan would have jumped, so she took a deep breath, armed herself with courage and changed her attitude and way of thinking.

" Beautiful car, *ghost,* it`s just you and me", she thought.

"Agent, tell me, how can I help you this time?" Alan Wilder pronounced in the doorway of his house, half hidden by the door that separated them. Katrine noticed a certain uneasiness in his voice and the posture he assumed in opening the door, she suggested that maybe that man had something to hide.

"I am sorry to disturb Alan, but since the last scene of the crime a test has emerged in a completely random way that has delivered us directly to the DNA of the murderer. We are comparing the new sample with the DNA of all your staff and there are few people left to probe. Here, the bomb had been launched. The consequences of her private initiative could have been catastrophic if Alan had asked for a mandate to avoid raising suspicion on him.

Uttering that lie, Kat got the desired effect: Alan seemed agitated, looked at him as he swallowed visibly and despite wanting her out of the way, he kindly invited her to enter the house; it was enough to throw the bait and the fish had immediately taken it.

With a ready hand and a firm grip on her 45-gauge M1911, she prepared to enter trying to never give her back to the landlord. " You have nothing to worry about Mr Wilder, two minutes and it`s all over".

Yeah, you're done for, murderer.

With a quick movement Alan put his hand on the cabinet just behind the entrance corridor trying to wield the gun he had prepared as soon as he saw Kat at the gate. Luckily the policewoman expected such behaviour and was on him almost immediately hitting him on the wrist with a kick and sending him to the ground with a straight left.

"Alan Wilder, known as the *Ghost,* I declare you under arrest for the murder of Melanie Andrews, Luisa Thompson..."

She could not finish the sentence because Wilder sprinted towards her trying to throw her to the ground using his weight but Katrine, younger and also prepared for this desperate attempt, dodged him and gave him a powerful knee-kick in the side that took his breath away and stretched him for the second time along his Persian carpet at the entrance of his living room.

"You bastard, another movement and I shoot you straight in front", Katrine roared, brandishing the gun and pointing it to his head.

From the floor the *Ghost* turned to her and after staring at her and coughing a couple of times catching his breath, gave a little chuckle, accompanied by others in the following instants, until it came to a loud, crackling laugh.

"Have courage Agent, I have nothing to lose...my marriage is a gigantic theatre, of which nobody, not even Neighbours suspects of anything. It's her fault, you know?", he said pointing to the photo where his wife was laying on a Cuban beach.

"Jill, that bitch, started fucking me right away, the day after our wedding. I understood that she only manipulated me for my position in the studios immediately after the return of our honeymoon, do you understand?"

Alan turned to Katrine looking for a kind of understanding, absolution or pity that on the other hand Kat seemed determined not to give him.

"It took very little to get my hands completely on my life, but the straw that broke the camel's back was that afternoon when I found her in bed with your friend, only, they didn't see me..."

Alan's eyes were now fixed on a distant point, though Kat, who was beginning to tremble with rage, knew they weren't looking at anything.

She was aware of the homosexuality of her actress friend, but this connection with the *Ghost's* wife was not expected and she cursed herself for the repeat times in which she begged her not to tell the details of her adventures with the fairer sex.

If only she had been more understanding and open with her friend Melanie, the first of the victims, she could have stopped him earlier, saved the other five victims and avoided that bloody trail of deaths, but fate had decided otherwise.

"So you're telling me that instead of divorcing, quitting work, start a new life like most people, you preferred to brutally rape and kill six women? Just to vent the repression your wife gave you? I don't care Alan, you're a psychopath, a sick man and don't try to justify yourself with me".

The *Ghost*'s gaze was now prey to the ecstasy of the memory of his actions, while he stroked his red beard he kept talking:

"Oh no. No, no, no. It was completely random to discover my Talent and my art. I was at Melanie's house to ask for explanations when I felt that extraordinary impulse, the inspiration that only an artist like me, in his heart knows he has.

I wanted so much the death and suffering of that person that I didn`t even realize what happened. I had violated her inside and taken her life. My wife never suspected me, that her husband could have taken away her happiness, as she had done with me.

The only image that came back to me was that face of terror and the satisfaction of knowing that nothing in the world could bring her lover back to life".

Katrine had a tear running down her cheek and her heartbeat seemed to accelerate as if she were sitting on a rollercoaster. The trembling of her hands increased and an adrenaline rush gave her a shiver that ran down her back.

"...So I grabbed the glue, I placed her in the way the vision had shown it to me and there it was, as perfect as I had dreamed it, in the posture that made it seem still alive and important; people should have found it that way and in no other way".

When Katrine saw the smile and the joy on the face of the killer in front of her, she decided that the meeting would end like she had dreamed it months before, from the first day she volunteered to hunt that monster.

At that moment she didn`t think about her career, her mother`s death, her ex boyfriend`s abandonment, or any of the thoughts that accompanied her and tormented her every day of her life.

Kat thought only about how Melanie would have wanted to take revenge on Alan Wilder, on the extraordinary career as an actress that was waiting for her, if only she had been alive, if only that maniac hadn`t killed her.

Then she imagined her approaching at that moment on her side, smiling in the most complete joy that had always accompanied her for life.

Katrine pulled the trigger.

CHAPTER 2

Summerville *March 17th, 2017*

Sarah Finningham opened her eyes slowly.

She felt excruciating pains all over her body and as soon as she tried to get up from her chair, she remembered the handcuffs that imprisoned her hands and feet.

While her body was desperately trying to eradicate that strong steel chair firmly anchored to the floor, her brain sent her the last memories of what had happened before her fainting.

Sarah did not know who the misty individual who had kidnapped her in front of her home was.

A middle-aged man who hadn't even had time to look in the face, had drugged her and taken her out of the house, with the simple excuse of a router check. She had been very naïve, a real fool.

Sure, it was she who had called the telephone company with which she had set up a meeting with a technician, but the fact that she was alone at home did not give her the right to let her guard down with any stranger entering her entrance, especially after the robbery occurred in the previous month.

As the panic began to show itself in her, a lighthouse aimed at her figure making the darkness disappear which had been her only company until then.

Sarah began to tremble. Whoever was the figure who interposed between her and the lighted building site light, knew he would have no intention of making her speak, free her, let alone leave her alive.

The tight gag prevented her from giving voice to the questions she had been asking herself for ten hours.

"Who are you? Is it you Robert? Why? What did I do wrong? Please don`t kill me…"

The stranger had only come to check if his prey had somehow managed to break free, apparently disrupted by the noises coming from his cell, because immediately after he turned and, intoning a tune unknown to her, he seemed to return to his occupations, without forgetting to make the room slip back into absolute darkness.

Sarah then breathed a sigh of relief, she would remain alive, at least for a while longer.

She then turned to concentrate on her miserable attempt to evade and to rethink who could she have bothered lately.

The only person who could have thought of killing her was certainly her husband Robert.

They had married a year after they met, and only then had the defects and obsessive compulsive nature of the man she had loved, emerged.

By now, five years after their marriage, Sarah had learned to live with the worst sides of her husband`s jealousy: checking emails, forced exit bans, innumerable quarrels and scenes of the worst kind due to the most trivial reasons.

Sarah was a beautiful woman, but she knew that what attracted men was her femininity and her sureness.

Although in the early years she had accepted or tried to understand the uncertainty that day after day devoured Robert`s soul, in the last period of that life, if it could be defined, had removed it and delivered it, unbeknownst to her husband, in the arms of another man.

Sarah began to imagine, Robert, in the guise of that technician who had easily drugged and loaded her into the car, and then tied her to that chair so resistant that despite the numerous beatings, it didn't move an inch.

"I found out you know?" he would have told her; You are pathetic, taken for granted. I had to understand it from the day I met you; instead, your slut side you pulled out just now, isn't it? Not enough for you, the beautiful house, your hubby or the comfortable life you managed, didn't you? You needed to take your boss to bed...you have not been able to restrain yourself, I already imagine the daydreams you had every day at work that I found for you, to be able to escape from the life that I always gave to you...damned. Today, however, it will not end up like the other times; you won't get away with simple barrel. Today I will kill you with my own hands".

This was the worst scenario that Sarah imagined every day; the mad jealousy of her husband , a nightmare that accompanied her even before going to bed with her employer Tom, the man of providence who had always treated her well and helped her.

And if it was himself, the man whistling downstairs and preparing to torture her, frighten her or more likely to kill her?

After all, even Tom hadn't been a saint and he would have had a reason to make her disappear from the face of earth.

She was not the only one of the two to have an extracogniugal relationship and maybe it was her lover, the individual who was climbing the stairs, and wanted to make sure to silence that story.

No, she really hoped it was not his executor: the man who had seduced her in the place where she worked and had saved her from life in a one-way direction by her husband, the most beautiful and powerful man she could only dream of having: she didn't want to destroy her best memories or ruin her life for the second time.

The light came on and an explosion of light partially revealed the figure. This time he carried with him an iron tank, containing a liquid that could be felt swinging inside here and there, while he was clutching a heavy toolbox in his other hand.

Sarah tried in every way not to think about what would happen to her shortly thereafter and despite the strong light and the sight blurred by the tears flowing from her face, she tried to focus on the person in front of her.

Those boots, the wide trousers and the filthy sweatshirt that ended in two large protective gloves, did not reveal any clue to the identity of the person and to make matters worse his face was completely hidden by a terrifying mask. As he approached she noticed that the gaze of those who wore it, could only cause horror and disgust in the eyes of those who would be in front of him: a blood stain covered the entire area around the eyes, nose and mouth.

Even if the shape was not particularly cured, the mask had something mystical, crystals of a material unknown to her covered all its surface in an asymmetric way and small cracks appeared here and there, along the marked edges of the cheeks and forehead.

Sarah did not understand how her owner could easily move his head, despite the heaviness of the protection she thought was made of stone or marble.

Her gaze lingered once more on the bloody spot; Despite having been there for a long time it seemed red and alive as fresh paint.

Without ceasing to whistle, the masked man turned the cap of the tank paying attention not to spill even a drop of its contents and got up and opened the toolbox he had placed on a cabinet a few moments before.

When Sarah noticed that he wielded a nipper she tried to scream very loudly, but any sound was completely dampened by the gag carried for ten hours now.

The mask slowly placed the nipper at the established point and without ever removing the eyes of the unfortunate woman's face, made one strong pressure with his hands.

CHAPTER 3

North Carolina *March 20th, 2017*

Kat opened the front door.

As soon as she had hung her soggy coat from the rain, she found herself in front of Zack who had just lifted himself from the leather sofa to get close to say hallo.

"Welcome home love," he put his arms around her in an affectionate embrace that eventually resulted in a passionate kiss, as he used to reserve her.

Katrine returned the kiss, but no matter how hard she tried to speak, she found herself unable to do so.

So it was Zack who started the talk, suddenly becoming serious and never taking his eyes away, staring her intently with his deep hazel eyes.

"We could order a pizza and relax in front of the TV, what do you say? Or I could suddenly leave with the pretty girl who works in that corner-bar where we have breakfast on Sundays and with whom I go out for months".

Katrine made to raise her hand and give him the strongest slap she could hit, but again she could not move, nor open her mouth.

"Are you not saying anything Kat? Don`t you oppose to my decision? But you certainly can`t....

Because it`s an idea that was born a long time ago and now the fact has already happened, but you were too busy, very, very busy.

Kat found herself reviving the various scenarios in which they had loved each other, as if she was looking at images scrolling on slides.

He who embraced her while she was cooking, she who put a blanket on him while he slept on the sofa, the times he had slipped in the shower, he who was busy at his desk and all of a sudden looked up and smiled....

Then she woke up.

"Excuse me miss, is this seat occupied?"

Kat remembered she was on the plane, she looked around as she summarized a correct position and, with a smile, she removed the laptop and the book she was reading from the seat on the side.

"Excuse me for waking you up, but my son has fallen asleep on both seats and I should finish a computer job. I noticed that you are travelling alone and so..."

*Imagine, please sit down as well", replied Kat, who was wondering if even with the arrival of a child she would have put her career first, in any case.

While wearing her headphones and listening to *Against all odds* from Phil Collins, her thoughts returned to the dreams she previously made, and had already appeared in her mind for the fourth time.

Concluded that it was not the abandonment by her ex-boyfriend that happened five years before the cause of those nightmares, or of the memories still alive and clear in her mind, to annoy her and make her suffer, but not having accepted that the person most dear to her had cheated her.

She was awake, very beautiful and intelligent, but the love for that man or the strong dedication to her work, had greatly clouded her vision.

She looked out the window; the sight of the sun and it's heat above the rain-clouds below lifted her spirits and seemed to wish her a serene future, after the sentimental storm that not even five years had been enough to appease.

The notes of an Elvis Presley album accompanied her in the following twenty minutes of flight and the landing.

After retrieving the luggage, she left the airport and was attacked by frost. Despite been late March, the strength of the sun was still typical of the winter months.

A light cold breeze forced her to lift her scarf up to cover her nose, as she walked towards the taxi rank and get on the first available.

After having indicated the address to the friendly face of the man driving, Katrine decided to contemplate the view of the town she was born and raised.

Although five years had passed, Summerville seemed not to have changed much: a small town surrounded by nature with the luck of being surrounded by miles of woods and forests, but also that of being directly facing the ocean.

Destination for hikers, surfers and lovers of tranquility, the town had evolved in direct proportion to the growth of tourism, making the fortune of rental agencies and some construction companies.

Despite this, it seemed that everything had remained the same as five years before even though the buildings and the main infrastructures had been modernized.

The memories made her relive some moments of her youth: the Gelateria where at fifteen she had given her first kiss, the multiplex cinema where she had spent many evenings.. she was even happy with the new style that the sports center had adopted where as a girl she had gained important recognition in the field of swimming.

Those years away from home had served her at least in part to turn page after Zack, but the nostalgia for that magnificent place had turned to make itself felt several times, despite Los Angeles had much more to offer.

After paying and leaving a tip for the taxi driver who gently took her luggage to the door, she took the keys to the apartment from where she had lived with her sister before moving to Zack.

She noted that the expenses they had incurred together during these years had borne fruit: the renovation and the new furnishing brought to the house followed to the letter the style that the two women decided to give.

She left the bulkier bags at the entrance and after turning on the huge wall-mounted TV in the living room, she headed for the kitchen determined to eat something, even though it wasn't lunch time yet.

On the island in the center of the room she found a note: "Welcome home! James and I are back in a week's time… enjoy our home XD I love you, Elisabeth".

Kat was happy to be able to count on her sister again and with a smirk that appeared on her face, she devoted herself to the cooking.

After lunch she unpacked, looked around the rooms, called Elisabeth and then went to the black leather sofa to take a nap.

As she walked she stopped to admire her own image in the wall mirror in the corridor.

Katrine was a thirty-six-year-old woman who looked ten years younger: her long slender and toned legs ended in two firm buttocks that aroused the interest of most male looks.

The pelvis, now deliberately discovered by the short black vest she wore, exhibited the fruits of a healthy diet and a favorite activity since adolescent age.

A pink sports bra held her abundant third and the skin of her face and neck she refused to show people that time ran for her too; her long black hair was loose in the evening and during the day it was free, but always gathered in a ponytail during work days and sports activities.

Kat liked herself and she also knew that she was part of the fantasies of most of the men she knew, but what she was really proud of and that people couldn`t help but notice her greenish eyes, the whole of her face and her person, gave her an alert and always attentive look. Nevertheless her sentimental life had been disappointing and victim of ups and downs because of her work and her hyperactivity or perhaps the fact that all men seemed to her equal and banal, bringing her to a total disinterest in that field for five years now.

Her contemplation was interrupted by the local news program that broadcast the news of her imminent return.

As she raised the volume she became aware of the nickname that the media had assigned to her: *The ghost Buster.*

After she had killed *The Ghost* she had to get used to having become a celebrity.

Despite the promotion and popularity received it was only she who knew the truth.

Alan Wilder had not died in a shooting like she had made believe with a perfect simulation.

She had executed a murderer without feeling any remorse: she had acted in the right way, she kept repeating herself, she would not allow that monster to ruin her life, nor to reap other victims and, above all, Melanie had finally been avenged.

So after shooting him by calculating a plausible shooting line that would have been verified by the forensic ballistics later, she had put on gloves and blown three shots at a column with Alan's gun simulating a firefight.

After all the commotion of interviews, invitations to television programs, she accepted the promotion from the Los Angeles police and decided it was time to return to Summerville to regain privacy and the anonymity she always had and loved.

Apparently she was very wrong. They had just renamed her with a nickname she detested and her e-mail box was always full of letters of admiration.

Suddenly her cell phone rang. On the screen flashed the name of Philip De La Cruix, her friend as well as head of the Summerville police.

"Hallo Phil, how are you? I'm dying to see you again tomorrow, so we can also agree on the date of my return to service".

The tone of her boss's response was not as serene as the one Kat was used to, but he seemed deeply upset.

"I fear you will have to reach me immediately, an anonymous package has just arrived for you and the attached ticket certainly does not make you think of a box of chocolates".

Kat saw her image on the TV screen and thought that the log-dreamed tranquility would have to wait for a while longer.

CHAPTER 4

Summerville Police Station

Kat took from her jacket pocket the electronic pass she had collected in the box labeled "AGENT STEWARD 2006/2011 SUMMERVILLE" together with her old uniform and other objects carefully kept by her sister while waiting for her return.

She noted with surprise that in spite of the modernization to which the police station had also been subjected, her old card allowed her access to the employee`s car park.

As soon as the metal rod lifted, her Jeep 4x4 of opaque black color, accelerated to the stand 16, the one reserved for her.

Philip De La Cruix was immediately at the side, in the empty space of stand 17 and seemed to be waiting anxiously for her.

Katrine gave three consisting kisses, but it was Philip who first spoke.

"Hi Kat, I am really happy about your return. I would really like to tell you about the news here at the station or to hear your Los Angeles exploits live, but a package for you came a little while ago and first I will know that it is a hoax, before I can say goodbye properly".

"Of course Phil, no problem. What does the attached message say so worrying?", replied Kat.

" You`ll see it for yourself, it`s waiting for you on your desk in your old office".

As they entered the station, Kat thought she had rarely seen her friend and boss so worried during the years she spent there, but she couldn't help but notice that he hadn`t changed a comma, the same elegant and charming man of all time.

Katrine quickly greeted some old colleagues and studied the face of some of the new recruits, remembering her period of setting at the dawn of her career in Summerville.

In reality, despite the tranquility enjoyed by her native town, she had seen firsthand several episodes that testified violence, the badness and the evil of man were present everywhere and they were also manifested in nucleuses of few inhabitants as they could be those of Summerville or of the neighboring Sparkling Bay.

This is Warren Valentine. He is working on the disappearance of some people at the moment and would be happy to cooperate with you, but first he is as curious as all of us to discover the contents of the anonymous package he did not want to touch in your absence".

The man who answered that name reached out with his right hand and tightened Katrine`s in a firm and sure grip: "I'm very honored to meet you Agent Steward. I followed your last case on TV and it would really be a pleasure for me to be your right-hand man.

I only allowed myself to make sure that the package was not an explosive device and to remove the attached ticket which unfortunately does not tell us much".

Kat noted with pleasure that she had a bright and confident co-worker who had taken steps rather than sitting around waiting for her arrival.

"Great Warren, I would have done the same, but please from now on call me Kat".

The agent replied with a gesture of understanding and handed her the note that had been attached to the box with a tape.

The letters had been cut from several sheets of newspaper and simply composed the words "WELCOME HOME".

Kat looked up not at all worried and turned to Philip: "You can`t imagine how many packages, death threats or letters from stupid bored kids I had to put up with in Los Angeles.

So if I were you I would not be too shocked even if this time a relative of someone I slammed in the cool, had sent me his underwear or some other souvenir".

Kat lifted the package and saw its extraordinary lightness as well as the oscillation of something smaller inside it.

"We`ve waited long enough", she said, as she was putting her latex gloves on.

The package contained a ticket and a small red box the size of a cigar sealed with a pink ribbon.

Sarah Finningham, 27 River Street, Summerville…guilty" read aloud to those present, pausing a little before uttering the last word. Philip De La Cruix ordered to a short , chubby guy to keep a Police car ready to go to the address indicated and urged Kat to open the other box, hoping with all his heart that it was another bad joke.

He immediately noticed the disgusted expression of agent Warren at the opening of the box, so he hastened himself to study the contents placed on the bottom of the package.

A left ring finger, revered brutally just under a wedding ring, rolled in its own blood.

CHAPTER 5

Journey to 27, River Street

The Police car driven by Warren was speeding along the busy roads leading to 27 River Street.

Kat glanced at her colleague who was concentrating on driving while checking the charger of her trusty M1911.

"What are you thinking of Warren? You look thoughtful..."

"Someone was waiting for you Katrine Steward, but it is good that you are here. Lately many people have disappeared in the city and its surroundings and excuse frankness, but most of our colleagues are not up to the task.

Although she was tense and worried about what she could find once they reached their destination, Kat tried to look more calm then what she really felt.

"I think exactly the same Warren and if we were too late once we arrived, I ask you to remain calm and strictly professional. Since I don`t know you well yet I`ll still try to trust you, so if you want everything to go smoothly, avoid getting me a bullet in the back, ok? It could also be a trap, for about a couple of months I involuntarily made many enemies, not counting the criminals that I captured in the past in Summerville and I have no intention of dying because of a thug, so always stay focused and try not to let your guard down if the situation should get worse.

You`re right about the cops, here most of them are locals used to handling paperwork and minor cases, but don`t doubt the boss, if he has chosen them there is certainly a good reason. I could say the same about you and I know I am not the superhero who suddenly returns and cleans up the city, keep it in mind".

Warren gave her a quick glance before getting over a truck that was slowing down the traffic: "I've been here for three years now, I'm sorry to be a policeman out of the choir, but I've found out that I have nothing in common with the others. The courses and the academy I attended at Atlanta were certainly better than those they do here in Summerville, most of my partners in the investigations seemed to have gaps in the ways in which they deal with cases that do not fit into their monotonous everyday life. Before I moved I worked in Rockford, I had my own office, good colleagues and together we solved difficult cases, certainly not at your recent level, but despite my request to move to this area, I felt uncomfortable, you know it's like a sort of downgrade. I don't know if I explained myself..."

Kat looked at her watch: It had been about ten minutes since they left. From the radio you could hear the voice coming from a police car on patrol that confirmed their arrival at the address."I understand you very well because I went the opposite way and I assure you, to go from here to a city like Los Angeles was not painless, but you know, the ambition and the desire to leave at that time have prevailed over everything. Why did you leave Rockford? "I will tell you another time, it's a long story and anyway we've arrived now".

"All right. I thought Philip would let me work alongside the donut-eater in all Summerville, not with the first of the Rockford class.

Kat managed to snatch a smile from her partner a moment before turning left and entering the ground on 27th River Street.

After traveling a short dirt path, Warren parked in the wide uncultivated land that was surrounded by a building under construction, next to the police car of colleagues who arrived earlier.

The building seemed half done and was surrounded by metallic wire and with entry bans to those not involved hanging everywhere.

The chubby guy who wore a plaque with the writing Williams seemed really upset: "I have never seen anything like it, there's a dead person in there, the smell is very strong, I'm sorry Agent Steward, I don't…"

Kat turned a knowing look to her partner, their predictions were unfortunately well chosen.

"Calm down Williams. Where is it? Did you and your colleague touch something?"

"Upstairs in one of the bathrooms to the left of the stairs. I found it, but I didn't touch anything; Johnson only glimpsed the body, but it only took the stink to make us run out and throw up here. We haven't done anything yet, sorry it's the first time that…"

Kat interrupted him again: "No problem, as soon as you recover you begin to make preparations for setting up a crime scene, but only after calling a scientific expert from the police station, I want it here as soon as possible".

Williams nodded with such a surprised expression that it seemed they had just asked him to leave for the moon.

Warren opened the trunk of the car and took out two masks and protective suits plus the shoe covers.

While they were wearing them Kat thought that this would not be the first body seen by Warren and at the expense of the other two, he would not have even thrown up.

"Be careful of anything you see, any detail. Everybody makes mistakes and leaves traces, especially the most inexperienced killers. So let's not forget or worse, compromise possible proofs".

Warren nodded from behind his mask and walked first up the stairs.

The scene that appeared to them was disturbing.

A person had been tied hands and feet's to a metal chair, or more precisely to it's remains, from which it would have been impossible to establish it's sex or age: the body had been completely dissolved with a powerful acid and what remained was a mass of bones and pieces of meat.

The only parts that seemed to have suffered less damage from that lethal liquid were the upper limbs since even the feet had been completely dissolved.

"Oh my God, the smell is really sickening", Warren said as he studied every millimeter of that "thing" that had once been human.

"It looks like we have Sarah Finningham in front of us, or at least what's left of her", Kat said, urging Warren to take a look at her hands.

Despite the burns and injuries caused by the reaction to the acid, it could clearly be seen that the poor victims left ring finger had been severed, to then be carefully sent, inside a small red box, with the pink flake for Katrine Steward.

Who could have done such a thing?

Of all the ways she had seen people die, this went far beyond her imagination and understanding towards a murderous mind.

Only a beast could have done all this and Kat mentally promised to give all of herself for the search and capture of that criminal, this time too.

"Come and have a look Kat, the jerry can is still here and in this room...well, you really have to see it".

Kat rose from her position leaving her thoughts behind her and, as soon as she crossed the not yet completed threshold of what seemed to have to become a bedroom, it was impossible not to notice the inner wall.

"We are dealing with an exhibitionist, apparently", she exclaimed with a rapt look.

Suddenly a flash lit the room and they both turned. A young man in his early twenties turned and went down stairs hurriedly to run away along the paths that led to the center.

"What the fuck..." she didn't have time to finish the sentence that Williams appeared out of breath.

"Damn Walter. I Know him, he works for the *Sunshine,* I didn't notice him, but apparently he followed us here".

Kat swore loudly; What would certainly not have helped this time was the involvement of the local press and Philip would have gone on a rampage.

Nevertheless, she gave up the episode and looked back at the wall.

The young Walter put down his backpack with all the equipment.

He washed his face with the icy water of the fountain located in the main square of Summerville.

The run-down the hill had taken his breath away and he was soaked with sweat.

He still felt very satisfied with the outcome of that afternoon: it would surely have ended up on the front page the following day.

As he turned on his digital camera, he smiled at the idea of his mother's face, when seeing his front-page article the next day, completely contrary to that kind of precarious work that her eldest son had chosen.

He also thought of bringing his girlfriend Madeline down to the dock at Pier's and offer her an oyster dinner because surely he could sell that picture even to top titles, he was sure.

Always with a smile on his lips, he scrolled through the photos of the policemen who were vomiting next to the building site, the ones that showed the arrival of the long-awaited women in the city, and then dwell on the last one, which he hadn't had the chance to examine carefully a quarter of an hour ago.

The photo depicted the two policemen who arrived later, intent on looking at a mural painted on the wall.

The subject of that grotesque work was a stylized woman wrapped in flames colored green and purple, perhaps a work of a hippie artist.

Walter noticed a writing a little lower down and adjusted the zoom to make it readable.

To the side of the figure the word "GUILTY" was reported and seemed to be written with blood, probably with that of the victim.

Walter suddenly found out he had lost his smile.

CHAPTER 6

27, River Street

On the card of the uniform of the newly arrived woman you could read, written in capital letters, the name of Judith Law.

The photo would have been taken a long time before, because cut and color of her hair did not correspond to those of the slender woman who had just arrived.

Kat just had a few seconds to study her profile while the forensic colleague opened the gray suitcase she had brought with her to be able to prepare her own instruments.

She would have been her age more or less, now that she had turned around, she noticed that her deep blue eyes were staring at her behind strange glasses. That particular frame gave it a true nerd look.

At the end of her work, Judith went to call Kat and Warren who were taking pictures of the mural in the room next door and other parts of the building.

"From a first analysis we can establish that the body has been here for two or three days at most, the victim has been completely dissolved by a very strong acid, of which later I will be able to tell you the name of it in the report.

The person who killed her has cleaned up very well, I can`t find traces of fabrics or clues, so I think this person was able to act undisturbed".

"Something else particularly?", Kat asked.

"The assassin has severed the left ring finger at its base with a pincer or tongs, but I think you already know this, by tonight we will have confirmation that the finger in the box and the body are actually Sarah`s as written on the ticket. Jesus, I have never seen anything like this in so many years".

While Judith gathered her tools, she noticed Williams interrupting Kat and Warren as they were deciding how to start the investigation.

"We found an open van nearby with the logo of a repair company and with the keys still on the dashboard, there are handcuffs and a purse in the rear compartment, I think they're the victims, come".

Kat gave a nod of approval to her colleague who immediately drove the two blocks that separated them from the abandoned van.

Judith would have resumed her analysis later, but as she watched Kat empty the contents of the purse, it was Warrens petrified stare that caught hers and the whole groups attention.

"What is it Warren, have you found something?" asked his female colleague.

The agent`s gloves took the photograph that sprouted from a work suit hanging from a wall of the van.

The two subjects turned out to be a smiling couple with a sunset behind them and the photo was taken from a well-known viewpoint of the woods around Summerville, even Kat remembered.

"Do you know them Warren? Is she Sarah Finningham?"

The man turned to his colleague and handed her the photo while with the other began to rub his forehead.

"I don't know. But I know who he is, his disappearance was reported just this morning".

It had been a long afternoon. Kat and Warren had decided to part ways to act faster; they knew that the hope of solving a murder case would fade more and more with the passage of time. Katrine should have investigated the site of the murder, the surroundings of the site and anything related to the van: it was her job to find any useful connection or information.

Warren had been asked to gather as much data as possible on the victim and to verify any connection with the missing man in the photograph: in their opinion it was the obvious choice since Warren was already aware of several facts about him and Katrine had landed in Summerville only ten hours earlier.

Philip De La Cruix had met all of the agents who had been involved listening first the two who first had come to River Street and then devoted himself to the story and to the data that Judith, sitting right next to her, was finishing to exhibit.

Warren entered the room closing the door behind him, saw a free chair right next to Kat and sat down.

"Did I miss something important?" he asked her.

"Nothing we already knew, only Phil's outburst when he discovered that the local press is already aware of the murder and has detailed photos".

The police chief invited Katrine to stand up and expose what she had discovered.

She didn't need to look at the documents she had in front of her because what little she had managed to discover was clear in her mind, so she cleared her throat and began to talk.

"The company that operated at the construction site declared that they had suspended the works about two months ago because the owner suddenly stopped financing them, so the killer was able to act undisturbed and to be able to make a graffiti of that size with all calm.

However the van appears to be registered under Nordtech and the company reported it stolen a month ago, exactly on February 25th, when it was stolen from one of its operators while working inside an apartment for a private client.

One last thing: Nordtech had set a date with Sarah for 5.00pm on Friday, but they didn't find anyone".

Phil slowly scratched his chin and got up to add elements on the blackboard on which he had marked notes from each of his collaborators.

"Can we establish the time or at least the day of the murder?"

"Some witnesses indicate that the van was parked there for at least three days so I would say that the murder took place on Thursday or Friday night".

"Friday without a shadow of a doubt".

It was Warren who talked and always with his arms folded, he looked from Kat to his principal.

"Sarah Finningham went to work regularly until Friday. She left work earlier at about 3.30 pm, as my colleagues confirmed she had asked for an hour`s leave to go home and arrive in time for the appointment with Nordtech at 5.00pm, but the fake operator must have seized her just before".

"It sounds very risky, but I think it could have been exactly like that, let's mark these times on the board. Can you tell me more about her or the man on the photo, Agent Valentine?"

"Of course. Sarah Finningham, 29, works as an employee for an insurance office in the Summerville center, the "Gray Insurance". The secretaries described her as a strange , almost asocial person, she never left the house as far as they knew and was never present at dinners and parties organized among colleagues. We will know more from her boss, tomorrow he should come back from New York: apparently he seemed to have special attention for Sarah.

Both parents lost their lives in a car accident two years ago, the neighbors were not very familiar with her. Sarah was a very lonely girl for her age, however, had a spouse: she had been married to Robert Hudson for five years, does the name tell you anything?"

"The missing person report we received this morning at nine, shortly before the package arrived", Philip said as he connected with arrows the names just written with chalk.

"Exactly. It could have been he who killed her, in most of the murders the victim is a woman, it was her husband who killed her".

It seemed that that version had convinced all those present, so Philip ended the meeting with a brief summary of the events and pointing to Robert Hudson as the principal suspect.

While the policemen left the courtroom, Philip stopped Katrine holding her by the shoulder and once the flow of people had crossed the threshold of the room he stopped to talk to her about the step forward that the police had taken in these years, listening to the stories of her service in Los Angeles and finally confessing her on how much he had missed her all these years.

When he looked at his watch, he noticed that it was almost time for dinner and to go home to his family, so he got up and put his elegant jacket on.

"Kat I'm going to put you in charge of the investigation. I want you to choose your partner and your collaborators, I had them prepare your old office down the hall, it's pretty much the same as five years ago and the one where he practiced, your…"

"…my father she finished.

"Thanks Phil you shouldn't do me all this favoritisms, but know that I really appreciate what you do or you've always done for me".

"You don't have to thank me, that's what he would have wanted and I do it willingly, not only on behalf of our old friendship that tied me and your father for many years, but also because his name here is pronounced as if it were a legend".

Kat sighed and held out her hand "Greet Rose, see you tomorrow".

By the time she left the Police Station it was seven o'clock: darkness had fallen on Summerville.

On the journey that separated her from home she reflected on life and unanswered questions that every so often arose.

Could one define fortune, simple case, series events not planned to direct our lives or was it something more complex, studied and wanted on which our existence was based on?

She liked to think that it was only a matter of good and bad luck: she could happen to know and fall in love with people like Phillip, her father, Warren or so many good men.

Or you could have been much unlucky, like she had been with Zack or worse yet, how fate had driven Sarah Finningham to marry the man who would have then killed her.

CHAPTER 7

Warren's Apartament, 11 Roxy Avenue

Warren entered his apartment with the day's mail.

Apart from a postcard sent from Trinidad and Tobago by one of his former colleague from Rockford, he placed the usual bills and advertising leaflets on the kitchen table, which were often the only contents of his letterbox.

Turned on the radio that broadcast the famous *Smell like teen spirit* from Nirvana and like every day he devoted himself to his quarter of an hour of free body exercises starting from the high abs.

He put a frozen pizza in the oven and after having programmed it, he allowed himself a long hot shower.

It was not his habit to make a summary of the day, especially in moments of complete relaxation like that, nobody like Warren Valentine loved to switch off from work and face private life with a mind completely free from the stress of work; today, however, it was practically impossible.

His mind reproduced the today`s movie before his eyes closed under the jet of water; the remains of Finningham, the late afternoon meeting and every single glance Kat had given him.

Came out of the shower, put his bathrobe on and prepared some comfortable clothes to wear that evening at home, he had already decided not to go out.

As he finished shaving, the oven timer went off.

A few minutes later he enjoyed his four cheeses accompanied by a can of beer while answering almost all the questions on a television quiz.

Warren liked his life, his job, and the apartment he spent his nights in; overall it could be said that Warren was a happy thirty-five year old man.

However, no one could know that his greatest desire was to create a family or that lately the libertine lifestyle so much appreciated so far, began to suffer from the lack of a companion with whom to build a future or simply make him feel loved.

Of course, women were not lacking: over the years many friends and lovers had entered and left his life or his bed, but since he had moved he had understood how he himself imagined, that none of these women had loved him so much that they go on to follow him to Summerville.

The phone began to play the notes of the soundtrack of *Game of Thrones* and on the screen appeared a number not present in his column.

"It doesn't make sense", said the female voice he had heard for the first time live that morning.

*What doesn't make sense, Kat?"

"If you were my husband, why would you want to disguise yourself and then eliminate me and disappear?"

"Well, it is assumed that the blame would have fallen on me, so maybe I would not have held up one or more interrogators giving me the escape".

He heard the sounds of pots or pans in the background as he held the phone in one hand and with the other clearing the table.

"Mhmm... maybe. I was thinking of a kidnapping of both".

"Don't rack your brains too much Kat. Most of the time the solution to the problem is the least complicated. Tomorrow we are planning another interrogation and I'm sure something will come up, you'll see".

"Most of the time you don't get packets with shear fingers, why should they look for me?"

"Well a part of some people's subconscious always works the opposite from another.

His repentance could come in the form of a message allowing his capture, while the other party is booking a ticket for Brazil".

There was a brief pause then Kat ended the call communicating to him that she was his new partner and giving him an appointment in a bar not far from the Police station for the following morning.

When he put the phone down he wondered how Katrine's private life could be, how she spent her evenings, the days off and the holidays, without being able to find an answer.

As soon as the call was over, Kat flipped through all the local web newspapers, then charged the phone and quickly zapped her five provincial TV channels where several times services had been broadcast on the forest trails or in the most frequented places in the area.

She discovered nothing, so she suggested she would find the news and photographs in the newspapers the following day.

She had spent the previous two hours arranging the house and phoning to her sister, then she had cooked the worst burger of her life.

Kat's talents and interests were numerous, but the kitchen had always been her weak point.

She tried to read her book, but she realized that she was too distracted and tired, so she turned the television to one of the many programs of culinary challenges that the television schedule was lately filled with. Followed the first twenty minutes trying to learn something new, then fell asleep on the couch.

Pulled hard on the rusted bolt of the hut, put the backpack containing the mask inside an old wooden wardrobe and sat down at the table.

Began to eat the meat-based meal eagerly, helping with a spoon only after removing the boots, carefully placed under the bench on which he sat.

Had seen the woman as it got on the taxi at the airport: would have wanted to see her face at the discover of Sarah's body.

Had studied the details in those few minutes of waiting in the taxi stand, and wanted to scream her name, say goodbye and run away, defiantly, to show her how close it was, and could almost smell the scent emanating from her jacket.

You hadn't had to try very hard to hide in the crowd even counting on the fact that you couldn't recognize a face that was completely foreign to it.

The game had begun, the mask guided and acted on the movements of the body and all this brought pleasure.

Moved the plate to make room for a white sheet, a pair of scissors and a glue then got up, picked up some old copies of newspapers and opened the wardrobe.

Took the mask with both hands and brought it close to the face.

It was still difficult to get used to the heavy beating of drums that buzzed in his ears, even more so to move around observing the world from the two narrow slits for the eyes.

Yet simply wearing it, trace of fear, doubt or uncertainty seemed to disappear, even tiredness ceased, leaving room for new, much more intense, sensations.

The perception of reality seemed to be altered, that of distorted time, in a unique sensation of its kind that no experience could possibly hope to describe.

Yes, wearing the mask was a unique sensation.

CHAPTER 8

Cafè Paradise   *March 21th, 2017*

The cold wind that morning had served to wipe out the clouds of the previous day.

Shortly thereafter the sun would have peeked through the surrounding mountains, raising the temperature by a few degrees and also the mood of the inhabitants of Summerville, moving at a brisk pace to get to work.

It would have been a splendid day if only there had not been that annoying breeze that did not seem in the slightest intention to cease.

Kat was sitting inside the Cafe Paradise, on one of the first tables at the entrance of the less crowded restaurant , when a young waitress took her order.

Once she rested her coat and purple scarf along the bench, she reached out to get a copy of the *Sunshine* to take a look at its front page.

One of her photographs had been placed next to the one with the graffiti on the wall; the reporter had fortunately played on her presence and not on the manner in which the murder had occurred as she herself had imagined. The bottom-of-the-page article showed the two agents completely unprepared and would surely have done bad publicity to the local police force and sent Phil furiously high.

The smiling waitress served her double coffee and the croissant just at the same time that a disheveled Warren entered the room.

"I'm sorry, two trees fell last night and the main road was closed to traffic and I had to follow the detours".

Katrine raised her eyebrows and frowned: "Don't worry, you are right in time, at least fix the Elvis tuft".

His surprised expression made her laugh and at the same time reflect the fact that Warren and the mirror didn't seem to spend most time together.

Despite this, the boy was physically enviable: his dry, toned and trained body was held by two muscular legs that could only have a cyclist or a runner.

"ten points in favor", thought Kat as she watched him take his parka off.

When the girl brought his cappuccino, the two had already decided to go to Tom Hackett, head of the "Grey Insurance" the place where Sarah carried out her profession.

Tom had scheduled an appointment by telephone the previous afternoon with Warren, claiming to return only late in the evening from a weekend trip that took place in New York.

The meeting would have served to learn something more about Sarah's life and, with a little luck, even that of her husband, now the main suspect.

The only one to be questioned was Robert's mother, the same one who had denounced his disappearance and who had a shock and went to the police station as soon as she learned of the death of her daughter-in-law.

Nothing interesting was discovered: the lady had fainted twice, cried repeating countless times that her son could not have committed what she herself had called an inhuman act, without ever ceasing to strangle the crucified Christ of the worn chain.

When they had finished, the waitress presented the bill and realizing she was not receiving any tip, she decided to offer the sight of her splendid teeth to the elderly gentleman as he entered the door.

Just before getting into the car, Warren allowed himself a cigarette, one of those four which he decided to smoke during the day.

"Minus one hundred points", thought Kat.

They would have found the building even without being aware of its address.

The gigantic complex stood along one of the main streets in the city center and the logos of the companies that exercised inside could be seen from any point of the main square or from each of the cars that ran along the large roundabout below.

From the windows you could see the inside of the numerous offices in full activity that fortunately could take advantage of the sunlight throughout the whole day.

In continuous coming and going of people were preparing to face the stairway placed in front of the main entrance: behind two powerful marble columns the two huge wooden doors had been opened wide at the opening time.

The two secretaries consulted by Warren the day before had been replaced by a man in his sixties and a young trainee who kindly indicated the floor and the office where the meeting would take place.

Mr. Hackett's office looked very neat and tastefully furnished: various files filled the shelves and were strictly in alphabetical order.

The man in his forties rose from his black leather armchair and presented himself with two energetic handshakes and then invited the two agents to sit in front of his desk.

"I am very sorry for Sarah's disappearance in that so horrendous way, so believe me I will do everything possible to help you arrest the culprit, you can count on me".

Tom`s face was visibly shaken: the deep circles brought Kat to think that he had hardly been able to sleep a wink during the night, only to start questioning him.

"Agent Katrine Steward, we would like to ask you a few questions to get to know Sarah Finningham and her husband Robert Hudson, if you don`t mind can we be informal Mr. Hackett?

"Of course, no problem. I knew Sarah from before her job at the "Grey Insurance", to tell the truth I entered her myself. One of our employee approached retirement and her husband Robert came to me to ask for a job for his wife.

Kat listened carefully as she looked at Tom's desk and personal effects: two silver frames held photos of him with his wife and their two children resting on a yellow Hummer and on the railing of a cruise ship.

"So you also know her husband?"

"Yes, we had been classmates in high school, two excellent students who shared the same room in college and attended the same courses, nothing more; in the future we would have taken two different careers, Robert teaches in a school not far from here".

"We are aware of this, please continue"

"Her resume was perfect for the kind of assignment we could offer her and so, after a short trial period I decided to hire her full-time: I was doing a favor to an old companion and at the same time the company inherited an efficient and extraordinarily dedicated employee".

"We also know this Mr. Hackett, what we are interested in is knowing whether the bond between you and Sarah went beyond the normal working relationship, there have been rumors of a possible approach from both sides, considering that their marriage was in crisis".

The question had been presented in a very natural way, but Katrine hoped she could reveal some uncomfortable secrets about the charismatic man who sat opposite her, so she kept staring at him with her inquiring look. She knew that Warren had turned to look at her, but if Tom had something to hide, his body would have betrayed him right now, or after such an uncomfortable and private question.

The question gave the result fired: Tom's dry denial was exposed in a too blatant way, waving and giving life to a frantic drumming with his fingers.

"If you could reveal to us something that we ourselves could not discover by analyzing you're phone records, you could really save us important time Mr. Hackett. You could give us a big hand in closing the case as you promised us at the beginning of our conversation".

Warren was not so sure what Kat could find in this man's life with an iron alibi, but he had noticed a loss of confidence in his voice and his posture: Kat had hit the mark.

There was a brief pause followed by new, uncomfortable questions that led Tom Hackett to get up to drink a glass of water, given the two the opportunity to exchange a quick glance of understanding.

Mr. Hackett collapsed as he turned his back on them.

"Do you want to know if I loved her? No. Do you want to know if we used to hang out together after work? Not even. I am a happily married man so I would prefer if what I am about to tell you remains within these walls. You know, it would be a scandal...the company would suffer...not to talk about my private life".

The two were all ears.

"Sarah confided in me on how her marriage was going to rookie, her husband's jealousy and so on: I was her friendly shoulder.

The meetings ended with hugs where she used to give vent to tears most of the time".

The two followed him with their heads as he moved around the room and articulated his story, frantically gesturing.

"Two months ago she suddenly kissed me and I did nothing to drive her away, in fact our meetings turned into business lunches, then into imaginary meetings in other places, naturally unaware of everyone, at least I thought so.

It was like been back as teenagers, two kids who met in secret outside the classrooms, do you understand me?"

No, the plastered faces of those two seemed not to understand, but on the other hand they certainly weren't the ones he should have given explanation to.

"Mr. Hackett, I don't want to judge you based on your actions, I am only interested in knowing if you were lovers and if her husband could have known about it".

*Yes, we were lovers. There have only been a few isolated episodes; here in the office I believe no more than three, but only she could have revealed it to him, which I guarantee you, she would have never done. Maybe because Sarah was afraid of her husband, but also because at the same time she understood very well by herself that our flirting could not continue. Believe me it would only have been a matter of time, I myself wanted to close the matter as soon as possible, the story would not have worked".

The words were interrupted by starting a silent cry: the tears streaked the tanned cheeks to then fall on the carpet.

"These two weeks have already been tormented enough for me, please don't say a word to anyone and please leave if you don't need anything else, I think I exposed myself enough".

The crying was triggered only by Tom's tensions and worries and had not aroused any emotion in Kat: that man seemed more interested in covering his own body than in contributing to the capture of the person responsible for the death of one of his employees as well as lover.

She remembered that metaphor from somewhere where the devil was portrayed as a person in a suit and tie and not in his monstrous form.

It's the same image of the man who hoped for their silence.

"You are lucky Mr. Hackett to have a great alibi for Friday night, otherwise you would be on the list of suspects. Your version, however, leads us to reinforce our suspicions on Robert Hudson who, from what you made us understand, was an acquaintance for you, not a friend.

Before replying to the policewoman the phone rang on Tom's desk, the intern's voice announced the arrival of the next customer with whom he had an appointment.

"As far as silence is concerned, I can't promise you anything, I will have to mention everything in the report that I will personally write. I will take a business card of his and I count on a future collaboration in case we need other details".

"Certainly agent Steward, on the other hand, I hope you will again be able to write what is strictly necessary for the investigation on your report and nothing that could damage my image".

Kat went out quickly and without turning around; she got what she needed and didn't want to waste one more second on that man's requests.

When they left Mr. Hackett closed the door and leaned against it with his back. He took a deep breath and realized he had a shiny forehead and beaded nose with drops of sweat: it had been years since anyone had cornered him that way.

He would never have thought of giving up his secrets to that policewoman who was as famous as she was charming, but he knew very well that his extra-marital relationship could ruin his life and he could only blame himself for it, for giving in to the advances of a woman under his command.

He cleaned himself up in the bathroom before letting the client in, aware that Katrine had already ruined his day and, probably in the future, would have ruined his marriage too.

Warren followed his colleague down the corridor towards the elevator: although she had marked an important point in favor of the investigation, she seemed to be very irritated.

"Remember me never to lie to you", he told her as he pressed the button that would lead them to the ground floor.

As the sliding doors of the elevator closed, she turned and smiling to him said, shut up.

CHAPTER 9

Mellow Park

After buying lunch from a street vendor, they gave a quick reading of the report drawn up together to be delivered to De La Cruix. Once finished they decided to eat together when they returned to the police station, as the force of the wind made a lunch break in the adjacent park impossible.

Under a porch Warren allowed himself his cigarette number two, then turned the car on and followed the path he would take back to the police station. During the return journey, they could not help but notice the damage caused by the strong gusts to the shopkeepers of the local stalls. Along the road that surrounded the historic center, once a week a market was held where people could stock up on products such as fruit, vegetables and clothing from local producers or retailers.

Lately the poor sellers did not seem to enjoy particular luck in the weather report: after the rain of the week before, today they were forced to pick up tents and stalls to avoid overturning of the goods, or even worse, the breakage or the serious damage that the structures and their supports could suffer from the fury of the strong gusts.

Around four in the afternoon Philip De La Cruix went to Kat`s office to take a look at the continuation of the investigation.

He had found and read the report on the desk, so he imagined that they would both dedicate themselves to follow the only sensible path: the one that led to her husband.

"Are there any news?"

Warren was leaning against his desk while Kat was on her computer, they both then sat up as soon as they heard his voice.

""So far nothing. We checked the properties of the Hudson family, asked friends of her husband of where he could be right now, not to mention the useless phone calls to his mother: of course with no results".

"Do you think he may have left the country?" Said Phil, grimacing.

Kat stretched her arms backwards rocking with her chair: "I exclude him. There is no purchase of air tickets, trains or withdrawals from his current account. Not to mention the phone that turned out to be off since Friday, just like Sarah`s".

The two men looked at each other trying to formulate new hypotheses or ideas to hold onto, but neither of them seemed to find anything logical to propose.

"I`ll let you work, I`ll call the press and inform all the districts of the country by forwarding photos and data on Robert Hudson, hoping someone will find him.

One last thing Kat…Today someone came to ask about you, it`s Zack".

Katrine sensed the increase in heartbeats in her chest. The shock caused by the news was partly due to the person who had pronounced it: she would never have imagined that sentence coming from the mouth of her superior.

She felt a flush of heat on her face: "Okay thanks for letting me know".

Phil hesitated for a moment on the threshold, watching her dive completely into the computer screen, then walked to his office.

It didn't take a degree to notice Kat's sudden change, her eyes had become shiny, her cheeks were flushed and her hands clutched at the mouse as if the latter wanted to get away from her.

Curiosity prevailed over Warren "Who is Zack?"

Everyone in the Police Station was aware of Katrine's past relationship and the way it had stopped, but it occurred to her that Warren had recently moved to Summerville.

"An asshole".

Dark blue sneakers hopped fast on the path of the fitness trail.

The color of the *Nike* logo and the carbon rubber sole were slightly faded, the dust of the gravel ground had taken off the bright red glow that stood out in the window where she had bought them.

By seven o'clock the wind had set in, granting Kat an evening run. She strode along the path that wound towards the mountain, crossing other runners from time to time.

To the tune of the Oasis *Roll with it,* she thought of as five years had not served to completely forget Zack.

She even believed that he had moved to Europe, more precisely to La Rochelle, a village from which the French hen for months had served breakfast for her and her ex-boyfriend.

"You gotta roll with it, you gotta take your time, you gotta say what you say don't let anybody get in your way" it seemed that the Gallagher brothers were attuned to her thoughts.

She found the reaction from her body that afternoon annoying, she could still fell Warren's searching gaze on her neck.

With a light pressure on the button of the headphones, she switched to *Stand By Me* to give free rein to the rock of Ac/Dc.

The live version enhanced the percussion and the electric guitar more, stimulating the production of adrenaline into Kat's body, which then undertook to increase the speed of the race.

The daily goal of 8 Km. had already been exceeded, but she wanted to be sure of falling asleep quickly that night, so she took a detour, extending the round.

She loved everything about the race, feeling the muscles of the legs push on the ground, feeling the contrast of the heat of the face with the fresh woody air, but the real pleasure was to prove to herself as to each race could be better and exceed her own records.

It was the same spirit with which she faced life, challenges and difficulties, anyone who knew her appreciated this quality.

The next day she would return to work reborn, twelve Km. were an easily reachable distance, but she did not want to exaggerate or find herself with pains in the knees, for which reason she added an extra stretching to the pre-established cool-down.

She took a slow and invigorating shower, the boiling water took away her sweat and fatigue.

Once she put on her underwear and a lace dressing gown, she walked towards the kitchen where she noticed the dirty dishes in the sink of the day before.

She began to wash them against her will; once finished she ordered food from a Thai take away restaurant then spent the rest of the evening thinking back to Zack.

The last thought when she turned off the light of the lampshade at 10.30pm was, however turned to Robert Hudson.

Who knows where he was hiding at this moment?

CHAPTER 10

Burrington Road *December 19th, 2015*

Dylan Roger had placed himself at his favorite post at the top of the hill. He would not have moved for quite a while, the military combat suit with applied vegetation would have camouflaged him among the bushes. A flash lit up the dark night over the helmet for a few moments and a few moments before the sound response, he heard the sound of fast footsteps in the vicinity, despite the radar did not highlight any kind of movement.

The enemy rushed past him, supporting a boot in the puddle located between them, but after a few meters he collapsed lifeless, dropping the gripped MP5.

Dylan reloaded the silent model P9 pistol and then put it back in the side holster, took his sniper rifle and aimed at the tool shed at the bottom of the valley.

The lattice moved slowly up and down, swinging on the left door post, in the hope that soon an enemy head would peep out of it.

About ten seconds passed when holding his breath, he fired a shot towards the bandana of the newly released mercenary, killing him instantly.

A bullet grazed the bark of the plant by his side, then quickly moved the view towards the wooden bridge and noticed the enemy laser sight coming from the dry river bed.

He was the fastest again: the bullet mortally hit his opponent in the chest, forcing him to jump back almost comically.

His MJ bullets were about to run out, he had to move to the corpse of the last target to refuel, so he got up and started running in that direction.

An enemy came out of the hut and fired a missile launcher in the trajectory of Dylan who, taken back, did not have time to react, knowing that the explosion would have killed him.

His body was thrown forward, ending up next to that of the other sniper; both rifles were collected by the survivor of the shooting who abandoned the now unloaded rocket launcher.

The timer on the screen reached zero, revealing the results of the game just ended.

His team had seen the death match and he had been the MVP (Most Valuable Player) for the third consecutive time, totaling twenty kills and five deaths.

The first chat notifications of the opponents began to appear on the TV screen; they insulted him by giving him a *noob camper,* referring to the game tactic he used which consisted in hiding in a point on the map and waiting for the opposing players to pass.

Dylan didn`t care much about their judgment, after all his strategy did not seem so stupid after all, as in reality, a soldier would have preferred to take shelter and not run towards the enemy fire.

He often accepted invitations and found himself arguing with video game players from all over the world, insulting most of the time the innocent mothers of those boys who vented their anger through vulgarity into the microphone or in the violence of the virtual war.

He took off his headphones while he pulled the copy of *Black Ops 2* from the console to put it in the green case: that evening he didn`t really want to answer to some stupid boy.

He looked at the clock hanging on the wall of his room: it showed exactly twenty-three, or the beginning of the party.

Opened the zipper of his sports bag to extract the few grams of marijuana left that were kept in secret.

He could not resist smelling the small package of tinfoil, as he loved that aroma more than anything else in the world.

Only his father had discovered him in the past, giving him a good groomed, telling him to get smart and invest his free time to meet girls.

That discussion had led him to listen to his father, at least in part: no one would have rummaged inside a boxing glove.

He put on his inseparable hooded sweatshirt and slipped smoke and wallets into the pockets of his wide rapper pants; he placed the strings inside the *Vans* at least two numbers wider than necessary, than in the mirror he checked the long black forelock that covered the entire forehead and his right eye.

His friends were right to call him "stoner" and he did nothing to hide it.

He went downstairs, said goodbye to his parents, busy watching a talent show on TV, and left the house.

He opened the garage and got aboard his old third-hand Honda Civic, turned the key, giving life to the engine and selected the third track from his new CD.

The music from Sum 41 accompanied him for the twenty minutes that separated him from the party to the old shed of the Sanders.

Once parked, he showed the bracelet purchased at school in the morning and entered quickly, under the silent gaze of the bouncer positioned at the entrance.

An unknown band played a cover of a Greenday song and a crowd of drunken boys danced staggering under the stage while another group huddled on the improvised balcony where alcohol was sold regardless of the clientele's age.

He caught a glimpse of the red eyes of his best friend Johnny among the line of people in the queue, as he dangled his head to the rhythm of music: he was completely done.

"You ugly bastard, you could have at least waited for me!"

There was a short break before his friend reacted to that sentence, recognizing him.

"Dylan! I'm sorry, I couldn't resist. I wanted to try the exotic herb I was talking about this afternoon, but don't worry, follow me in the bathroom, there is enough for three people".

"What is it; a challenge? I bet there will not be a shred of it left within two hours", he said as he opened the door of the men's toilet and made sure it was completely empty.

Two hours later Johnny had collapsed on an old sofa together with four perfect strangers to whom he had manage to sell part of the drug.

Dylan, after the initial adrenaline rush that had made him unleashed for over an hour in the ballroom, had suddenly gone into a state of strong malaise and dissatisfaction. The group had stopped playing and left the stage to a techno-loving deejay, who in a short time had managed to empty the room and make him a headache. So, since he was now alone and hated that music, he decided that for him the party had come to an end.

When he came out he was hit by a freezing gust of wind and noticed how some snowflakes had settled on the remaining cars and started to whiten the ground.

As he stared at the hot stream of urine, he thought undecided whether to spend the rest of the night playing video games or browsing his favorite porn sites, but as he approached the car he noticed a familiar face in the center of the square.

Lucy Reign stood in the center of the parking lot and spun around as soon as she noticed that he was staring at her, trying to hide behind a red wool scarf. Her beautiful blonde curls were covered in part by a nice cap, her long slender legs ended in a pair of black ankle boots with studs and were kept warm by black leather leggings that enhanced the perfect curve of her back.

Dylan knew that that girl felt a crush on him from elementary school, but he had never given her importance until then because he would never have imagined seeing her at a party, much less dressed like that.

Lucy was the classic girl that males of that age snubbed, the know-it-all of the first desk always attached to a book during the break and arm in arm with the teachers during school trips.

The boys preferred to spend time with girl like Jenny, who after having drained and smoked everything that was offered to her, could reciprocate by letting their hands stretch all over her body, or by giving the lucky person of the evening a private appointment.

However, a long time had passed since then, Lucy`s body had developed, growing quite tall and giving her a generous breast. Since she did not stop giving him hidden glances, Dylan decided to follow his father`s advice in full and approached her firmly.

"Hi Lucy, do you need a ride by chance?"

"I'm waiting for my mother, the shift ends in ten minutes and she is going to pick me up here", replied the girl, blushing in her face.

"Come on jump up, I'll take you home, send her a message, I'm sure she will understand, after all you are no longer a child, aren't you?"

The girl swallowed and undecided looked for words to assemble in order to formulate a sentence of complete meaning, but the emotion of that invitation only managed to make her nod with a nod of the head.

Of course she could not refuse him after years in which he had not lent her the slightest intention and together they went towards the car.

Spent the first few minutes asking her questions followed by quick and vague answers, it almost seemed like the girl was dosing the oxygen she needed to breath, so Dylan started to compliment her and to give her explanations on how in those years he had never been brave enough to invite her to go out with him: the drug had completely erased any trace of insecurity present in his body.

He continued to talk to her as he moved his hand away from the gearbox and began to rise up her leg without encountering any obstacle.

The girl responded with a slight tremor in her voice and clutching her sweaty hands inside her thighs.

Then without ever taking his eyes off the road he took her hand gently and placed it on himself, making her feel the erection that she had procured him.

"Enough Dylan, I don't want to…"

He unhooked her seat belt and with one arm dragged her towards him, sensing the fragrance of her clothes and the scent of her hair, then turned to look into her eyes and asked her if she was really sure she didn`t want to.

The desire prevailed over common sense and Lucy brought her shiny lips up to touch those on which she always dreamed.

Dylan felt her tongue enter his kneaded mouth and play with his; with one eye he watched the snow hit the windshield and with the other he studied the serene expression of the girl who, without ever opening her eyes, was abandoning herself to him.

He felt her panting as he held her breast with the palm of his hand, but suddenly something caught his attention a little further on the road.

Two eyes full of terror shone in the light of its headlights and as soon as he saw the deer make a leap in the woods to the side, he made the unforgivable mistake of pressing the brake pedal fully.

The car tires lost grip due to the thin layer of snow that had become ice in no time, the car steered disobeying the steering wheel controls while dangerously approaching the edge of a curve.

The next few moments would remain etched in his mind forever: Lucy squeezed his hand tightly as the car rolled down the slope ending up violently crashing into a tree.

CHAPTER 11

Sunset Hill   *March 22th, 2017*

Dylan Rogers slowly opened his eyes: he panicked as soon as he realized he was sitting behind the wheel of a car.

More than two years had passed since the accident with Lucy and since then he had never been able to get into the driver's seat of any vehicle and had avoided traveling by car most of the times he had had the need to move.

Therefore, when he realized he had both hands tied to the steering wheel and the body wrapped by a rope on the seat, he began to cry and shout, but the adhesive tape dampened any sound or lament in the bud.

In the previous days he had been kidnapped, he had lived in the darkness of a room where he had been regularly fed; he could not know who had been or for what reason the person had done it, but he hoped for a ransom request or for his accidental discovery by the police.

He repeated the same identical mantra: "you will not die, you will not die, you will not die"

That situation did not indicate anything good, maybe he had been left and someone was about to come and free him, perhaps a person passing by would noticed him and set him free.

He tried to find calm within and forced himself to think and find a solution or an escape route, so he looked around himself.

He had already seen that place as a child, in an educational walk organized by the school. He recognized the picnic tables to his right, but he couldn't connect where he was.

The darkness of the night made visible only the starry celestial arch above him and the silhouettes of the trees that seemed to be able to touch him.

Suddenly he saw a figure approaching slowly towards the car, he tried to hit the horn in any way, even with his forehead, but for a few centimeters he failed in his aim.

"Please, I'm here, please look here, turn around, he thought.

As soon as the person passed by the door on the opposite side of the car, he recognized the mask that he saw daily for the few seconds needed to lay his ration of food and water on the cell floor.

He stared at it while his breath clouded the window and the seat under him began to soak with his own urine.

He trembled like a leaf when he saw the person wearing it, open the passenger seat door and recline on it.

The mask tilted his head to the side and looked at him, it seemed to enjoy the sight of that boy so helpless and full of terror.

From the right pocket of the dirty work overalls, pulled out a cordless bone saw, then with a glove lifted Dylan's left ring finger and after having forced him to open his fist, with a light pressure the circular blade of the tool started to spin around.

A splash of blood turned the windshield dark red and excruciating pain struck the young man who was now frantically leaping under the gaze of that terrifying mask.

Before leaving the vehicle, the individual lowered the handbrake then whispered something in his ear, then finally went out and closed the door.

The rear view mirror showed the individual intent on pushing the car towards the descent in front of them: the time had come.

After two years, several sessions by the psychologist and an endless process, Dylan Rogers was reliving the nightmare: the speed of the car was increasing more and more, while his trajectory was about to project him beyond the edges of the ground in front, without being able to do anything.

In the few moments in which the car was pushed, he remembered that he had already heard that voice and managed to connect it to a known face, only when all four wheels were detached from the ground.

Then he saw the rocks getting closer and closer until it turned all black.

CHAPTER 12

Kat's Apartment, 25 Elm Street

The electronic clock on Kat's bedside table said seven o'clock when the phone started to ring.

She took it in her hand without looking at the photo of the incoming number, pressed the reception button and with her eyes still half closed she brought it to her ear.

"Hallo?"

"I'm Phil, Robert has struck again, this time near Sunset Hill. The others are already heading there, reach them as soon as possible".

"Did he hit again, so early? I'll be right there".

She got up, took a quick fix in the bathroom, then after having done a ponytail, she took a pair of jeans and a light white sweater from the closet and quickly got dressed.

She went downstairs , put a banana in her pocket and ate a diet bar while wearing her jacket, then put on her boots.

Once the door was locked, she got into the car and started: exactly ten minutes had passed since her awakening.

The thermometer on the dashboard marked 4 degrees, the wind of the day before had stopped, leaving a clear cloudless sky.

When twenty five minutes later she reached the dirt parking lot at the foot of Sunset Hill, her colleagues had already fenced a wooded area a little further on with yellow tape.

She noticed the car carcass popping up between the rocks in a vertical position, perfectly embedded in a rocky inlet.

She looked up estimating a height of about ten meters from the ground to the point from which the car had crashed.

When she approached she could notice the lifeless body inside the cockpit: the bleeding face of a man was turned towards her with an unnatural neck angle, as well as that taken by the arms and legs.

She noticed that one hand was missing a finger and that the victim's body was still tied to the seat with a rope, just like his hands were tied to the steering wheel.

The legs had been almost pulped and now formed a whole with the sheet metal of the car that had not caught fire after the fall.

"The tank was completely emptied, it fell with the engine off and the victim died instantly, as you can imagine, about seven hours ago", said Warren behind her, as if he could have read her mind.

"What else do we know?"

"I'll tell you everything I know as we reach Judith up the hill, she's looking for possible tracks. I can already tell you that she did not find anything here in the car".

Kat took a further look at the scene then turned around and followed her colleague, however, she would have looked at the photographs that were taken at that moment once they returned to the office.

"Follow me, let's go up to the top along the path. This way will take us only five minutes".

Warren walked towards the narrow and steep road traveled by hikers and lovers of tranquility that led to the panoramic point of Sunset Hill, from which you could admire the whole city.

"We received an anonymous phone call, the signal of which could not be traced, which informed us of a corpse near Sunset Hill.

If you hadn't already noticed..."

"...it's the same place where the photo was taken, the one we found in the Nordtech van".

"Exactly, but we could not have imagined it, because until this morning we thought of a passionate crime, assuming that Robert Hudson had learned of the relationship between Sarah Finningham and Tom Hackett".

"Avoid the summaries, so far we had all gotten there, go on".

"The victim turns out to be a certain Dylan Rogers, 21 years old, residing in Summerville in the house with both parents, who reported his disappearance a week before your arrival".

"Any connection with Robert Hudson?"

"Yes. Dylan was a student of his, for three years now he and the whole class had taken English lessons from Hudson, but other than that there seemed to be nothing outside the pupil/teacher relationship".

The steep path between the conifers had almost come to an end: another team of agents could be glimpsed in the rest area just ahead on the asphalt road.

They also saw Judith in her white scientific police suit.

"About two years ago, Dylan and a girl named Lucy Reign had a car accident exactly over there, in those trees".

Warren pointed with his index finger to a point far from the other side of the river that flowed further downstream, where a road immersed in the woods and turned sharply to the left, following the edges of the mountain.

"The road was frozen and after losing control of the vehicle, the two crashed into a tree. Dylan claimed to have seen a deer in the middle of the roadway, but blood tests showed he was under the use of drugs; the fact is that the girl lost her life.

Apparently our Robert's thirst for revenge or justice, went far beyond our imagination...here we are, we arrived in the area that interests us".

Judith was grappling with an instrument that measured footprints and recreated a precise copy on a plaster cast.

Probably later they would have compared themselves to those found near the construction site on River Street.

When she noticed Kat's arrival her giant glasses turned towards her.

"Good morning Kathrine. I was waiting for you to show you something. Could you come a second this way?"

The two women walked until they arrived near a table with two wooden benches, where a family could have lunch outdoors on a beautiful sunny day.

Warren followed them, eager for additional details about the accident, but limited himself watching Kat find out what he had discovered a little earlier.

A finger had been nailed on the table (probably belonging to the body found in the car) and an incision made with a pointed object clearly showed the word "guilty", easily legible on the wood.

"Do you know what it means Kat?"

"It means that we are dealing with a serial killer, the same modus operandi as last time, he wants to make fun of us, of me. No matter how he kills the victim, he is interested in letting us know about his guilt, then leaving a severed finger as a signature.

He wants to demonstrate his superiority towards us, first he sends us a package, and now he leaves this message in plain sight just for us.

"Yet, I want to clarify that the killer is not killing at random, on the contrary, he seems to be following a precise plan.

Dylan Rogers turned out to be missing on Monday, four days before his wife".

The three turned their gaze to the same point, that is, to the nail that pierced the phalanx exactly in the middle of the finger.

It was Warren who broke the silence: "We have underestimated the case, we have to do everything in our power to stop him, I'm sure he has no intention of stopping here".

Kat moved towards the tracks left by the tires, two tessellated strips sank in the ground, like the footprint left by an athlete's skis before tackling the jump from the trampoline in the famous winter competition.

"Tell me Warren, how many people have disappeared in Summerville lately? I should have asked you before".

The man took the last cigarette out of a pack of Marlboro Light: "As many as four people in the past month: three during this last week, including Robert Hudson. Philip called you back from Los Angeles for this, to investigate these chain disappearances with me. We could not have imagined that they were connected, Summerville is not a Metropolis, we all know each other".

"Four people? Christ Warren, excluding Robert Hudson, means that in addition to having this death on consciousness, another person is in serious danger. I want to have a list with all the names as soon as possible and know everything about their life, ties, interests, even where they spent their holidays twenty years ago. This time we need to know anything useful to be able to anticipate his next move".

"I'm going now, I'll see you at the police station, he addressed a quick greeting to Judith then went back to the path from which they had climbed, going almost to collide with the photographer.

"As for you Judith, try to analyze anything that can confirm the identity of the murderer, so far nothing has been found that can indict him".

The woman was rummaging in search of a transparent envelope where she could put a cigarette butt she had seen just before. "Of course Kat, It's my job, but the killer was very careful not to leave any trace. If I will find something, I will call you immediately. You can count on me".

Kat left with a "Thank you", then went down on the ground following the tire tracks.

When she reached the edge she looked down, clinging firmly to the branch of a tree; it would have been impossible to think of surviving from such a leap.

A slight disturbance of balance and a sensation of rotation made her retreat.

She walked along the edge of the precipice until she reached a rock that protruded for a couple of meters directly into the void.

She climbed easily among the cracks on her side and managed to reach the top, located three meters above the ground.

The sun rose in front of her just at that moment, partially illuminating the city and heating her face skin, now wrapped in its golden light.

She put a hand on her forehead to shield her eyes from direct light and took a few steps forward: she seemed to have seen something.

She knelt on the smooth and flat stone and managed to focus on what seemed to her a drawing made with white chalk.

Then she got up and waved an arm towards the forensic scientist.

"Judith! This way. Maybe I have found something", she screamed to make sure she heard her.

The woman proceeded briskly and then helped her colleague to climb up the rock.

Once in front of the drawing, they both took their cell phones to photograph it.

In the drawing appeared a spiral sun circumscribed by a circle of rays of equal size and just below two hands seemed to want to enclose it.

The two wrists touched each other until they split into the two open palms of the hands pointing upwards perhaps in a gesture of prayer.

*Have you seen this symbol anywhere before Judith? Do you know what that could mean?"

"Actually I seem to have seen it before, but to find out more we should ask a symbol expert. I know there is one in Rockford, we have already contacted him in the past for an archaeological discovery that unfortunately proved to be of little importance.

"I will try to get in touch as soon as possible. Do you think that…"

"Yes. The rain and the weather would have canceled it long ago so I can already confirm that it was done last night".

"As I imagined, Kat said as she stared at the remains of the car beneath them.

CHAPTER 13

Katrine Steward's Office

When Kathrine entered her office, she slammed a copy of the Sunshine onto her desk.

In large letters one could read the word "scandal" on the title of the first page.

Someone had leaked the story between Tom Hackett and Sarah Finningham and she had gone on a rampage as she was sure she had only reported it to Philip and her team.

The article traced the career of one of Grey Insurance's most prominent member and shareholder, as well as chief of staff of what would later be described as "a close collaborator" and how the police had exposed their clandestine relationship.

Of course the journalist had thought well to support Katherine's photo to add depth to the scoop, a scapegoat already known for Tom Hackett.

The day had not started in the best way, but she could not allow herself to waste precious time: there would have been a lot of work to be done.

Warren was inserting sheets into some transparent plastic bags, he managed to glimpse some photos among them, including that of Sarah already present in the folder concerning her case.

"I'm almost done with, Kat. I'm going to fix everything on that wall so I always have the information at hand. You don't mind if I detach the David Bowie poster, right?"

"Do you know what I was thinking about? That word that our killer likes so much to write: guilty".

Warren turned as he rolled up the image of the white duke and placed it on the desk.

"Well yes, even if one could inadvertently say that Dylan Rogers killed that girl two years earlier, that would have judged him guilty, but I think the boy didn't deserve such a severe penalty: from what I have been able to discover, he has spent the last two years between a session in court and that of a psychologist, then developing a total phobia towards cars".

Kathrine entered the ICECUBE password and waited for the program to start "That's right. Our Robert could have fun using the so-called Dante counterpoint, have you already heard of it?"

"No, I'm sorry".

"I will try to explain myself quickly. Dante placed the damned in different circles of hell according to the gravity and nature of the sins committed. Minosse was the judge who assigned the infernal circle, the further he went down to the center of the Earth, the more serious the sin in earthly life had been".

Warren followed the speech carefully, assimilating any information on a topic unknown to him so far.

"I'll give you an example: the ignorant, that is, those who never made a decision or position on earth, were forced to chase a sign for eternity, while they were stung and injured by wasps and flies. This is counterpoint by contrast, do you follow me?"

Warren nodded slowly.

"By analogy, the retaliation makes the penalty resemble the sin which the damned must make up for eternity.

For example Paolo and Francesca let their bodies be overwhelmed by passion, in their group the souls are condemned to be overwhelmed by strong incessant storms".

"A sort of an eye for an eye then?"

*Exactly. These reasoning's are only hypotheses, but let's say that our Robert is punishing his victims following this criterion. The flames of his wife's passion would have been extinguished in the acid until she melted…"

"…and Dylan's accident would have been punished with the same coin. The speech holds even if there is never a right part in a murderer.

Kat shrugged and sighed "I disagree with your last statement. Many people rejoice to see a multiple murderer as he walks the green mile that separates him from the lethal injection".

Warren's eyes widened "Kat, what are you saying? We are cops. We must act according to justice, it is not up to us to set the penalty, but to judges and magistrates, otherwise we would not be very different from the criminals we arrest".

Kat turned her chair to look at her colleague and, while trying to formulate an answer, the image of *The Ghost,* who she executed two months earlier, intruded on them.

*You're right Warren, sorry. It is only difficult for me to feel pity for a murderer. He may also have had traumas in the past, not being completely sane in his head, but nothing will give life back to his victims and no excuse would serve to fill the void of their loved ones".

The conversation ended as soon as Judith entered the office.

She brought the brown tuft to one side, highlighting the side shave that was now in fashion at that time.

"Here it is Kathrine, I managed to retrieve the number of the expert on symbology, as I promised you".

She placed the note with the telephone number on the desk and placed her index finger on the Sunshine article.

"Some people deserve this type of treatment, they will be deprived of everything, you will see".

Warren watched as she sat in the chair next to Kathrine.

"I'm dealing with two ruthless women", he said, leaning a cigarette on his ear that he would later smoke.

In the afternoon, after having lunch in the office with mixed salad and a savory pie that Judith had brought with her for the whole group, they were repeating the cards of the subjects hanging on the wall for the umpteenth time.

The names of Robert, Sarah and Dylan had already been probed and as soon as Judith's turn was over, it was Warren's turn.

"Only Eric Preston, 37, missing on March 1, whose complaint was made by his girlfriend Courtney Afford, with whom he had an appointment in the afternoon to arrange the last suitcases of a holiday that would begin the next day, is missing.

As we already know their relationship was booming, engaged for a year and a half, under both of their names there is not even an unpaid fine in the police records.

Together they run a tattoo shop near the university and apparently they had no enemies".

Judith took her glasses and started cleaning her lenses, she really looked completely different without them.

"Maybe there is no connection. Just because it's on the list of missing persons doesn't necessarily mean being the target of a serial killer, especially with such a clean criminal record".

Kathrine started to move her feet to relieve the tension: "Sure Judith, but for now that's all we have. We don't know Robert Hudson and we do not know what exactly he has in mind, so we assume that he is punishing the victims who have disappeared till today. What can we notice?"

"First he is acting undisturbed despite being wanted and his face has already appeared on TV and in most newspapers", said Warren as he blew to chill the coffee from their machine.

"We have to understand how he does it. Tomorrow we will be able to trace the images taken at the time of the theft of the Volvo crashed last night. If we are lucky we can trace his movements or his hiding place by retracing the images taken by the traffic cameras".

Kat dialed the number written on the ticket in front of her for the fourth time: "Later I will ask Philip to intensify the nightly rounds, but for the moment I would like you to do more detailed research on Eric Preston. If we could find a possible connection with Robert or something strange in his past, we could perhaps track him down or, at best, save his life".

Both colleagues nodded and took their seats behind their computer screens as she delved into Dylan Rogers.

After several searches nothing significant emerged about the man and only the old articles of the accident that occurred two years earlier on that of the boy.

The only connection that emerged between the four names on the list had been car insurance with the same company, that is Grey Insurance. This was not a significant discovery given that

90% of the people in possession of a car preferred to take out a policy in the nearest insurance office and Grey Insurance was the only company present in the Summerville area. For two of them then, it would have been an obvious choice, almost obligatory.

Before going out at the end of the shift, she knocked on the door with the sign De La Cruix, impressed in plain sight on the glass.

"Come in", her boss said to her as he finished tidying up his desk.

The caramel-colored skin shone on his forehead and the two patches of sweat under his arms stood out in the yellow of his shirt.

"The press is tearing me apart, they always want more names and details about your case. Of course people need to know as much as possible in order to help us with the possible sightings, but do you have the slightest idea of how many fake reports I have already received in these days? The mother of the idiots is always pregnant".

Kat put a hand on his shoulder and a comfortable look.

"Tomorrow we will resume the investigation, unfortunately there is not much hope of catching him, but there will be possible evidence that will confirm the identity of the murderer".

She heard him mumbling something in what she believed was a variant of the French language he spoke on the island of Martinique where he was born almost fifty years earlier.

"I should ask you if it was possible to intensify the night patrols, it would probably be of little use, but it would give citizens a little more confidence. The fear of going out in the evening after these news will skyrocket".

"I'll try to do something", said Philip, sinking into his armchair and rubbing his eyes.

"Perfect. So good evening Philip", Kat said turning to the exit.

After a few steps she turned to face him "One last thing…why did you reveal to the press the betrayal of Tom Hackett? I don't think there was really a need".

The man stood up showing all his 190 cm. and looking her straight in the eyes: "Tell me Kat…do you really think I'm so stupid?"

CHAPTER 14

Trevor's Pub

Warren Valentine threw the cigarette butt over the railing on which he was leaning.

He followed the red dot describing an arch in the dark of the night and going out contacting the icy waters of the river that flowed fast beneath him.

It had been a busy day, but he had no intention on spending it at home in front of the TV.

He would eat something at Trevor's Pub, probably a hamburger with fries, under the notes of some tracks by the Gun's or the Rolling Stones.

The new sign illuminated his face in red at regular intervals: an intermittent neon had taken the place of the red yellowed coat of arms that the wind of the previous day had made to end up in the river.

The Trevor's Pub had recently been his second home: an almost always very crowded place, frequented by young customers, mostly made up of single women looking for adventure.

There was nothing he could do, he felt alive and full of energy only in places like this, where a cross of glances was enough to put him in a good mood.

He left the jacket to the cloakroom clerk immediately after passing the entrance and received a colored key ring with the number 34.

He sat down at his favorite table, where he could have a good view of the entrance and greeted the waitress with a quick nod.

The wooden benches creaked under his weight as he sat down and unrolled the napkin, placing the cutlery on the paper placemat on which the menu was printed.

He thought of Kat, the scent she emanated, the authoritarian way in which she gave orders and her graceful physique.

"The usual?", Said the maid with the lip piercing and the white shirt of the staff of the restaurant.

"Yes thanks Cindy and a medium beer, as soon as you have time", he replied with the good manners that the girls liked so much.

He could not help but take a quick look at the green and black checkered skirt that the owner had chosen as a uniform for his employees.

Unfortunately none of the waitresses, secretaries or students present in the club could attract his interest or distract him.

Those green and deep eyes had bewitched him, but he didn`t have to allow himself the luxury of falling in love, he preferred to maintain his rationality and light-heartedness that for many years had saved him from uncomfortable relationships and embarrassing situations.

No, he had to find a way not to think about her or that madman of Robert Hudson, to get distracted and stay in peace, he had full right.

Although a part of him strongly desired her, he made a promise to himself: forget her as soon as possible.

He decided that the girl that just entered, with riding boots, could have given him a hand or if nothing else, would have explained to him the reason why such a beautiful girl was around on her own.

The foam of the beer in the glass went up quickly, to then overflow from its top and be able to form a dark spot on the tablecloth.

"Shit", thought Judith as she lifted the glass and moved her napkin under it.

The news on television had just broadcast the report on Dylan Rogers, which meant that from then on, people would talk about the presence of a serial killer who was wandering the city's streets.

The oven timer rang behind her, as soon as she turned around, she could ascertain the perfect state in which her blackberry tart appeared.

After taking it out and serving it on a dessert plate, she waited a couple of minutes while the guy on TV listed the sport results of the recovery session played by the basketball teams unknown to her.

As soon as she placed her half-empty plate of lasagna on the floor tiles, the muzzle of a black Labrador appeared from under the tablecloth.

The dog began to lick the plate and Judith could see his joy manifested through a wagging of his tail against her knees.

"Piano Sharky, piano", she intimated caressing him. Sharky licked his snout showing for a second the sharp teeth that had suggested Judith to give him that name, then slowly dragged his four legs to the bowl of water.

That old dog was the only company on Judith's evenings, excluding the monthly visits of the mother who wanted to ascertain the conditions of her second child.

She had made a reason, men didn't seem much interested in a clumsy girl who was already wearing her floral pajamas at six o'clock in the evening.

Men in the past had been able to appreciate her cooking and her company, but had run away as soon as they learned of her oddities.

First of all her collection of statuettes depicting the characters of any film, TV series or cartoon released after the 80s. There was certainly nothing wrong with decorating the house with some personalization, but finding the look of *Chucky,* the killer doll or the *IT* clown mask while sitting on the tablet, was not something that normal people seemed to appreciate.

Others did not like the small barn just behind her house: the sounds of her animals seemed to ruin the atmosphere typical of spicy moments.

Now Judith was not making any problems, in fact she also never had any. She claimed her sword -I have to like it as it is- despite her mother and whoever had entered that house, they would have insisted on making some changes to her lifestyle.

She put on her windbreaker and worn-out sneakers, then waved the leash to get the dog's attention. Once the door was locked, she walked towards the public gardens.

After cleaning Sharky's needs, she could see how the moon was about to be swallowed up by the gray clouds directly above them. Maybe the next day it would rain, which would not have affected her life in any way, except for Sharky`s two daily strolls.

She heard a rustle in the hedges behind the two empty swings on the playground to her right. She decided that with a free killer on the streets, she and Sharky would go straight home.

She turned the key until it made a complete turn in the lock and heard the sound "click". She went back to the kitchen and turned on the tap, waiting for the water to be hot enough to dissolve the food residues left on the bottom of the dishes.

Kat began to rinse the glass of wine, then put it in the dishwasher and then switch to the fork and knife used for the meat just earlier. She had prepared a cut of beef with mashed potatoes following the instructions of the video on YouTube saved the previous evening and the result was pleasant.

She turned to the table half occupied by the photocopies of the files of missing persons that she had had prepared in the afternoon and tried again to get in touch with the expert in symbolism. On the third ring she heard Alessandro Zaretti`s voice answer the phone in a calm but serious tone.

"Good evening, doctor Zaretti, I`m Kathrine Steward of the Summerville Police. I have tried several times to contact you about a symbol that appeared at a scene of a crime.

There was a short pause, the words police and crime scene were never auspicious, which is why people took a couple of seconds to assimilate the sentence.

"You have to excuse me, but I`m just leaving from a conference right now, I just turned my cell phone back on. Please, what can I do for you".

"I wish to talk to you in person and show it to you personally, do you think it is possible to meet me tomorrow at the Summerville police station?"

"I'm sorry, but you will have to wait until Friday, I'm full of commitments in the next few days".

"Mhmm... okay, let's make an appointment . My number is the one I'm calling from. Can I send you a photo of the symbol? Maybe you can give a quick look".

"Of course. Good evening, see each other on Friday". Kat put down her cell phone and went back through the folders. Two and a half hours later she lay down in her bed , where she fell asleep after a few seconds, exhausted.

About fifteen minutes later, the mobile phone screen lit up without vibrating or ringing.

A text message appeared in full among the notifications of her IPhone: "I don't understand how this story has to do with an African tribe dating back to 1000 years ago".

The mask called to action, it's bright interior did not stop attracting it's attention. The streak of blood yearned for it again, but that wasn't the time to act yet. The policewoman had to be given time to assimilate the information, so that it could continue with the plan.

He decided to turn his gaze to the prisoner's room so that he could resist the strong temptation to wear it and go out for another hunting trip.

CHAPTER 15

Cafè Paradise   *March 23th, 2017*

The sky above Café Paradise was completely gray; the clouds shielded the pale sun just below greatly reducing the heat emanating from its rays.

A disheveled Warren Valentine hastily entered the bar, spotting his colleague at the same table two days earlier.

"I seem to have a sort of déjà-vu", she said sipping her black tea.

"Sorry for the delay, did you get my message?", said the boy trying to fix his matted hair.

"Actually… no".

Warren locked the keyboard of his cell phone and noticed that the message was still being written.

"Oh shit… sorry I had a busy evening". The girl looked at him from head to toe.

"What is it about? I managed to get in touch with Alessandro Zaretti, I will tell you about it later when Judith will be present".

*Yesterday, around 02.45, I got a call from Ardinson, on the night shift. Another person's disappearance appears to have been reported".

Kathrine put her cup down, interrupting the sipping of her hot tea and giving him a stern look.

"It's Dr. Olivia Palmer, 44, her department manager called after trying to get in touch with her. She should have started the night shift after taking a week's vacation, where no one has had contact with her anymore. He decided to call us for a checkup at her home.

"So she may have disappeared long ago, like the other names on your list?"

"Exactly. That is between the night of Friday 10 March, her last day of work, or the first day of vacation, Saturday 11 March. Tonight they sent a patrol, the front door was not locked. The neighbor said she hadn't seen anyone enter or leave the house, she believed she had always been inside since she had seen the lights on in the living room for the whole week".

" This shouldn't be, the list is getting longer...Any connection with Robert Hudson?"

"None, but the same cannot be said for one of the victims".

Kathrine clenched her fist and showed it relieved, a sign that she did not like to stay on thorns.

"Olivia Palmer was the mother of Lucy Reign, the girl who lost her life in the accident two years ago. We tried to get in touch with her yesterday to find out more about the accident of her daughter and Dylan Rogers".

*I know, I knew her by sight despite not being my doctor. Her father ran a shelter north of Summerville and as a child I crossed paths with her on summer walks up there; I didn't know she was Lucy's mother".

Kathrine put her hands on her face: that nightmare seemed destined to get worse.

After updating Judith and Warren on Dr. Zaretti's message and adding a folder to their office wall, Kathrine was called by Sam Wickett, a colleague of her in the surveillance department.

Sam informed her that the video where the person driving the Volvo from a week earlier appeared was ready and had been transferred to her desktop.

It was not possible to go back to the exact moment when the killer parked the car near Sunset Hill, as the area was without cameras. Even during the theft in the city center car park it was not possible to obtain images, since the internal cameras had been tampered the day before.

The three then followed the development of the video showing the Volvo driving along the main road until the turning of the intersection leading to the ascent of Sunset Hill.

On the recording of the analog clock showed one and forty-two minutes.

"Turn onto Pause Judith. Can we enlarge the images a little?"

"I'm sorry Kathrine, but we can only restart the slow motion video. This format is obsolete and changes such as enlargement or better resolution cannot be made."

After the third slow-motion view Judith pointed to the screen:

"Look here, just as it turns".

The image reflected in a shop showed a clearly visible detail of the person driving the stolen car.

"What is it?" Warren asked, reducing his eyes to two small slits, in an attempt to see better.

The two women looked at each other before inadvertently replying at the same time: "A mask".

In the afternoon they went to review any suspicious sightings reported by the citizens and dug even deeper into the lives of the two faces , whose photographs had been framed on the wall.

Both occupations gave unsuccessful results, the killer seemed to have chosen people with a solitary life or with few emotional ties and had somehow acted without making mistakes.

Eric Preston's girlfriend had only made herself available for a meeting in the next few days, engaged in an important exhibition at the tattoo fair that was going to take place in Indianapolis.

Dr. Olivia Palmer, according to the statements made by her colleague, had dedicated body and soul to her work at the Central Hospital in Summerville after the death of her daughter.

Palmer worked as a general practitioner, since her microsurgery studies were rarely needed in that small town.

So her job had become to assist patients in her office within the hospital, even though she occasionally served to help other doctors with more complex intervention, wherever her help was requested: first aid, operating rooms or complicated interventions that required her presence.

At the end of the working hours Kat's group broke up and everyone left taking different directions.

Kat's thoughts that night were very negative: they hadn't been able to find out much, but she didn't want to get more killer addresses because that would meant dealing with a new victim.

On a poster of a newsstand near her, you could read about the accident of Dylan Rogers caused by a possible serial killer and two elderly people animatedly discussed it among themselves.

While walking towards the historic center to go to the grocery store, she decided to make the phone call she had in mind to make from the day before.

She dialed the number on the card by copying it from the business card she still had in her right jacket pocket.

"Hallo?"

The voice on the phone seemed sad and tired, Kat was about to hang up, but decided to go all the way.

"Hi, I'm Kathrine Steward. I wanted to ask you a couple of questions that buzz my head, if I can".

*Since when do you ask me if you can ask me questions? What makes you think I'm going to answer you, miss Steward? It seems to me that I've already done enough for you and I'm not going to help you.

"Mr. Hackett, I wanted to inform you that no one on my team has said anything personal about your account to the press, including myself. There must have been a leak".

Kat perceived the anger of the man on the other end of the phone, who had began to speak through gritted teeth and raising the tone of his voice more and more.

"A leak? Damn bitch, what else do you want from my life? I spent two hellish days, my wife took the children and left, the shares of Grey Insurance suffered a drastic collapse, not to mention my associates and employees who struggle to even look at me! All this because of you and your fucking leak!"

"I wanted to know if any of these names mean anything to you, it would be of great help for…"

The sentence remained suspended in the middle, Tom Hackett had interrupted the line, not having the intention of collaborating, as she had imagined herself.

After arranging the shopping, Kat put on her running gear, attached the headphones to the phone and started the application that monitored the route and the speed with which she ran, in order to calculate the calories burned.

Went out in the freezing air just in time to admire a fantastic sunset: the cloud accompanied the descent of our star behind the mountain, tinged with various shades of red and orange.

She decided to walk the road around her neighborhood, she would later choose whether to go down to the heart of the city or move to the woods.

The usual thoughts immediately jumped to her mind, accompanied by a song of which she did not remember the title or the name of the artist.

During the afternoon the three had come to the conclusion that the next target of the killer renamed *The Mask* would have been Olivia Palmer and not Eric Preston.

This is because the murderer seemed to be going backwards compared to the timeline in which those five people had disappeared.

She turned left on a wooden bridge reserved for pedestrians only and noticed a black SUV following her at a walking pace just beyond, on the roadway where motorcycles and cars could pass.

She saw him stop in a rest area immediately afterwards: that case was making her paranoid.

According to her reasoning, Robert Hudson first kidnapped four people, and then killed them one by one following the order of disappearance in reverse, starting with his wife.

What she just couldn't explain was the reason. Jealousy, hate, revenge, love? What had gone into his brain to involve other people in his diabolical game, and by what criteria had they been chosen? What were they guilty of?

She looked on her mobile phone screen: she had now reached the half-way point of ten kilometers when she turned onto the dirt road which, before the construction of the tunnel, had been the only way to reach the other side of the mountain.

She realized she had an untied string, so she stopped to bend over her running shoes.

The program automatically went into pause mode and with it also the music production.

This allowed her to hear wheels rub on the gravel where the road separated from the main path; her breathing became even more labored when she saw the headlights of the SUV previously encountered pointing towards her.

She ran with her heart in her throat, as fast as she could, leaving her earphones dangling against her shirt: nobody lived along that road and as far as she knew, she had never seen a car drive it.

The eyes and throat began to burn, the leg muscles were brought to the maximum effort, even if she knew all this could not last long; she was beginning to feel the production of lactic acid and the consequent drop in speed.

She knew of the presence of an old tunnel just ahead, and if she remembered right, the entrance was protected by a rigid steel bar. There was no alternative: she absolutely had to reach it.

The SUV gained meters, Kat forced herself to point the road in front of her, resisting the strong temptation to turn around. Very little was missing, she ran awkwardly and unevenly, but the old tunnel began to appear behind the curve.

With a leap she jumped the metal rod recalling all the energy left in the body, just before the car stopped, turning literally with a steering, raising a cloud of dust a few meters behind her.

As soon as she saw no man or mask opening the door to chase her, she slowed slightly, while continuing to walk the tunnel in search of a way out.

Immersed in darkness and terror, she proceeded for about ten meters, trying to catch her breath and glimpse something, now that her eyes were getting used to the darkness.

About twenty seconds later, a lamppost illuminated the arch and the side which marked the exit of the tunnel and the end of that suffering: once outside she would have reached the petrol station going straight for another hundred meters, saving herself.

A figure positioned itself exactly where light and shadow met, with a rapid movement it appeared from the rocky wall next to the exit of the tunnel to meet her.

Kat stopped to quickly turn on herself, ready to retrace her steps.

Immediately discarded the idea as soon as she saw the beams of two torches illuminate her face: she was trapped.

She decided to face the only individual who separated her from the freedom for which she started in her direction.

The person in front of her raised his hands and stepped back, until the white light of the neon could fully reveal his identity.

She had seen that man before, though she didn`t remember exactly where.

"Kathrine Steward! You have to listen to me, I need your help", he said making his echo loud inside the tunnel.

In that instant she recognized the man: he was the rich Russian tycoon present on numerous covers of *Forbes* Magazine. What was he doing here?

He approached her until she noticed his sad look, while his henchmen slowed the race down.

"My daughter is missing. Only you can help me".

PART TWO

Sin and Punishment

CHAPTER 16

Summerville Spa   *One day before, March 22*th*, 2017*

Victoria Varichenko hated Summerville.

It was for this reason that she had chosen to spend the whole afternoon in the largest and most expensive wellness center in the whole region and not to follow her father in those tiring and useless unhinging in the woods.

For the same reason one of those typical father-daughter discussions was born where the same digs were thrown each time, the same opinions expressed and always ended in the same one, identical manner: her abrupt exit from the scene in which she deliberately slammed the door of the room, with such force as to make the glass of the veranda vibrate.

She pushed the button to start the whirlpool and the heated pool started to jump and fill with bubbles.

Victoria leaned her head against the edge, causing her thick golden crown to fall out.

Her straight blond hair were arranged in a radial pattern on the marble tiles, under the irritated eyes of one of the attendants and of numerous customers forced to wear a cap.

Certainly no one would have opened their mouth to make comments or would have approached her.

Anyone who had turned on the TV at least once in the past six years, would have learned of her bad temper and the haughty manner in which she gave orders.

Because Victoria Varichenko wanted and could afford it unlike the other subordinates she dealt with on a daily basis.

Her parents had always spoiled her like a princess, given up the use of the word "NO" for too long.

The problem was, that satisfying the whims of a six-year-old girl meant covering her with toys, while fulfilling the wishes of an eighteen-year-old girl, meant allowing her to do anything that went through her mind.

The fact that her father was the founder of HiRuski, the largest Russian telephone company, made it difficult, almost impossible to restrict the limits and funds necessary for Victoria to be able to express her power and demonstrate her superiority.

Unfortunately she had been forced to follow him in that stupid remote town, in order to carry out the photo shoot for the next advertising campaign.

Her face would appear in the insignia of the tallest skyscrapers in Moscow, but the compromise to be able to realize her new dream was to spend two weeks in the company of her father, in a house that could not even remotely satisfy her tastes.

The promise made to her father, however, did not mean to spend her days removing cobwebs from her face or ruining her pedicure by traveling kilometers of slopes and slopes with her feet locked in heavy mountain boots.

Therefore Victoria had thought of doing what she did best, namely swiping her credit card in the most exclusive places in town.

She was still undecided on how to spend the evening, but for now the local casino, disco and gourmet restaurants had deeply disappointed her.

The girl got out of the tub to head towards the sauna revealing the two-piece colored swimsuit she had advertised last spring.

The Russian beauty was enchanting: the slender body was highlighted by the posture and the walk typical of high fashion catwalks, adding an additional touch of class and femininity that made her untouchable and confident. The fine and straight hair was actually very black and well hidden under the platinum blonde tint and reached exactly at the edge of the costume, perfectly proportioned to the 185 cm inherited from the father.

The skin did not have the classic pallor of Eastern girls and her eyes were light brown, warm and unique, in stark contrast to the gray-blue irises of the majority of her peers in Moscow.

The genetic makeup left by the Spanish mother made it a unique and atypical beauty in the entire Soviet territory.

She noticed with pleasure that the wooden docks of the sauna at 80 degrees were empty, so she took the towel, delivered at the entrance, and lay on it, returning to her thoughts.

She loved her father, so after the divorce she chose to stay in Moscow with him and not to move to Barcelona as her mother had done.

Despite the quarrels and misunderstandings, she had a profound esteem for that electronic engineer who alone had had the courage and the ideas to give rise to such an important undertaking at just 27 years.

Small drops of sweat were now beginning to run down her smooth, red skin, but the hourglass on the wall was only half empty, which meant another five minutes of stay.

She still had to buy a birthday present for her father, soon they would celebrate dinner in one of the most elegant restaurants in the Russian capital surrounded by the stocky faces of his minions and those of his associates jackals, Is it possible he did not realize it? How could he not despise them and treat them so well? Sometimes she would have liked to have a more cynical and ruthless father, but in retrospect, only one with those qualities in the family was enough.

When the last grain of red sand passed through the narrowest part of the hourglass, Victoria Varichenko was exhausted from the sauna.

The next day she would be able to involve her father in another activity so that both could spend time together, but not to reveal that fragile and needy part of love hidden in her soul, she decided she would spend the evening getting drunk in Summerville's premises, just to make him feel a little apprehensive and not let him have won too easily.

On the other hand there was nothing she could do: a Varichenko always gets what they wants.

CHAPTER 17

Gas Station, North of Summerville   *March 23th, 2017*

The ticking of the Rolex on Ivan Varichenko wrist was the only sound Kat could hear inside the gas station. A grave silence reigned supreme after the Russian had finished recounting the events of the day before.

The shop assistant had gone out to refuel the two cars as soon as they arrived under the watchful and attentive gaze of the two bodyguards sitting in the black SUV parked just outside.

The watch and the two gorillas betrayed the alien appearance that Ivan had been forced to take on to conceal his identity.

Sitting at the far corner of the table at the back of the room, dressed in a red and black checkered shirt, a pair of camouflage pants and mountain boots, he could very well be mistaking for one of the twenty-thousand hikers who explored the surroundings of Summerville every year.

Now the man in front of her silently waited for a reply, showing her an imploring look, under the visor of the Lakers hat.

What I can't understand, Mr. Varichenko, is why you don't want to report the disappearance of your daughter to the authorities, limiting the research involving only one person.

I'm already working on missing people and believe me, I find it difficult to find them even working in a close-knit and efficient team. We have chosen to divulge what little we have discovered to the press, in the hope that some citizens will help us in the research. The fact that you contacted me..." she said, glancing at the SUV"... in private, does not imply that all my research, without counting the help from my colleagues, can be moved to your daughter, you understand me?"

The Russians big hands fell on the table making the two empty coffee cups tremble.

"Nobody needs to know. Not even your colleagues", he began to say in precarious English, characterized by a strong Russian accent.

"I received this at eight o'clock this morning in my mailbox. There is no problem, Agent Steward, I will pay any amount for my daughter's release, and I will give you any necessary reinforcement. Victoria and I often quarreled, but she is my only daughter, do you understand?"

Kathrine continued to stare at him as she opened the sheet of paper that was given to her.

"If there is any news, my phone number is at the bottom. Call me at any time of day or night, while I will think about paying on the bank account".

When Kat read the ransom note on which a bank account and a short computer-written text appeared, she realized that it would be impossible for her to refuse the requests made by Ivan Varichenko.

A twenty-four-hour ultimatum ordered the payment of a large sum in exchange of the girl`s life.

He had five million good reasons to hope he could negotiate with the Mask.

CHAPTER 18

Eric Preston's Tattoo Shop   *March 24th, 2017*

Warren Valentine was leaning on the bench in front of the tattoo shop.

For once he was ahead of Kat and Courtney Afford, with whom they had an appointment for nine in the morning.

He was at the mercy of the cold on that cold and sunless morning for a quarter of an hour reading a copy of the *Sunshine*, waiting for at least one of the two women to show up.

He did not know what effect this article would have on people but he hoped, like everyone in the police station, in close collaboration with the inhabitants.

The murders and disappearances of the previous days were attributed to Robert Hudson, whose smiling photo stood out over those of the four faces who disappeared in that period.

The author of the article had nicknamed it *The Mask,* inspired by the photo showing Robert with his face covered and driving the Volvo, printed on the second page.

Once finished the article he felt the vibration of the cell phone in his pants pocket.

"Hallo?"

"When you`re done studying, can you join us at the bar down the street? We have been waiting for you for at least twenty minutes".

"Shit…"

Courtney Afford was sitting on the bench in front of the policewoman and timidly sipping her fresh orange juice with every question she was asked.

Her outward appearance would never have made one think of a shy and reserved person like the one with whom Kat had talked for about ten minutes.

The first thing that stood out was certainly the skin of the arms and neck entirely covered with tattoos, probably performed by her boyfriend. The battle between angels and demons took place from arm to arm under the watchful eye of the trinity painted along the neck. It was difficult to look away from the ring piercing placed between the nostrils or from all those that ran along the contours of both ears, but one could easily get distracted even by studying the hair.

Kathrine would never have been able to even look in the mirror with that fiery red bangs or with that hairstyle, in her opinion horrible, with the Rasta typical of cannabis lovers.

She didn't have any kind of prejudice, but the thing she really couldn't stand in people was exaggeration, like in that case.

After the ritual presentation Warren moved his chair to join the interview.

He appreciated the way Kat conducted the interrogations, that is, the choice of the place where a person could feel more comfortable and exhibit their versions more easily; it was much more likely to get something useful in a bar or in the homes of the people questioned, than in the aseptic room at the police station.

Yet the girl did not seem calm, but it could be understood, as recently her boyfriend and business partner had disappeared into thin air.

"You say he was kidnapped by *The Mask?*"

The two policemen looked at each other: inevitably the involvement of the press had fed the citizen's fears.

"Don't worry Miss Afford. We are following a track that will deliver *The Mask* to us shortly and it is not certain that your boyfriend must necessarily be involved", Katrine lied.

"We are from the missing persons division and we only contacted you now, because last week we know you were at a fair in Indianapolis, can you confirm this?"

The girl nodded and calming down, after shelving the idea of Eric's kidnapping by a murderer, she started talking.

"Yes I had to go there with my cousin, a young apprentice who just entered this world, being unable to back down; you know, me and Eric had to pay a lot for our participation in the event and sponsorship of the shop".

"I'm just going to ask a few short questions to find out more about your past, do you mind?"

Only Warren could have known that his colleague was investigating a possible connection or reason why Robert Hudson would kidnap her boyfriend.

"Of course, if I can help, willingly".

"We understand that your relationship has lasting till now for more than a year, can you confirm that?"

"Yes, one year and seven months to be precise".

"Very well. When did you decide to open your business?"

"Last September and towards October we managed to open the shop".

Warren noticed that finally the girl had stopped fiddling with the straw and started talking more easily.

"How did you manage to finance the license, the equipment and everything you needed in such a short time?"

"Well, Eric thought about everything, he had some money aside, it didn't take long to set up the shop. I remember that while the various companies made changes to the structure, the couriers came to deliver the necessary items in the warehouse at the back of the room".

"We can see that your boyfriend has several years of unemployment , how is it possible that he had so much money aside?"

The girl assumed a doubtful expression: "To tell the truth I don't have the faintest idea He spoke to me a lot about that period without work, but towards August he told me about the sale of one of his paintings at an exorbitant price; it may be that the proceeds from that deal pushed him to realize his dream".

"Eric did anything to make a living, he really wanted to create and work. A misunderstood artist, discarded from any warehouse or carpentry shop only for his physical appearance. He saw people throw away his curriculum and heard comments on his tattoos as soon as he left the premises, until he lost hope and gave up looking for a normal job. At the beginning of summer he had already made about fifty works that he could resell in the summer markets here in Summerville: bracelets, paintings and wooden works. He reinvented himself several times until he succeeded. The shop is booming, you know? Only that …well he…I miss him terribly".

Courtney's eyes became shiny and after a few moments the two policemen began to see the tears flow down her face and fall on the demon face engraved on the back of her left hand.

"I'd say we stole enough of your time. The customers of your shop will be waiting for you, but please do not lose hope: we will do everything possible to track your boyfriend down.

Warren glanced quickly at his colleague, the questioning had seem too short.

They said goodbye to Miss Afford after thanking her for the help in the investigation and as they walked down the sidewalk to the parking lot, Katrine answered Warren's questions, without being asked.

"We have discovered enough Warren, it made no sense to go further, we would have done nothing but worry her further".

Warren turned the wheel of his Zippo until he lit it and brought it closer to the end of his cigarette: "So, a hole in the water, yet another, I would say".

"I don't think so Warren. A boy does not buy the walls of a room and spends more than fifty thousand dollars of equipment with a sale of a simple painting".

"And how do you know about these figures? The shop may be for rent and the material leased".

"I got Judith to do some research. Apparently someone takes their job seriously, operating out of service hours, without arriving late the next morning.

Warren stopped in the middle of the parking lot "Today I was on time".

Katrine pointed the accusing index towards him "Almost Warren, almost…"

After asking a few questions at the Summerville Spa reception, Katrine got into the car to reach the place where she had an appointment with Alessandro Zaretti, the expert in simbology.

She had entrusted Judith and Warren with the task of sifting through the August newspapers in search of some significant event that could enrich Eric Preston in Summerville or within a radius of fifty Kilometers.

In reality she should have participated, but in doing so she could have carried out investigations in private on Victoria Varichenko.

Investigations that had brought only confirmations on the temperament and the haughty ways of the young model.

Once she found a parking place, she crossed the wide open gate of Mellow Park and saw the Italian standing near the fountain. Alessandro Zaretti presented himself with an energetic handshake and a funny smile under a short black mustache.

The dark curls reminded her of an African-American TV host and gave an eccentric appearance in contrast to the serious face and elegant clothing of the young doctor.

Hallo Agent Steward, I arrived as soon as I could".

"Hi Alessandro, let's call us by name, if you don't mind; I prefer to be called Kat unless it's a problem for you".

"That's fine with me, for once I won't have to be called a doctor. Would you mind if I show you what little I know about that symbol, while we walk in the park?"

Kat nodded and together they walked on the road that bordered the artificial lake.

Even with the absence of sun, the temperature had slightly risen in the afternoon and many people were taking advantage of it to take a walk in the park.

"I had to puzzle a lot to remember where I had already seen that symbol, but then finally I remembered where to look, so I rummaged through the notes of the first year of university".

Katrine listened carefully: It would have been a one-way conversation.

"The symbol in question belongs to one of the first populations of men who populated the Earth about 10,000 years ago: the Akkrasa.

The data in our possession are very few and not detailed; most of them are hypotheses developed during the discoveries of pictograms and ideograms found in ancient underground caves of central Africa.

This nomadic tribe was initially composed of a few individuals, but once it reached the Niger valley it managed to establish itself and expand, creating a real community, made up of more than seven hundred units.

Unfortunately the weather conditions and the clashes with other tribes decimated most of the men. About two thirds of the entire Akkrasa tribe lost their lives in just five months.

Dr. Zaretti stopped to buy a bottle of water at the park kiosk.

After drinking nearly half of it in one sip, he continued his speech.

"From here on, everything I will tell you is considered legend; we pass from real historical sources to ancient myths and legends, handed down from generation to generation, so I will not be able to guarantee any truthfulness".

Kat looked at him perplexed; that Italian did not seem exactly the type of person who relies on stories or fables to analyze the past.

"It would seem that the Akkrasa chieftain during a nocturne assault on an enemy population, ended decades of clashes and abuses in one night. The legend tells of a magical weapon, but the versions of its shape and power are manifold: a fiery spear with its own conscience, a stick capable of domesticating ferocious beasts to its advantage, a mask foe seeing on darker nights. There are those who believe in the existence of all these three objects…"

"Wait. Did you say a mask? Do you have any pictures to show me?"

"Unfortunately no. Everything I am telling you can be the result of the imagination of some of our ancestors".

"Come on Alessandro, don`t tell me you still believe in magic or the X-Men superpowers?"

The doctor took a small parcel of candy from his breast pocket, offered one to Kat and then took two for himself.

"I am a historian, so I am not allowed to base my conclusions on mystical events without a plausible explanation.

However none of my colleagues can understand how so few individuals have been able to exterminate an entire tribe made up of about a thousand men in one night and how a tribe of shepherds has been able to expand throughout the African territory in the following years".

Not even Kat could understand what the choices and motivations were, that pushed *The Mask* to act the way he acted. And what were they based on.

The two looked at each other silently. Both looking for answers that could solve their questions.

CHAPTER 19

Summerville Police Station   *March 24th, 2017*

Judith Law smiled contentedly as the result of her research slowly came out of the office printer.

After discarding the various articles selected by Warren, she had found one dated 30. August 2016, that immediately had aroused her curiosity.

Two and a half hour later the pieces of the puzzle seemed to fit perfectly, just in time for the arrival of the colleague in charge of the investigation.

"So Judith, Is there any news?"

"I would say yes, Warren is out smoking a cigarette, but he should come very soon. I think we finally found something.

Katrine noticed that the colleague's words were pronounced with the typical pedantry of the nerds of the class and smiled imagining a young Judith locked up in the school locker.

Warren entered the office greeting Katrine and taking a seat in his chair with a cup of coffee in his hands.

"Did Judith update you on Eric Preston's news, yet?"

"We were just waiting for you before we could start…Warren", she said approaching the desk.

There was no doubt, the Judith of fifteen years ago had certainly been the main target of the school bullies.

"So, it took more than two hours of research to find something relevant, it seems that last August all the criminals thought it well to go on vacation, but....on August 30, 2016 something happened that attracted my attention, at Bridgestone, about 30 kilometers from here".

The blue irises behind the thick lenses of Judith`s glasses controlled how the audience in front of her reacted to that moment of suspense, but since they both seemed slightly irritated, she immediately started talking again.

"At around half past nine in the morning, the Bridgestone bank was robbed of about 150,000 dollars. A man with a covered face entered with a toy gun, managing to deceive the young clerk at the counter, who filled his bag with banknotes, but not Gary Hoffman, a brave citizen who attempted to disarm the thug.

After a violent scuffle, the robber managed to extract a knife and stab Gary in the stomach, collect the duffel bag with the money and flee.

Gary Hoffman was rushed to Summerville Hospital, where he lost his life two hours later.

The security guard who had just delivered the money to the bank come back for a forgetfulness, just as the masked robber was leaving the main entrance.

The van managed to keep up with him up the hill above the station, when the man chose to launch rather than get caught, rolling down the slope until he easily disappeared among the crowd of commuters".

Katrine turned to both colleagues "What makes you think it`s really Eric Preston?"

Warren tried to speak, but was preceded by his exhibitionist colleague. "We are not really sure of his identity, but we contacted Courtney to ask her why in the late summer photo`s

Eric carried plaster on his arm. It appears he broke his arm in a domestic accident.

"And you think he may have broken his arm during the fall from Bridgestone Hill, right?"

The two agents nodded satisfied.

"We can say we found the reason for Eric Preston's guilt that guaranteed him a place among the people kidnapped by Robert Hudson. Adding this to that of Sarah Finningham and Dylan Rogers it would seem that *The Mask* is selecting people with rather serious skeletons in the closet.

Katrine crossed her legs as she flipped through the papers that Judith had just given to her.

"Great job guys. Later we will inform Philip of the progress. The meeting of the professor did not bring much, but if we want to believe the legends, then listen to what I have to say. The mask worn by Robert Hudson could be the same used by a primitive tribe 10,000 years ago; it is not known for what reason but its creation has allowed them to conquer the entire African territory.

What's up, why do you look at me like that?"

Once De La Cruix was informed, the three set the program for the next day, that is to know as much as possible about Olivia Harris. Unfortunately, the team was aware of the low probability of finding those two people left alive, as it had been impossible to predict the moves so far and the place where the killer decided to punish the victims he selected. Actually Kat knew there were three remaining people involved in Robert Hudson's plan, But even if she could not discuss it with her colleagues, the truth is that she could do little to find the hideout of *The Mask*.

This time the killer had left no clue at the previous crime scene, unlike the photograph showing the location of the next crime. Although it was difficult to admit, the chances of a new murder were very high as two days had passed between the discovery of Sarah and Dylan's corpse and two more days had passed since then. Katrine knew that, very soon *The Mask* would hit again. However, investigations into the past of missing persons revealed their hidden side. The killer did not kill innocent people haphazardly, on the contrary, he seemed to follow a purification plan for victims already designated for some time. The choice of that *Mask* was a further unknown factor that could not be answered.

These thoughts accompanied Katrine on the way home, as darkness returned to take over Summerville. Once parked, Kat stayed aboard her jeep keeping the engine running, and making a call enjoying the warmth offered by the heating aimed at her feet.

"I'm Katrine. As I imagined for now, no great news has emerged. Her daughter left no indication as to where she might have spent the evening. Listen to me carefully Mr. Varichenko, I believe that the only way to capture *The Mask* is to establish a safe place where the exchange between your daughter and the requested money can take place, as soon as she will contact you".

"Agent Steward, my only interest is my daughter's life, I don't care about her capture. For this reason , tonight I will make the payment to the account indicated to me".

"Mr. Varichenko, you contacted me to help you, and I'm telling you that this is not the right solution. Nobody can assure you that after having paid the money, you will be able to see your daughter again, perhaps given the timeliness with which you make the payment, They could ask for more money, I ask you to wait just another day. *The Mask* has never made ransom requests before, we have to take advantage of it".

There was a short pause, then the Russian spoke again after talking to other people on the other end of the phone. "The last deadline is twenty-four hours. Tonight I will pay the ransom. Continue your research and keep yourself ready for any developments, Agent Steward".

Katrine stared at the number disappearing from the screen and put Ivan Varichenko's business card inside the bag, then got out of the car cursing to herself.

As she was approaching the front door, she noticed a figure trying to peek inside one of her side windows, so she pulled her gun out and silently approached with slow and suffused steps. She removed the safety from the weapon and pointed it towards the center of the man's body in front of her, to be sure not to miss the target with all that darkness surrounding her. "Raise your hands and turn slowly if you don't want me to shoot you in the head. I have a gun and I intend to use it if you don't tell me what you are doing outside my house". The man obeyed raising his hands slowly and turned around.

Katrine lowered the weapon leaving her arms along her body.   "Zack?"

CHAPTER 20

Kat's Apartment, 25 Elm Street   *March 24th, 2017*

"What the hell are you doing here?"

The adrenaline experienced until recently had given way to old, uncomfortable feelings as soon as the scent of her ex boyfriend was perceived by the receptacles of her sense of smell.

Five years hadn't been enough to forget the fragrance emanating from his clothes, his confident walk and his hazel eyes.

He hadn't changed at all, the tanned face had remained the same, as had the well-groomed Chuck Norris beard and mustache. The only difference with the American actor was the color of the hair modeled with gel and the new hairstyle that reminded her of a young Bradley Cooper on the set of *Wedding Crashers*. Kat recognized the beige sweater she had given him for Christmas. It was still very beautiful, as was his owner, and it was able to highlight his powerful chest and the muscle mass of his arms and shoulders.

It was difficult to change a person's style, she thought as soon as she saw the pair of light jeans ripped on the knee, the latest purchase of numerous identical models that had filled Zack's closet over the years.

She felt her body melting and her brain go haywire, it was incredible how in critical situations she managed to maintain the necessary calm and concentration, while with Zack in front of her in flesh and bones, her hands seemed not to want to stop shaking.

"Katrine, finally. I tried to look for you everywhere. Did Philip tell you I was at the station?"

Kat could not open her mouth or move the muscles needed to escape Zack's embrace: she was completely dazed, but this time it was not a dream, she was sure of it.

After abandoning herself to that embrace, the cause of the end of their relationship came back to her mind and suddenly reason managed to prevail over the feelings, giving her the strength to push him away.

"Answer my question. What the hell are you doing here?"

"When I heard about your return to Summerville, I came to the airport to see you, but you didn't notice me. Then I went to our old house, believing you had gone back to live there, but I was wrong. So I went to Philip who didn't want to tell me where you were and advised me to leave you alone…"

"I'm indebted to him for the umpteenth time", Kat thought.

"In the end I came up to the apartment where you and Elizabeth lived before you moved to me… and here I am".

Katrine could not hide the fact that she was happy that Zack had looked for her, but this time his gaze would not have deceived her as in the past.

"Why did you come looking for me? Listen Zack, it's over between us, you know that very well. Where is your beautiful French girl, the reason you left me?

"Katrine, you know very well that I only loved you, with Nicole it couldn't work, I fell in it because you were never there, it almost seemed that I didn't exist".

History repeated itself. Of course the blame laid on her, despite the fact that Zack's betrayal was clear: that man would never change.

"Listen to me very carefully: you know very well that you were my point of reference, the only one I could truly trust, but it is only now that you no longer exist for me, can you understand? you betrayed me, you have to take responsibility for your mistakes, as well as all adults: we are no longer teenagers at the mercy of our hormones".

"But Katrine we could try again, give me another chance I…"

"Stop that! you must leave now, leave me alone!"

Katrine had raised a hand to settle the slap that she had wanted so much in recent years and in the dream she had during the flight, but was blocked by the energetic grasp of the man's wrist.

Zack's pleading gaze changed expression becoming very serious. The force in which he applied the pressure of that grasp was greater than necessary and Katrine felt strong anger in the eyes of her ex.

"You prefer that Italian to me, Is that so Kat? I saw you today walking with him in the park, believe me, that man does not deserve you".

Kat lifted the boot and hit him vigorously between his legs, managing to free herself from his grip: no man came out unscathed from that move.

"Get out of here and if you show up again, know that I will not be so good as to lower the gun", she said as he writhed in pain in front of her feet.

With her heart in her throat, she stepped over him and after entering her house, she closed the lock and pulled the chain, feeling finally safe. She could not believe what she had just done.

A part of herself still wanted him, it was not easy to enter in his heart, just as it was not easy to get out of it, and their story had been the only one really relevant in her life.

But the other Katrine, the one who was struggling to get out of that relationship now over, had finally won, prevailing over old memories of a love that had come to an end.

So it was that happiness and a sense of liberation that invaded her heart, allowing her to do something that she hadn't been able to do for a long time: cry.

The metallic noise in the other room was starting to get annoying.

Eric Preston had not yet resigned himself and consisted with his futile attempt to escape: it consisted in rubbing the steel of the chain that joined the two rings tight around the young man's wrists, again the rusty tube to which he had been handcuffed.

Fortunately no one within two kilometers could have heard the noise and complaints from the refuge and the person in the center of the room could even afford the luxury to listen to the CD inside the stereo.

The *Killing Me Softly* melody of the Fugees came out of the speakers and spread through the corridor where the tool case and everything needed to complete the next passage of the prefixed plan was placed.

Once he put on his overalls, he covered his face with his balaclava, leaving only the colored contact lenses visible, then put on his boots and tied the strings as tight as possible.

He took the mask from the table and put it on, than put everything he needed in a black bag and carried it on his shoulder. He put the volume louder and started to chuckle: The song was just the right one for its situation.

CHAPTER 21

Kat's Apartment, 25 Elm Street *March 25th, 2017*

The ticking of the rain against the windows, woke up Katrine three minutes before the alarm programmed on her alarm clock.

She slowly opened her eyes and after checking the time on the electronic clock, moved the covers and sat up on the edge of the bed.

She took a sip of water from the bottle on the bedside table and unplugged the cell phone from the charger, checking if there were any messages.

She found one from an unknown number which arrived about an hour ago, but the only active vibration on the device, had not been enough to wake her.

After unlocking it she pressed the key to read the text message "Road to Sunset Hill number 43, I thought you were more awake Katrine Steward, you are disappointing me".

Forty minutes later Katrine parked behind one of the police car with the flashing light still on. After calling Philip De La Cruix, she contacted Judith and Warren to inform them of the new hit by Robert Hudson.

The address indicated a factory that had dealt in the past with the processing of ceramics, bricks and other different types of materials. When Kat had left for Los Angeles she had read about it`s possible closure, which occurred about a month before her return to Summerville.

The factory was an old building dating back to the early twentieth century built entirely of brick. The front door had been forced with a crowbar, while the internal one consisting only of a wooden frame and two large windows, had been broken through so as to make the entrance easily accessible to her and to the other law enforcement officers present. The height of the walls quietly reached five meters and barbed wire invited strangers not to climb over; the chimney stood like an ancient obelisk towards the sky, but for months now the dark smoke that indicated the operation of the structure was no longer escaping.

I the surrounding area the few houses that lined the road had been bought and then transformed into warehouses where the finished product could be stored, thus leaving the building surrounded by woodland only. Kat opened the umbrella and went to the woman in the white cape with the "scientific police" script, and immediately identified her as Judith, despite having part of the face covered by the hood and not wearing glasses.

"Have you already entered Judith?"

"Yes, I took a quick look, but I was waiting for you to start taking fingerprints, even if I think there is no need; the severed finger has enamel, so it must be Olivia Harris".

The rain managed to hide the panic from Katrine`s face, only she could know that the women involved were two.

"Compare the DNA with the samples taken at her home anyway, can you tell me something else?"

"She still carries the faith with her name and that of her husband, otherwise I prefer you make a first impression without my hypotheses influencing you. Here is Warren".

The policeman got out of the car and walked towards the two women, regardless of the flood.

"What is it about? Eric Preston?"

"No. The ring finger found belongs to a woman. I could get there, you know? In fact I should have gotten there before", Warren put a hand on her shoulder. "How? We did everything possible Kat, no clue was left the last time".

"But yes, you see up there? That is the rock with the Akkrasa symbol. Thinking about it, when I went up on the rock and found the symbol, I concentrated solely on that. If I had looked further, I would have noticed how the first structure that leaps out of sight, is the factory chimney. Behind it, if you look towards the city, the most imposing structure and closest to the place where Dylan Rogers was killed is the Summerville hospital, where Olivia worked. Not to mention that Dylan`s finger was nailed to the table pointing in this direction, in short, only now have I been able to get there".

"Don`t be too hard on yourself Kat. Now let`s go in and do our job properly. If this killer is playing to get caught, let`s satisfy him.

As soon as you entered the factory you could perceive a strong smell of burnt meat, like that of a chop left on the grill for too long.

In the largest room several industrial ovens were lined up along the walls, Katrine could count six of them. The ovens were dusty and all had the hatch sealed except the one at the far end in the left corner of the room, that had been polished, recently turned off and left with the door open.

The three approached positioning themselves in front of the opening, looking inside.

"Empty", said Kat, as she pointed to the muddy footprints of a boot leaving the room and entering the adjacent closet. Even the small closet was empty, except for a steel cart placed in the center, from which drops of blood slowly fell on the ground. The upper surface of the trolley was covered with blood and a ceramic vase with the same symbol found on the rock could be seen, imprinted on the side exposed in their direction.

Kat came over to lift a scalpel from the pool of blood and show it to colleagues, so she thought it was appropriate to lift the lid of the jar. With one hesitant hand she lifted the lid of what seemed to be Pandora`s box, containing the evils of the world, then helped by Judith she inclined it to pour the contents into a plastic bag.

The bag was filled with still hot ashes and all three realized that they had what was left of Olivia Harris in their hands.

While Judith was drawing blood to make a comparison, Katrine and Warren had returned to the industrial oven to recreate the events that occurred during the night.

"What do you think happened? Let`s compare the hypotheses".

Warren sighed as he glanced at the pressure and temperature gauges located on the outside of the oven pipes.

"Let's see, given that the internal capacity of the oven is 5 cubic meters, for me Robert cut Olivia`s ring finger on the trolley with the scalpel, maybe he inflicted injuries to punish her with the same criterion as Dante, as you said the other day, and then forced her into it. These ovens reach temperatures between 1000 and 15000 degrees capable of dissolving any tissue and I believe also the bones of a human being, until pulverized".

"Yes, even for me it went like this, but there is one thing that just doesn`t come back to me".

Warren studied the corners of the inner chamber of the oven, finding some remains of ash:

"What`s all this about?"

"Well there are no blood leaks along the floor, only in front of the oven and on the trolley in the other room, how can you explain this to me?"

"It would have been difficult to find them inside the oven because the heat would have certainly evaporated any type of liquid inside, once brought to such high temperatures. The killer may have simply cut her finger in front of it by resting it on the trolley and then moved it while the oven was running. Or knowing how clean and precise he is, he may have laid a cellophane or a sheet".

"What are you saying Warren, I think highly unlikely , what is the point of not staining the floor?"

"Katrine, we are dealing with a maniac. As far as I know this is the way he wants to express his design, his vision. In the past we have been dealing with very scrupulous cleaners. One woman spent a whole night cleaning the floor where her partner had been killed, while the neighbor called the police after finding his pieces inside the black bags visible in the home garden. Even the animals found it hard to get close to them because of the smell they gave off".

"Okay, maybe you're right, so we agree as to how the murder took place, a bad, bad way to die…"

"Yeah…I think it's the worse way to be able to leave, do you agree?"

"I believe that the death that scares me the most is that of drowning. Especially when you're trapped- Imagine the water going up, while you realize you have no escape…brrr I have the chills. Listen Warren I'm going over to Judith to figure out what the next clue is. We hope to anticipate it at least next time".

"Okay, I'll stay here, then I'll go out and smoke a cigarette. Ah Katrine I forgot…"

"Yes Warren, tell me?"

"I was wondering if you'd like to go out to eat something tonight or tomorrow if you prefer. So to distract you for a second from this trail of corpses, and tomorrow is Sunday, if you don't mind seeing us out of service, noticed that both are not on duty".

Kat looked at him in amazement, While Warren's cheeks turned red; Had he just invited her to dinner while they were at a crime scene discussing ways to die?

"Warren, I will think about it, tomorrow my sister probably comes back from her vacation, I haven't seen her for almost two months. I'll let you know. Agree?"

Warren watched as she joined Judith.

"I'm an idiot", he thought.

Judith had almost finished gathering the items to compare, when she noticed Katrine's presence behind her.

"Found something?"

"The only thing that doesn't come back to me is the absence of blood on the floor. Can you tell me exactly where the finger was cut?"

"I believe not in this room, nor in the vicinity of the oven. Robert must have cut it elsewhere. I believe with a nipper, you also know very well that it would not be possible to cut bones with a scalpel, right?"

"Yes Judith, please also tell Warren later. Why the scalpel and the blood on the trolley then?"

"I don't know, you say they can be part of the next clue?"

"I don't think, the scalpel is a clear reference to Olivia's work, maybe it's not her blood, it's still too early to draw conclusions. In my opinion, the real clue is the ceramic vase. Can you tell me something more?"

I'm sorry, it's a simple ceramic vase, probably produced here some time ago. The only relevant thing is the symbol on it, so far it has always been present on the crime scenes".

Katrine frowned.

"No. In the room with Sarah Finningham we didn't find anything Judith".

"Actually this morning I wanted to inform you of this detail that I discovered just last night, while I was looking at the photos of the graffiti on the wall".

Judith pulled out her cell phone and showed her the zoomed photo of the graffiti found at 27 River Street.

"You're right, even if really well hidden in the flames, this would seem to be the drawing on the rock. I hadn't noticed".

"Impossible to notice. This image has been enlarged and during the first investigations we did not give much importance to the drawing".

"It will mean that we will be more careful this time. Look Judith, nothing significant has emerged about Olivia's past, right?"

"Exact. Olivia Harris is the doctor to whom most of Summerville's inhabitants turned to. As far as we know, Harris career is a Nobel Prize winner, no mistakes or braking the rules. An Agent is studying her Agenda, but if she knew Robert or Sarah, I repeat, it would not be a relevant detail".

"So no connection other than that with Dylan Rogers. Last morning, however, I reread the articles related to his trial. The woman granted him forgiveness when insufficient evidence was found to arrest him for driving under the influence of drugs or in a drunken state, as initially suspected. The lawyer hired by the wealthy parents convinced the judge to analyze the case better, describing how the incident actually happened, or because of an external element, probably a deer, which forced the boy to steer suddenly and to swerve the car until it ended off the road and against a tree.

After a first sentence, the judge decided to change his mind, simply condemning him to house arrest, perhaps also because of his young age".

" Yes, I remember those articles and also Olivia's declarations against Dylan: she understood that it was an accident mainly due to the road conditions and the presence of the animal".

"We have to find out why the killer killed Olivia and at the same time try to save Eric Preston, before it's too late, based solely on this ceramic vase".

"Exactly Katrine, and like the rest of the investigations, it won't be easy to get something out of it".

"I say you two can end up here. I take care of the vase, I will send you and Warren looking for something useful at Harris's House and in her office at her hospital, call me as soon as you discover something, okay?"

"Of course Katrine, I'll let you know something as soon as I'm done, call later".

Katrine gave Warren new directions, then went out in the pouring rain when the cell phone rang.

"Hallo?"

"Agent Steward, I'm Ivan Varichenko. I just got another message. My guards stopped a young boy, he only received directions and took money to deliver me an envelope with a letter".

"What was written on the letter?"

"Indications of a place I do not know, I need you to go and save my daughter, I'll see you at the gas station like last time, okay?"

"I'll be right there, Mr. Varichenko, I don't want you to go alone and unarmed, I'll see you there in twenty minutes".

"Okay Miss Steward, but don't worry…I'm never unarmed".

Kat's jeep drove off, lifting the muddy ground under the startled eyes of her colleagues.

CHAPTER 22

Gas Station, North of Summerville *March 25th, 2017*

The black SUV waited with the engine running in the parking lot of the service station north of Summerville. Once the jeep was next to the passenger window, she waited for the glass to slowly lower, before she noticed the Russian's worried face.

"Do you know this address?"

Kat slightly stretched her neck to see more clearly the address indicated on the card that the trembling Russian showed her.

"Yes, it should be the square where commuters leave their cars to take the train. They stay there all day, it's a nonpaid public parking and I don't think it's even controlled".

Lightning lit the sky above the two cars and the immediate noise of the thunder that followed, indicated the immediate proximity of the point where it had fallen.

"You go ahead, we will follow you".

The black jeep made a U-turn and as soon as the SUV got into its trajectory, it got out of the stop and started towards the exchange point. The rain increased and Katrine was forced to increase the speed of the wiper; it looked like someone up there was throwing buckets of water on the windshield.

As soon as the jeep crossed the gate of the parking lot, Kat noticed very few cars parked inside.

On the other hand it was Saturday, many people did not work, so she stayed in the car while he was walking along the fence that bordered the ground.

The SUV seemed to have read her mind because she made the same maneuver, in doing so the drivers of the two vehicles scrutinized scrupulously outwards symmetrically, looking for a car or a place where the mask could have hidden Victoria.

Once they reached the end of the huge square the two made contact by phone, avoiding exposure to that incessant downpour.

"I don`t see anything, do you think they deceived us Agent Steward?"

"I don`t know, we will keep looking, but I don`t like this".

The cars crossed and walked the paths in reserve, giving a more accurate look as far as possible, keeping cell phones at hand, in case one of them noticed something, but even this attempt proved in vain.

On the third lap Kat`s gaze rested on the rubbish bin at the center of the square.

"Holy shit, don`t tell me that…"

The jeep accelerated by steering , to get as close as possible to the dumpster, then Kat pulled the handbrake and went out to open the umbrella.

Ivan imitated her and began to run quickly towards the dumpster, crying and cursing something incomprehensible in Russian as he reached her.

A small box hung along one of the metal edges of the dumpster and when Ivan opened it, he dropped a cut finger in the mud under his feet.

The Russian knelt down crying, while one of his bodyguards tried to console him and the other held the umbrella over his head to protect him from the rain.

Kat put a hand on his shoulder and was seized with a sense of melancholy and a lump in her throat that prevented any word of comfort. Then she went to the waste container and pressed the pedal, thus lifting the lid.

Inside there was nothing but rubbish bags, but Kat did not have the courage to open one to check its contents, so she let a furious Ivan approach to the thankless task, after removing a snap knife from the pants pocket. Kat noticed something inside the box, grabbed the end of what appeared to be a messy note and when she read it, she knew that maybe they would have another chance.

Even if the yellowed and sodden paper was about to melt, the text on it was legible, "If you want your daughter back in one piece , you must make a final deposit of 10.000.000 dollars by Monday, on the same account as last time.

Kat put a hand on her forehead and started to catch her breath while a wild Ivan Varichenko vented his anger against the garbage contained in the black bags.

CHAPTER 23

Centro commerciale di Summerville   March 25th, 2017

After lunch Katrine decided to look for information on the vase found at the brick factory at the ceramic and objects vendors in the Summerville mall.

Katrine and Ivan Varichenko had agreed to make the payment as far ahead as possible, to avoid other games by the killer and to have more time to devote to the investigations.

She knew that Varichenko would pay, she believed it was the only way to hope that he would see his daughter alive, but that morning had served her to frighten her cuts out and to make another important decision: she would have involved her colleagues.

It wasn't fair to them, much less to Eric Preston's and she knew she could trust them, surely they would have avoided talking to someone about it. She leaned against the bar counter and ordered a decaffeinated coffee, looking for *Sunshine's* copy.

She found it in the hands of an elderly gentleman and as soon as she was able to read the title she approached it and took it from his hands.

"Excuse me sir, I`ll give it back immediately".

The old man was about to reply, but after seeing the neckline of that young girl, he gave up and continued to examine her curves in silence, while she was intent on reading the newspaper.

The front page article revealed important details of the police investigations known only to her team and Philip De La Cruix.

"Are the police groping in the dark?" It was the title that could be read on the front page and in detail it was told how the *Ghostbusters* had been interested in an ancient African legend instead of investigating the dangerous serial killer that circulated free on the streets of Summerville.

But it was not the article itself that bothered her most: in the article was written the identity of the author of the robbery that took place last summer in Bridgestone, Eric Preston.

Kat decided to repress the instinct that was suggesting her to blame one of her comrades, but decided to take note of the journalists name and change her mind again about involvement in the Varichenko case.

She left the paper on the table and went back to the counter to finish her coffee, under the curious gaze of the man she knew he was studying her rear.

The cell phone rang and Katrine answered promptly after seeing Judith`s name on the screen.

"Tell me everything".

"Here I am Kat, I`ll list you the various news. First of all the cell phone from which you received the message was made out to Olivia Harris, we sent a patrol to follow the signal and the result was disastrous: those poor were forced to chase a goat under the flood to the top of Mount Turson, and then find it tied to the body with adhesive tape".

" That bastard is really fucking us".

"Yeah…later I can confirm that both the severed finger and the blood on the cart belongs to Olivia Harris. The footprints are the same found at 27 River Street and the killer did not leave any traces or fibers that could help us further".

"So no news".

"No news. I'm going to reach Warren, for the moment he has not found anything in the house, I hope it will be better once he probed her office at the hospital".

"Okay Judith, we'll talk later".

Kat hung up with a new question buzzing around her head. Who had passed the information on to the *Sunshine* reporter? It must have been a person between Judith and Warren.

As soon as they had passed the sliding doors of the hospital entrance, the two policemen were hit by a jet of hot air. After showing the police badges to the woman sitting behind the reception desk, Judith and Warren were accompanied by a young nurse to Harris's office.

"I'll try and look for something on the computer, you browse every single medical record present in this room".

Warren nodded and, after taking the first of several binders placed in the closet behind the desk, began to leaf through it while Judith fiddled with the computer's keyboard.

"Maybe I found something, look at this Warren".

Agent Valentine closed the file in his hands and placed it on the pile of other documents previously probed, then leaned towards the screen, approaching Judith, so as to allow her to inhale the scent of his delicate aftershave.

"See, there is a folder hidden among those created automatically when a new program is installed and it has been renamed "letters of apology".

"What are you waiting for? Open it Judith!"

"I can't, access is protected by a password and it's the only time I've been asked since I turned on the computer".

"Mhmm…usually a password must contain a capital letter, at least a number and a length of not less than eight characters".

The policewoman seemed surprised by her colleague's computer skills, from which the proximity began to make her feel slightly uncomfortable: it was centuries that a man was not so close to her.

"We just have to try it, let's see…let's try Olivia250573, it's her date of birth".

Judith pressed the keys on the keyboard and an error message appeared on the screen.

"Damn. Some idea?"

"Try with the date of birth of her daughter Lucy, in the accident file I seem to remember it was reported on June 18, 97".

Judith pressed the keys until Lucy18697 appeared, but the error message appeared again before their eyes.

"Warren if only it were possible to call a hacker or a brain capable to…"

"Press Lucy191215, it's the date of the accident in which the daughter lost her life".

Judith composed the password on the screen and subsequently opened a Word document under the astonished gaze of the forensic scientist.

"Bingo!"

When Katrine left Philip De La Cruix's office it was six o'clock in the evening and after that afternoon spent in shops for housewives and other various items, storming questions with the salesmen about a very common decorated ceramic vase, she decided to go home.

Her Team probably felt more frustrated than she was and she was already thinking about how to enjoy the weekend, since she hadn't received any messages from Judith nor Warren during the whole afternoon.

"Their probably be at home taking a hot shower to forget yet another day spent groping in the dark, I should do the same", thought Katrine as she opened the umbrella to shelter her from the pouring rain.

As soon as she pressed the unlock button on the keys, the four arrows of her jeep lit up and Kat was able to open the trunk to lay the handbag and the umbrella down.

At that moment the uninterrupted sound of a horn caught her attention and after recognizing Judith's old Renault, she caught a glimpse of Warren driving and on his side the smiling face of his colleague, intent on waving the sheet she was holding in her hands.

Five minutes later the three of them were sitting at the only occupied table of the Café Paradise, while the waitress was starting to move forward with the closing work.

Katrine took the sheet of paper out of the plastic bag and began to read the contents aloud.

"Hallo Mrs. Andrews, I am doctor Olivia Harris and today is February 22, 1997.

I am writing this letter to try to alleviate the huge boulder I have on my conscience, although I know that perhaps I will never have the courage to give it to you.

Believe me, I can`t even look at myself in the mirror and it pains me deeply what I`m going to tell you.

Her husband's operation two weeks ago didn`t go exactly as I told you.

Your Husband did not die immediately after reaching the emergency room, but because of a serious medical error.

You see, when I had to open the neck injury that your husband suffered in the car accident, I accidently cut an artery, I can`t explain how it happened, believe me, but the truth is that your husband lost his life because of my medical error.

Nothing can ever justify my mistake, but I will try to explain them because I have never been able to reveal anything to you.

A month before the surgery, my husband had to give in to the disease that had been devouring him for some time, leaving me and my daughter Lucy alone. We had to sell our house to pay the expenses necessary to buy my husband`s survival equipments, in addition to everything we owned before.

I could not afford to lose my license or go to jail because of the accident caused to your husband, my daughter needed me and so I preferred to act in the most petty way: keep silent and mask my mistake, releasing a bogus medical report and hiding the truth from you.

I know that you can never forgive me , but one day I hope to be able to tell you the truth and have the strength and courage to deliver this confession.

I'll probably burn in hell for what I've done, but if I had to go back I think I would make the same choice.

I am truly sorry, I am a horrible person, selfish and a liar, but first of all I am a mother, just like you, so I had to act that way for the sake of my daughter, I hope you can understand this, I am not asking anything else, Olivia Harris".

Kat looked at her colleagues as she placed the letter inside the transparent envelope.

"I would say we can understand why an industrial oven was chosen to punish Harris's hidden faults. The mask wanted to anticipate the suffering of the eternal flames of the underworld.

I am very proud of you, I just want to remind you that this information must remain confidential, so Philip must not know, at least not before Monday".

Katrine stared both colleagues in the eyes until they both nodded.

"Gentlemen, we have one, maybe two days to anticipate the killer's next move, so I'll spend Sunday studying the case and I'd ask you, Warren, to do the same. Judith, you are on duty tomorrow, so if there is any news, do not hesitate to contact me".

The small team said goodbyes, heading towards their cars, under the incessant rain.

When the two left, Katrine was able to notice an individual standing on the sidewalk on the opposite side of the road, just as she was entering the lane.

She seemed to have seen him even in the open-air parking lot of the shopping center, at least the umbrella with the Grey Insurance logo looked exactly the same.

She rolled down the window after slowing down: "Hey you, are you stalking me? What the hell do you want?"

The individual moved the umbrella slightly, so as to allow her to see his face.

"You should stop behaving like this, otherwise I will be forced to report you, do you understand me?"

A car behind her honked her horn and Katrine`s black jeep was forced to leave in order not to clog the evening traffic.

Across the street, Zack Ebbott watched her leave as he stood motionless under the storm.

CHAPTER 24

Kat's Apartment, 25 Elm Street   *March 26th, 2017*

Katrine got out of bed, went to the bathroom and turned on the shower tap.

She had slept very little since she had spent the Saturday evening, again leafing through the files concerning her case.

She dropped her underwear and bra on the floor and, still dazed by the awakening, she entered under the jet of hot water.

The meeting with Zack the previous evening had slightly disturbed her; in the past he had never behaved in such ways.

She had heard about stalkers, but never imagined she would find herself in such situations.

She decided that if she caught him stalking her again, she would talk to Philip and maybe file a complaint.

As she closed her eyes to avoid irritating them with shampoo, her thoughts passed suddenly to the other unpleasant events that happened that week: in addition to the three murders and the disappearance of Victoria Varichenko, The thing that most pressed her at that precise moment had been the betrayal by one of her colleagues. Yet the previous evening they had both shown enthusiasm for that small step forward that the team had been able to take in the investigation.

When she had finished removing the foam from her body and hair, Kat put on her fuchsia bathrobe and went downstairs to make preparations for breakfast. She placed a bamboo placemat on the edge of the island in the center of the kitchen, inserted the capsule into the coffee maker and subsequently heated a cup of milk in the microwave.

At that moment, for the first time in a week, Kat heard the sound of her bell, so after having fastened her robe tightly to her waist, she headed for the front door.

When she opened the door she thought she could look in the mirror.

She and Elizabeth looked alike like two drops of water, even though her sister was six years younger.

She had chosen to apply red streaks to the ends of her hair, in order to distinguish herself from Katrine, even if this problem had not arisen for five previous years.

"Hi little sister, how are you doing?"

"Elizabeth! What a surprise, I didn`t think I`d see you before tonight".

The two sisters hugged each other and Kat seemed to experience, for the first time in a long time, a great joy in seeing her sister again. The last time she saw her, it went back to the previous summer, Elizabeth had flown to Los Angeles to be able to keep her company for a couple of days.

"Come in, I`ll offer you a coffee. Where`s James?"

"I left him in Amsterdam, now I have a new boyfriend from Spain".

Katrine watched in astonishment at her sister, taking a loose step towards the kitchen and taking a place in one of the raised stools…she followed her on a rampage.

"But what's on your mind? You and James have been married for almost eight years, I don`t understand how you…"

"Calm down Katrine! I was just kidding, he went to see his family, calm down".

Katrine handed her the cup of coffee and refilled the machine's water tank before preparing one for herself.

"Ha ha, If only I could see your face Katrine. You know perfectly well that I wouldn't be so happy without my James. By the way, what about your private life? Any man on the horizon?"

Kat thanked herself for turning her back while she waited for the coffee to come out, so that she could hide her embarrassment to her sister.

"Except for Zack who is literally stalking me, I am talking to a Russian millionaire over the phone, but my mind is literally obsessed with a married man".

"Wow Kat! You have to be careful with married men, you know, they promise you things that…one moment. Don't tell me you're referring to one of your cases".

Katrine sat down, holding her cup in her hands and rolling her eyes.

Katrine, you have to stop thinking only about work, they don't even pay you well…life is also made of relationships, friendship, love, hobbies…you have to come out of it, I am saying this for your own good".

"Elizabeth, don't start with your speeches. I don't have a husband who keeps me and even if it were I would not be able to spend my days between yoga, tennis lessons and complaining about how much noise the neighbors make, so don't attack this speech".

"Sure Kat, sure. Do you see yourself getting slaughtered by some fucking psychopath, who else would care if not me?"

Katrine stared straight at her; it was like seeing herself in a parallel life, a life she would hate.

"Okay Kat, sorry, this was heavy. Listen to me, I am just trying to show you the world from another perspective. I don't want to fight with you, at least not today. Would you like it if we go to the hockey game later? Not even on purpose, today is the derby. It will be just you and me like in the old days, what do you say?"

Katrine emptied the cup with one last, very long sip.

"Okay, but first I'd like you're point of view on the case I'm working on. Sometimes it has proved useful in the past".

Her sister raised her arms in surrender.

"Holy Christ Kat. You will never change!"

Victoria Varichenko saw the door open and her eyes were struck by a blinding light. After a long time spent in complete darkness, they struggled to stay open, but she managed to glimpse the bowl that was being pushed close to the ground and ended its run a few centimeters beside her.

She reached out and heard the tinkling of the chain behind her when she tried to turn around to help herself with the other hand. The chain was very short and ended in a steel collar that did not allow her to stand up or move around a lot.

She had never felt so weak and humiliated, forced to do it and live with the smell of her feces all that time. Her survival instinct forced her to bring the bowl closer to her mouth in order to feed herself. She had skipped the first two meals that had been delivered to her by her kidnapper, for fear of swallowing a poison or the same drug he had used to be able to easily abuse her, but then she understood that there was not much better to do chained in that way, if not to try to survive and continue to hope.

In those days of captivity she had had the opportunity to reflect on her behavior and the mistakes she had made, but nobody deserved to feel what she was now facing.

Once she finished what she thought should have been Sunday lunch, she threw the bowl towards the door and started crying, as she emptied her bladder in the same position she had been forced to since the day her tormentor chained her.

She had never been able to see him well, but she had heard a voice complaining in the distance the previous night and she had not been able to understand, whether it was her kidnapper or another prisoner.

"Who`s there? Who are you?", she repeated several times, but only getting silence as an answer.

A few seconds after pronouncing those words, Victoria heard the sound of footsteps approaching the door of the room and subsequently felt someone repeatedly hit her with a metallic object to lead her to silence. Victoria would have liked to shout and insult her jailer as she had seen in some television series, it would have been the most obvious reaction on her part, but for fear of suffering further violence she decided to remain silent. After the abuse she had done nothing but eat her meals, without hearing anything but the sound of silence.

She endeavored to think of beautiful things, so she decided to relive happy and carefree memories of her life that happened long before her arrival in Summerville.

It was incredible how quickly the transition from exclusive parties, driving of breathtaking vehicles or carefree holidays, to the icy floor of a dark and lost cell had been rapid. Or how a stranger had taken possession of her body, when she herself had discarded the most beautiful and wealthy boys in all of Moscow, sometimes only because she could afford it.

Maybe this was the punishment for her bad behavior towards others.

She laughed at the thought of a sentence she had addressed to a maid while the poor woman was forced to clean the place where she had vomited the previous evening, returning from a party.

That's discusting, you have to be really shitty to do this job", she said proudly, while fiddling with the key ring of her Porsche.

Evidently Victoria would never have imagine that those words would come back to her mind very soon, but in different circumstances.

The crowd present at the exit of the stadium where the hockey game had just ended began to thin out. Katrine and Elizabeth were still in the column at the turnstiles and stared at the flood of colorful umbrellas scattering in the streets of Summerville.

"Well we lost, but ours fought well, didn't they Kat?"

Katrine seemed slightly distracted: she watched people leave with her eyes, but in reality she was lost in her thoughts, as in most of the time spent watching the game.

"Yeah, it was….fun. Listen to me Elizabeth, as far as the photo of that vase is concerned…don't you really remember where you could have seen it?"

"Mhmm no, at the moment I don't remember, but as I already told you I thought I saw a similar one a while ago. Do you have any plans for tonight? Would you like to come over for dinner at our place? I will kook you a nice dish and I will be able to show you photos of Amsterdam, Stockholm and Madrid in complete tranquility.

"No thanks, I already have a commitment", said Kat imagining the three of them sitting at the table eating the only dish that her sister could cook, scallops with beer.

Evidently the kitchen was not in the Steward's DNA.

"What is it about? A boy? Indeed no, I understand, I don't want to know".

Katrine gave a friendly shoulder to her sister who stepped back.

"But what are you insinuating?"

"Nothing, it will simply be the usual dinner where you and Philip or an ugly and full of pimples colleague will only talk about corpses and how evil the human being is. The usual things: bullets 18 caliber found at the crime scene…traces of semen found on the victim and therefore possible sexual violence and blab, bla bla…".

"Stop fooling around with your sister. Bring respect for the profession I do, at least once".

"Let's not start again Kat. you're right, then now that you've become famous…also you and your team have discovered the reasons why the killer is chasing those people. All four are guilty of past crimes, you have been really smart, this I have to admit".

Katrine stopped suddenly and was hit by the man with the Summerville Tigers uniform behind her.

"And how do you know that we have discovered the faults of all four people involved?"

"Wake up Kat! Internet. While you were at the toilet a little while ago, I started to look at the facts of the day and I read the first page of the *Sunshine* of today.

Elizabeth took her cell phone out of her bag and started the application, showing Katrine how *Sunshine* had informed her readers of the letter found by Warren and Judith on the afternoon of the day before.

"Sorry Elizabeth, I'm running away. Thanks for this afternoon and please, let me know if you can think of where you saw that vase".

He sister was amazed as Katrine started running straight for the jeep.

"Hi Warren, I'm Kat…I was wondering if you were still available for that dinner tonight".

Katrine heard the background voices and the clinking of glasses typical of crowded bars that showed the live hockey game just ended.

"Of course Kat, just give me half an hour to get ready, see you at Sergio's, I'll reserve a table. Do you know where it is?"

"Yes Warren. See you there in half an hour, see you later".

She had avoided telling her colleague that this was the restaurant most frequented by her and Zack during their relationship, but it did not seem appropriate to make fun of or point out a very relevant detail.

She had to clarify that matter once and for all and as soon as possible, in a face-to-face meeting with her colleague.

CHAPTER 25

Sergio's

The Italian restaurant overlooked the main street of Summerville, but the summer terrace was facing the river almost full, avoiding, for the customers, the smog caused by traffic and the noise.

The restaurant is run by Sergio and his wife Cristina for more than thirty years, since the two newlyweds had decided to move from Naples to Summerville in order to transmit their passion for cooking to the city`s customers.

Katrine waited under the shelter across the street, safe from the rain, dressed in the same denim skirt worn in the afternoon. The pantyhose ended in a pair of rain-soaked ankle boots that were freezing her toes. Therefore, since Warren had once again exceeded the time of their appointment, she opened her umbrella to walk the crosswalks so she could warm up inside the room.

"Cristi, come and see who has returned from the city of angels. My favorite detective, Katrine Steward".

Sergio greeted her with a wide smile hidden under his thick gray mustache, then, having put a hand on her side, a bit too close to the maximum allowed limit, accompanied her to the kitchen pass.

"What a pleasure to see you, you are in excellent shape. Let me give you a good kiss, wait for me to come out for a second".

The corpulent Cristina took off her apron and went out through the sliding doors of the kitchen, then kissed Kat`s cheek, sprinkling her with a strong smell of French fries.

"I too am very happy to see you both, I have been waiting for five years to taste my favorite pizza again".

"Sergio`s four seasons, excellent choice my daughter, but tell me...who is the lucky knight who reserved the table a little while ago? I didn`t understand on the phone, Valentino o Valeriano?"

"No Cristina, he must have said Valentine, that's his last name. His name is Warren and he`s just an office colleague".

Her sweet eyes narrowed until small wrinkles appeared over her plump cheeks.

"My dear, even if it is a colleague, when a man invites you to our restaurant, it can only mean that he has a soft spot for you, trust Aunt Cristina".

At that moment the doors of the restaurant opened wide and Warren made his appearance, while trying not to wet the doormat with the tip of the umbrella with the words "Welcome" and greeted Katrine with a nod.

The lady winked at Kat and then disappeared into the kitchen, while Sergio directed them towards the table next to the window.

"Sorry I`m late, I went home to change".

Warren looked different in his shirt and elegant trousers and Katrine regretted not having specified the reason why she had accepted his invitation.

"I have to talk to you about something, It's very serious and I'd like you to be totally sincere with me".

Warren picked up the menu, but after hearing those words he put it down immediately.

"What is it about?"

"I need to know if I can trust you. Look at me in the eyes and tell me that you haven't revealed any details of our investigations to anyone".

"Warren seemed taken aback, but was very relaxed in answering her.

"Of course Katrine, you can trust me not only as a colleague, but also as a person".

"Oh no". Dinner was taking an unexpected turn and Katrine wanted to avoid given false expectation to her colleague, but just as she was trying to formulate the right sentence, she was interrupted by Sergio.

"Do the guests wish to order?"

Warren ordered a simple Margherita, as he had not been able to open the menu, while Katrine was preceded by Sergio's good memory.

"I don't mean to delude you, Warren, I would just like to know if you are the mole who provides information to the *Sunshine*".

Warren straightened up on his chair and looked at her curiously.

"That's all? Are we here to talk about this? Katrine, I thought you would have liked to spend the evening in my company, while instead you accuse me of having betrayed not only you, but the entire police force. Maybe I'd better go…"

Katrine stopped him by placing a hand on his arm.

"No! Sorry Warren, you're right. I was too direct and believe me I am very happy to have dinner with you".

The smile reappeared on the man's face the moment he sat down again.

But I have a big doubt that haunts me and, if you too have browsed today's newspapers, you may have noticed that the press is too well informed about the results of our research".

Sergio put Kat's sugar-free drink and Warren's beer on the table, than the policeman started talking again.

"You're right, but how could you have thought badly of me?"

"I only asked you the question. It is hard for me to believe that you or Judith could have done such thing, but the facts are clear".

"Well it could have been someone else at the police station".

"No Warren, last night only the three of us attended Café Paradise and I don't think the waitress was interested in our topics".

Warren thought back to their meeting the previous evening:

"You are right. But this means that…"

"Judith is passing information to the *Sunshine*. Please keep it to yourself and act as if you don't know".

"Wow…what a bomb. Don't worry, I will be as mute as a fish".

Katrine took a sip from the glass, then placed the napkin over her legs.

"There's another thing I need to talk to you about, hold on tight at the table. Of course, I trust that Judith will never find out".

"Well, tell me".

"There is a fifth missing person, the father does not want to leak anything and wants complete confidentiality, contacting me in private but, to be able to hope to do it , I need a hand".

"Oh Christ…are you kidding?"

"No Warren, unfortunately not. There is a ransom note expiring and I am afraid that if we do not find this person by tomorrow morning *The Mask* will decide to kill her before Eric Preston.

The father assured me of the good faith of the girl and I myself could not find anything that could call her guilty of something big.

Yesterday her father and I found her finger inside a box, exactly like Sarah Finningham".

"Do you have a photo to show me? I will help you Katrine, I promise you".

Katrine took the bag and began to rummage in search of the small photograph received by the Russian during the first interview. After finding it, she was interrupted first by Sergio who was approaching with the pizzas and then by something that had attracted her attention outside the restaurant window.

On the other side of the street she saw Zack motionless under the bus shelter that shook his head as he saw the two inside the restaurant.

"Kat, did you hear me?"

Warren shook her and she turned to Sergio.

"Sorry Sergio, what were you telling me?"

"I was wondering if you wanted a pinch of our chili which my cousin kindly managed to bring from Italy".

"No thanks, that's okay".

Kat looked back out again, but only saw the bus leave, leaving the opposite sidewalk empty.

"What is it, have you seen someone you know? It looks like you've just seen a ghost".

"No, it was nothing Warren. This is the photo of Victoria Varichenko".

Warren could not hold back the bite that fell on the plate and began to beat his chest and cough continuously.

"Yes Warren I know you know her, she is the daughter of the Russian tycoon, she appears in most fashion magazines".

Warren caught his breath and looked straight into Katrine`s eyes:

"It`s not about that. I spent an evening in her company a few days ago at Trevor`s Pub, the day before Dylan Rogers was found".

Katrine put both cutlery on the edges of her plate.

"The same day she disappeared…"

Both suddenly found themselves without appetite.

CHAPTER 26

Ivan Varichenko's Vacation Home

Ivan Varichenko stared at the clock on the wall above the kitchen door.

That policewoman would not have been able to discover the place where his daughter had been locked in for days, neither now nor ever.

He looked out the window: in a short time the river would overflow, the water level almost reached the wooden pier, where in the summer the kids from the area spent whole afternoons competing in diving competitions.

His daughter was out there somewhere and he could not help but wait for news that would probably never come.

He thought for a moment about what to do, while on TV they broadcast a commercial where his daughter smiled happily lying on a white sandy beach in Hawaii.

In the end it occurred to him to do the only thing that would make him fell a little more peaceful. He got up and took the phone and dialed his office number at the headquarters of the Russian-owned telephone company.

On the other side a female voice greeted him and asked him what he needed.

When he hung up Ivan Varichenko laid down on his sofa trying to rest his eyes for at least a few hours; by now the pupils were strongly red and the tiredness was felt more and more, since he had slept little and badly in the previous days.

He texted and placed his cell phone behind the sofa cushion, to be able to hear it in case the policewoman would have contacted him.

He had just transferred another ten million dollars to his daughter's kidnapper. After a few seconds Ivan finally fell into the arms of Morpheus.

Warren and Katrine went down the stairs to Trevor's Pub, leaving their dampened jackets to the cloakroom attendant.

"Excuse me, can I ask you a question?"

"Of course, just a second and I'm immediately with you".

Katrine felt the vibration of her cell phone and read the message in which Ivan Varichenko claimed to have paid the ransom.

As the cloakroom attendant returned to the counter, Katrine thought of the Russian's suffering and the huge amount he had been forced to pay for the second time.

"Tell me, what do you need?"

"I just wanted to know if this place is under video surveillance".

"I'm sorry, but the only day we have troubles in here is Saturday and that's why we have two bouncers come in to maintain order, but for the rest we don't need a similar system, if you want to speak to my boss…"

"No, thanks I was just curious, there is no need to bother him".

The two entered the room crowded with people and took place on the only free table, the same one occupied by Warren on the evening of his meeting with Victoria.

"Shit, the pictures would have been useful. From what you told me, Victoria left to go home immediately after your meeting, so Robert Hudson must have then followed her. Can you remember the time?"

"Yes, I also thought the same thing. I told you it does not happen so often to spend time with Victoria Varichenko. Time just flows, but I can't remember exactly the time, it was probably after midnight".

Katrine took the tourist map of Summerville out of her bag, then after opening it on the table, she scored a couple of spots in some areas.

"So are you telling me that Robert managed to steal a car in the nearby car park, seize Victoria Varichenko, travel the road to Sunset Hill and kill Dylan Rogers in two hours, without being noticed by anyone?"

"Well it was Tuesday night if I'm not mistaken and it only takes half an hour, forty minutes at most to reach Sunset Hill from here, so once Victoria was picked up he could have loaded her into the Volvo used for the murder of Dylan. I don't think it took him long to tie him behind the wheel and cut his finger off, so I feel like saying that the facts should have happened in this way. We also add that Hudson is very shrewd and attentive to what he is doing, following a precise plan without ever having to make a mistake. You forget that the cameras in the car park were tampered the day before, probably by himself".

Warren ordered a double coffee while Katrine asked the usual decaffeinated coffee to the amused waitress who was watching them discussing, probably exchanging the scene with a banal quarrel that she had witnessed with others in the past.

"Mhmm...and once the car ended off the precipice?" How did he transport Victoria to the hiding place where he is currently taken refuge?"

The two reasoned silently and then came to the same conclusion at the same time.

It was Katrine who highlighted the route, calculating several times with the tip of her pen.

"The hideout must be on this path, Robert Hudson stole the Volvo and while he was going to the refuge to take Dylan, he was able to kidnap Victoria. Once in the car he went to an unspecified point in this area where he hides and holds the kidnapped prisoners. He dumped Victoria and took Dylan to the top of Sunset Hill, to then get rid of him and the Volvo, after which he was able to escape on foot, passing the path in the woods. Once at the bottom of the hill he found a way to be able to safely return to the refuge, perhaps using a new vehicle".

"It could have gone this way Kat, but why kidnap Victoria? I mean, I don't think the kidnapping of the girl with subsequent ransom demand was part of Robert's original plan, don't you think so?"

"Mhmm...yeah. I don't think Victoria committed particular crimes or that the killer thought of kidnapping her, but then why stop to kidnap her and not go straight on continuing with his plan?"

Warren rubbed his eyes: it was now a week that they were making hypotheses and not getting concrete results necessary for the capture of Robert Hudson and he was starting to feel tired and very frustrated.

Katrine closed her eyelids trying to imagine the scene in which Victoria, walking her way home, was forced to board the stolen car.

The only explanation can be the amount of the ransom. Robert knows that he will need a lot of money once his carnage is over so he can start a new life, change area and recreate a new identity without problems. When he saw Victoria, walking alone on the street, he realized that he could very well get a good pension fund by blackmailing her father".

"It must necessarily be so. So maybe she doesn`t risk her life entirely, once he receives the money, Robert might decide to free her".

Katrine stared at the empty glass in front of her as she answered her colleague.

"The last payment only served to get us her ring finger back Warren, a murderer remains a murderer".

Both looked at the map: the circle previously described by Katrine restricted searches to an area that was still too large, even excluding half of Summerville.

The woman's cell phone vibrated on the table and her sister`s number appeared superimposed.

"Hallo Katrine? I`m calling you because it occurred to me where I saw that vase. Last summer I went around the markets and while I was trying a dress on, I caught a glimpse of James talking to a seller of handmade products. On the stall were wooden sculptures, vases, bracelets and other types of merchandise; James was holding a vase like that on the photo, but in the end he decided to give up and left without buying it".

Katrine swallowed as she felt a shiver run down her back.

"Could you describe the seller to me, Elizabeth?"

She heard her sister take a short break and the resume the speech.

"If I can remember right, he was a tattooed guy from head to toe, but I don't remember other details , I was somewhere else and I only looked quickly at James and the stall, I'm sorry".

"Don't worry, you have been very helpful. Thank you sister".

Katrine hung up and pulled a small pocket diary out of her bag.

"The vase is a work of Eric. My sister remembered seeing him at his stall last summer. Maybe we are there, I just need to make another call".

Katrine dialed a number on the keypad of her cell phone and waited for an answer by leaning it against her ear.

"Hallo?"

"Hello Courtney, I apologize for the time, I'm Katrine Steward. I need to have bits of information that only you can give me".

"Okay, tell me"

"I need to know if your boyfriend worked in a particular place; where he created the products to be resold, in particular the vases made for the summer markets".

"Eric modeled the clay pots in an old shed owned by his grandfather. He stayed there all day, he liked the view of the river and at the end of the day he went swimming before returning home. He cooked the pots to turn them into ceramic with a small gas oven purchased at a low price online, at the end I have to say that people did not practically appreciate the finished product. For this reason he preferred to switch to paintings and wooden works, always taking advantage of the space offered by that shed".

"Could you please give me the address?.

"Of course, just a second, I`ll look for it. If you would like to go and have a look at the place, I could accompany you early tomorrow".

Katrine waited for almost a minute until she heard Courtney come back on the phone.

"Here it is. 42 Drive Road, you have to take the first road on the right after the cemetery, listen Agent , for that story of the robbery ….I knew nothing, I would have told you".

"But of course Courtney, don`t worry, I believe you…go back and enjoy the evening without worries".

"Okay, resend".

Katrine hung up and looked for the address on the map: as she had thought, it was not very far from the marked route and it was in the area of the circle drawn just before.

"Half past eleven…Robert could hit this same night. Warren, I`m going to the address, I`m not going to have another corpse on my conscience, and please don`t make a fuss about the search warrant that I don`t have. There is no time to lose".

Warren saw her jump up as she picked up her bag and cell phone.

"I`m coming with you".

The two left the club and hurriedly boarded Warren`s pick up.

CHAPTER 27

Journey to 42, Drive Road

Warren's pick up turned right, onto the bridge that would take them to the other side of the river.

The speedometer hand marked seventy kilometers per hour and began to rise faster and faster. Until recently Warren had had to go at a low speed despite the road being busy, because huge puddles forced the vehicle to slow down every two hundred meters, due to the danger caused by the aquaplaning phenomenon.

"Never seen so much rain in Summerville in my life. Damn you can't go faster, now?"

"I'm trying. Here it seems the city is drowning. Send a message to Judith, at least someone will know where we are going in case something goes wrong".

Katrine kept her eyes fixed outside the misted windshield: "Don't worry Warren, you'll see that everything will turn up fine. Take this road, it will save us time".

Warren took a narrow one-way descent as suggested by his partner.

"As a first date it's a bit too busy for my taste, Kat".

The woman smiled amused while checking the magazine of her gun.

"You`re right Warren, if we catch that bastard tonight, I promise you that the next one will be much better. I also wanted to clarify your past in Rockford".

"Did you investigate on my person?:

"Of course Warren, you told me it was a long story, but in reality it was enough to tell me that you asked for a transfer after discovering the truth about your office colleague: Kevin Smith if I`m not mistaken, right?"

Warren clutched the handle bar and accelerated to undertake a steep climb:

"I could have told you about it personally. Kevin and I grew up together, he was my best friend until I found out that he was one of the three corrupt cops from the Rockford police. I never understood the real reason that pushed him to sell himself, but if he is now in prison, it`s because of me. Since then I started to look at my former colleagues with different eyes, until I can no longer know who I can trust, so I thought maybe it would be better to change air. I would have told you without the need for research on my account, why did you do it?"

Katrine turned to look at him.

"No, Warren is not your fault, but your merit. If there were more policemen like you, the world would be better, I can assure you. As for your past, I only checked yesterday and the reason why I did it you already know: either you or Judith was cheating on me. When I discovered your story in Rockford I decided to accept your invitation to hear from you in person: I knew I could count on you from the beginning".

Warren turned for a moment until he met Kat`s gaze, then in the distance he glimpsed the shed on Drive Road.

"I hope you will be forgiven for even doubting a second about my fairness Kat. Here it is, it must be that old building over there".

The pickup stopped in the dirt parking lot in front of the main entrance.

The building must have existed for a long time and although Eric had used it up to one year earlier, it appeared in a decadent and untreated state.

The ivy covered the entire wall around the old rusty blue door and the windows near the ceiling were mostly broken or so dirty as to not allow you to see anything through.

There didn't seem to be any lights on inside, but Katrine didn't let go of the weapon and pointed to Warren to check the side entrance as they proceeded briskly in the pouring rain.

"Fuck it's locked with a padlock Kat!"

The woman raised the hood over her head and motioned for Warren to leave.

The policeman watched her as she turned on the flashlight and positioned it under her gun.

"We didn't come here to go back Warren, are you with me?"

The man nodded, then Katrine pointed the weapon at the lock and fired.

Eric Preston was lying on a cold metal cart, the same where some of his works had been positioned until just before.

The drug that had been injected made him stay awake and conscious, but completely immobile and forced to look at the figure with the mask located in front of him and the five knife handles sticking out of his body.

The individual had drilled three small holes on the trolley and positioned him supine, then he had taken six very sharp kitchen knives from a briefcase and he was inserting them in non-vital points, making him suffer in silence, denying him any kind of movement.

He felt the drops of blood fall from the trolley and end up in a basin, but he could not know of the marker writing imprinted on it and not even that his finger was floating right there.

The writing read "guilty", just the way Eric Preston felt as life left his body. He understood that he would die in the same way he killed Gary Hoffman the previous summer during the robbery, but what he could not explain was, who was the individual behind the mask.

Before taking the last knife, the person who had observed him suffering with such interest, decided to take off his mask and balaclava revealing his identity.

He knew that person, but he couldn't imagine how he could have understood that it was he who carried out the robbery and killed that man.

While the mask planted the last knife in his right thigh, he seemed to pass out and feel a gunshot behind him.

Katrine entered the door and passed through the boxes covered with tarpaulin, while Warren pointed the light into the room in front of him.

Both heard sounds, so they moved quickly without ever lowering their guard until they could see a light source.

Once turned around a pile of bankers they were able to see in full what was happening right in front of their eyes, on a raised landing.

Eric Preston was lying, motionless, on a steel cart, with six knifes impaled at various points on the body.

Behind it stood an individual, covered with a hideous stone mask.

Now that they could see it live, the constellation of amber fragments that covered the surface of that disguise was incredible.

A strip of what appeared to be fresh blood and the empty gaze coming from the two small slits, instead of the eyes, contributed to make his appearance even more terrifying.

The only sound heard in those brief moments was the tinkling of Eric's blood which was falling into a large plastic basin; the liquid accumulated inside had filled it almost entirely. The poor fellow was bleeding to death, under the gaze of the *Mask* and the upset one of the two agents who had just entered the shed.

Katrine raised the weapon resting her head on her shoulder to take better aim.

"Stop where you are, Police! Put your hands up and well in sight Robert, you are now trapped".

The guy behind Eric Preston spun around and ran, quickly vanishing into the hallway behind him.

"Stay here Warren, call for help and see if you can find Victoria, I'll take care of him".

Katrine climbed the steps and passed Eric, quickly beginning to walk the path taken by the *Mask*. The corridor ended in a secondary exit, the door of which had been left wide open: she could see silhouette running towards a warehouse several meters in front of her.

Kat's boots were not exactly suitable for a pursuit of that kind, she felt them sinking with every step in the mud, but her training and the adrenaline rush, helped to reduce the distances considerably, under the incessant midnight downpour.

The fugitive entered the warehouse by knocking over some boxes in an attempt to slow down the pursuit of his pursuer, then entered a room by moving aside the curtain that protected the entrance.

Immediately afterwards Kat managed to avoid the boxes and enter the same entrance.

The room in which she found herself was completely dark so she felt the wall looking for a switch to illuminate it; when she could find it she pressed it several times to no avail.

"Shit, there's no current here", she thought.

She tried to proceed slowly without being able to see where she was going, holding the gun firmly and listening to every little noise that indicated his opponent's position.

A distorted voice echoed in the echo of the room: the killer used a vocal distortion to camouflage his identity.

"Agent Steward, finally. I was wondering when we would be able to meet in person".

Katrine listened to the words trying to understand their place of origin, but the echo of the room and the total darkness made the task even more difficult.

"Let me go, if you don't compromise my mission, I'll save your life".

The policewoman decided not to answer to avoid revealing her position as she took small steps in the dark: if only she had taken her cell phone or Warren's flashlight, it would have been much simpler.

"I admire you Katrine. Since the TVs did nothing but talk about you, I wanted to take advantage of it by launching a challenge. It doesn't happen every day to enjoy such an advertisement to spread my message".

Katrine approached a few meters, advancing with her back against the wall: she was now close, she could feel it.

"We are not very different, you and I. We both work to achieve justice, only in a different way, do you understand this? Let's say I'm doing you a favor by helping you get rid of Summerville's scum.

Katrine raised her weapon and pointed the barrel at the temple in front of her.

"You're wrong, but you will have plenty of time to think about it in a cell of a maximum security prison".

Behind her the killer knocked over a shelf to hinder her, so that he could have the time to escape from the opposite side. When he opened the door to go in the outside, the light revealed everything inside the room.

Katrine removed the weapon aimed at the head of a mannequin and launched herself again in pursuit towards the outside, losing a few precious seconds in overcoming the obstacle.

She ran out again, under the storm, along the pedestrian road that boarded the river until she could see *The Mask* turn right and disappear behind a wooden fence.

Katrine gritted her teeth and tried to follow him without ever stopping to run, but the killer seemed not to suffer from that effort and the weight of the mask worn, slightly increasing.

After about half a kilometer, running incessantly at maximum speed, Katrine reached the center of a crossroads, without knowing which of the two directions the fugitive had chosen.

On the right the road went up to the first houses that marked the border of the industrial area, while the one on the left followed an unknown path, where the high vegetation partially obstructed the passage.

Katrine opted for the second street and proceeded as fast as possible to what turned out to be a dead end.

"Shit!"

The woman stood in the middle of a wasteland surrounded on two sides by high stone walls, while to the right of the point from which she had come from, the passage was blocked by an iron fence hidden by a hedge.

Katrine turned on herself to resume her way to the inhabited area, when she heard a noise attracting her attention. She looked down and managed to notice a very narrow passage where the fence had been cut to allow a person to pass through.

Katrine stretched out on the wet grass and began to crawl until she could see beyond the obstacle.

The Mask had managed to climb a wall beyond the fence and was about to take the body to the other side when he noticed her.

"See you soon, Agent Steward", he said as he lowered himself to the other side, leaving only his hands and hideous face in stone visible.

Katrine raised the gun and exploded a shot, she would not allow him to escape now that she had him so close.

The bullet hit the right side of the mask, producing a spark and causing its owner to fall beyond the wall.

When Katrine managed to get over the fence she went to the rubbish bin and used it to help her reach the top of the wall and be able to climb over it.

When her feet landed on the ground, she could see the killer emerge from the icy waters, on the opposite bank of the river.

As the rain lashed her face, she noticed the figure on the other side raising an arm in greeting and then vanishing. Katrine bit her lower lip: after all that pursuit she had managed to let him escape.

As she approached the river bank she hit something with the tip of her ankle boots, realizing it was not just a simple stone, she decided to pick it up in order to observe it better.

One side of that stone was still hot, so she realized she had a fragment of the mask in her hands, worn by the individual who she had been chasing for a week now.

The shot must have hit his owner's right cheek, but the mask stone had been strong enough to save his life.

CHAPTER 28

42, Drive Road *March 27th, 2017*

Around half past one in the morning, two ambulances and several police cars had rushed to 42 Drive Road. A sleepy Judith also managed to go with one of the police cars, and was now studying the room, with the rest of the team, where Eric Preston had been found.

"So you're telling me he managed to escape despite you shooting him in the face?"

Katrine nodded as she held out the fragment she was holding in her hands.

"Okay, I can't give you precise indications about this type of stone, it seems only a very light but resistant mineral, at least based on the facts that happened a little while ago. Robert Hudson has managed not only to run faster than you, but even to cross a swollen river and sow you, all without ever taking off a mask that is apparently bulky and uncomfortable. Okay, I'm really starting to believe the story of Alessandro Zaretti's magic weapon".

"Judith, don't say nonsense. I wasted time in the warehouse behind here, he tricked me into attracting me to a blind spot in total darkness; by the way, he's using a voice distortion".

"But for what reason? A mask, a vocal distortion…it is now clear that Robert Hudson is behind all this mess".

I know, believe me there is something that does not come back to me…I leave you to your research, I'm going to Warren, I saw him come out a little while ago".

Judith continued to analyze the steel trolley and the rest of the surrounding environment. Katrine went outside to find Warren under a canopy, intent on smoking a cigarette.

"Is there something wrong with you Warren? I see you very shaken".

The man made a long cigarette shot with his fingers still dirty with Eric's blood.

"I think I can't manage it Kat. After looking for Victoria everywhere, I went up to Eric to ask him if he knew anything about a missing woman and do you know what he did?

He opened his eyes as much as he could, blinking quickly. Katrine, he wanted to help us, he knew of Victoria, only that the drug completely paralyzed him and he could not show us where she was, if only…".

"Nothing if and but, Warren. Eric is alive, got into that ambulance and he will be able to tell us exactly where he and the other victims were being hidden. Evidently this hut was only the place for his execution".

Warren threw the butt on the ground and stepped on it with his muddy shoes.

"Katrine, the doctor has estimated a blood loss of around 4 liters. The amount of blood present in a human body is around 5 liters. When the rescue arrived, I saw Eric lose consciousness and I know very well that the chances of survival for an attack of this type are very low. The killer positioned the knifes at pre-determined points to prolong his suffering. Unfortunately, also this time we arrived too late".

Katrine put her hand on her colleague's soaking wet shirt.

"We did all we could Warren. Don't take all the burden, you will see that Judith will find some clues that will allow us to get to Victoria in time".

"Hey Katrine, take a look here".

The forensic scientist appeared behind them.

The two looked at each other, hoping that Judith hadn't heard the last part of the speech.

"This time the killer did not have time to clean up the room properly from possible proofs. I checked Eric's clothes, it seems that under the soles there are traces of some animal excrement, the whole sole is covered with them; I also found hay in one of the trouser pockets".

"Mhmm...interesting. Maybe he was being held captive in a stable, or on a farm. There must not be many farmers left in the countryside just outside the city, this is a big step forward Judith".

"Yes, within a day I will be able to establish which animal they belong to; unfortunately there is no one left to save, but if we are quick in searches, maybe we will be able to capture him, what do you think?"

Katrine managed to avoid Warren's gaze and pretend that she knew nothing about the missing Russian model:

"We must hurry up and not waste time. You're right Judith, those victims deserve justice and we will be able to catch the murderer, I guarantee you".

The girl hidden behind thick lenses smiled.

"I will get you the results as soon as possible Katrine, I will start with the fragment you have given me".

"Perfect, I'm done here, I will try to sleep a few hours to resume searches as soon as possible, Warren, you should do the same".

Warren doubted he could rest after the events of that evening, but he replied by showing the raised thumb of his right hand.

When an hour later Katrine parked the jeep in front of her house, after being escorted to the restaurant by Warren, it had finally stopped raining.

At nine in the morning, she was awakened by the ringtone set on her cell phone.

Outside the window she saw the sun peeking out of the mountains as she pulled on a white turtleneck sweater and black skinny jeans.

After putting the coffee in preparation, she called Mr. Varichenko to find out if there was any news and to tell him personally about the series of events that took place the previous evening.

The Russian had not received any message that morning and this seemed quite evident: at that moment Robert was probably licking his wounds.

After having calmed him down and updated on the new track, she hung up, they would contact as soon as one of the two had had news.

She had omitted the fact that she had shot the only person who was aware of his daughter's position: at that moment she had only thought of stopping that chain of murders.

Her impulsiveness had allowed her to capture the *Ghost* in the past, but Katrine found herself thinking about the fact that lately she had had a little too much of the easy trigger.

As she stared at the postman intent on filling the letterbox of her neighbor, Katrine remembered the coffee being prepared: the woman cursed seeing the dark liquid overflow from the cup and dye brown the wooden top of the kitchen.

After cleaning quickly, she took the bag and once she had her boots on, went out in the sunlight. The strength and warmth of the typical spring sun were slow in coming, but at least the day could have been tackled without the need for an umbrella.

Katrine got into the jeep and started towards the police station, but after about ten meters she was forced to slow down and then to stop because a person had placed himself in the middle of the road.

Zack stood on the white strip that separated the lanes with his arms spread to force Kat to stop the car.

The policewoman checked the closing of the doors and slightly lowered the door window:

"What do you want Zack? Get out of the way".

The grim look of the man managed to inspire a pinch of fear, despite the fact that she had always been the dangerous and irascible one between the two.

"What are you doing Katrine? Do you refuse me for that idiot?"

"Here I imagined it, get out of the way Zack, I have to go to work, by the way: shouldn`t you be down at the carpentry shop?"

"No, no stop for a moment, please…I took a week off. Believe me Katrine I thought about us and…"

"Zack stop it with this bloody story! Did you take a week off to be able to stalk me? Put your heart in peace, between us is over, over! Get out of the way now and stop behaving this way, you only make the situation worse".

The shot was unexpected and Katrine saw the man attempt to open the door of her side of the jeep, fortunately closed from the inside.

"Curse Katrine! I will not allow anyone to take you away from me, no one, do you understand?"

Katrine instinctively pressed the accelerator pedal, starting the car at full speed.

She had never seen her ex- boyfriend behave in such a violent way, she just couldn't find another solution on her way to work: she would have reported him that morning.

Judith was sitting in front of the computer, waiting for the analysis of the elements found in the shed, rethinking the interview asked by Katrine to Philip De La Cruix.

From that little she was able to hear, the woman in charge of the investigation asked for advice regarding the request for a restrictive order against her ex-boyfriend.

"Give him time Katrine, Zack is a good guy, everyone knows him. Do not do actions you might regret, going to court is not the best solution, believe me".

The woman replied by telling him the previous episodes of stalking, which occurred during the week, but in the end she decided to follow the advice of her superior and wait a little longer.

Black and white pages began to leak from the old printer. Judith collected them and then compared the data relating to the excrement sample found under Eric Preston's soles with those of numerous poultry.

Despite her personal experience with animals such as rabbits and chickens, which Judith jealously kept in a room just behind her house, she had not recognized the very common goat dung.

She took out her cell phone to send the result to her colleague, but was interrupted by the policeman of the office next to hers, George Trevors, who communicated her bad news: Eric Preston had died around noon, despite the desperate attempts of the doctors at the hospital.

The team had failed to save any of the missing people and could not count on the valuable information that Eric Preston could have had revealed.

When George left, Judith finished composing the text of the massage, adding the last sad news, then went back to the analysis of the fragment of the mask.

While Warren took the dirt road to the fifth and final farm, Katrine read the text of the message just received.

"Shit…Warren you were right, Eric Preston lost his life around noon. We arrived too late".

Warren stared at the road in front of them, to make sure he avoided the huge potholes on the rough ground, without saying a word.

Katrine was able to perceive the deep regret of her companion who hovered in the air of the cockpit for which he tried to change the subject, while the pick-up stopped her race.

"Judith has analyzed the excrements, we must try to understand if the owner has goats or if he knows someone who works there in the surroundings.

"Okay, leave it to me. Ah, listen to me Katrine….promise me we will get him. I mean *The Mask…*"

Katrine leaned against the pick-up and noticed a sturdy man with a cowboy hat on his head coming out of the barn.

"Of course Warren, I promise you".

Warren turned to be able to introduce himself to the man, which turned out to be very disturbed of the presence of foreigners in his territory.

"Hi, I`m Summerville police officer Warren Valentine and she is my colleague Katrine Steward. We would only need to ask a few questions, if you don`t mind".

The man was very intrigued by the beautiful woman leaning against the pick-up, while he did not seem to even notice the presence of the policeman a few steps away from him.

"Gregory McQueen, very pleasure to meet you young lady. Aren`t you the policewoman who often appears on TV?"

Katrine moved away from the pick-up to get closer to her interlocutor, then raised her sunglasses, resting them on her forehead.

"Exactly, very pleased Mr. McQueen, We are not going to steal much time from you, I promise, so you can go back quickly to what you were doing".

Katrine looked at the bucket containing freshly milked milk, supported by Gregory.

"Tell me beauty. I always find time to devote to a beautiful woman like you".

The wink of Mr. McQueen`s eye did not seem to provoke any reaction in Kat, who began to address the ritual questions to the old breeder.

The error message appeared again on Judith`s computer monitor. For the umpteenth time the exact same word in flashing red "No match found" appeared on the wall screen and the scientist began to reposition the stone inside the scanner in order to facilitate detection by the laser pointing system.

The rays coming from the projector examined the surface of the object, covering it with red light very slowly, like the light beam of any copier.

Once the lasers had finished, Judith hit the "Enter" command on the computer keyboard, as she had done in all four years in which she had made use of that device.

Once again the same error message appeared, so she decided to call a colleague from Sparkling Bay to get some clarifications.

The machine was perhaps broken, the system went haywire, or she herself was wrong with the positioning of the stone. On the hand, what the computer was trying to tell her was unthinkable and nobody would have believed the outcome of those analyzes.

She put the phone to her ear and dialed the Sparkling Bay colleague`s number. Probably later she would have composed that of the technician who carried out the overhaul and maintenance of those machines, solving the problem.

Warren felt invisible for the duration of the conversation; evidently the inventor of the term "weaker sex" had never had anything to do with woman of the caliber of Katrine Steward.

"Thank you Mr. McQueen, It was a pleasure, goodbye".

"I really hope Miss Steward, if you happen to come back here, show up: I would gladly accompany you on a horse ride".

This time the man nodded a greeting to Warren, while he was arranging the package without having a lot of problems.

"So even from this playboy we didn't get a spider out of the hole".

Katrine closed the door and fastened her seat belt:

"Yeah, and he was the last one within several miles. I really don't know where to go to parry Warren, I confess it. We have to invent something to discover Robert's hiding place, losing Victoria would be too hard for all of us. Let's go back to the police station, I hope that Judith's research has give the desired results".

After a few seconds the ringtone of Katrine's cell increased its intensity, just as Warren inserted the first gear and accelerated along the winding road.

"You talk about the devil...tell me Judith?"

Warren studied his colleague's expression: the astonishment expressed by her eyes was evident.

"How do you mean? Okay I'll read the email you sent me...no, another hole in the water, we still grope in the dark. See you tomorrow Judith, as always if you find something...exactly, good evening".

Katrine hung up and immediately opened her inbox.

"Something new? You shouldn't keep me on thorns Kat..."

"Shhh, a moment. Let me read then I'll explain the absurdity of the matter".

Agent Valentine turned to take the freeway that would take them back to Summerville and after about ten seconds he glared at the policewoman, intrigued by the outcome of the analyzes.

"Then? Any clues?"

Katrine moved her cell phone so that the content of the email was visible to Warren, or at least the sentence underlined at the end of the email.

"As far as I could understand, there is no such mineral present on the earth's soil, at least not at this time".

"Are you really sure? I remind you that Judith is a serious scientist who is based on…"

"Warren, do you think I want to joke? Here is the confirmation by several people who guarantee the strangeness of this type of rock".

"Jesus Christ…"

CHAPTER 29

Serenity Lake, North of Summerville   *March 2th, 2017*

Jeremias Bailey parked his car along the dirt path that led to Serenitz Lake. He put his airplane-style sunglasses and opened the trunk of the car.

The dawn of that Tuesday morning seemed to have been painted especially for him: the sunlight was beginning to coat the surface of the calm and dark waters in front of it.

When, the day before, his business partner had proposed to take a free Tuesday, Jeremias had quickly prepared the tools to carry out his favourite hobby and had warned his wife of his imminent departure to their cottage in the countryside.

He extended the telescopic fishing rod and pulled out a jar of worms from the designer shoulder bag, together with the briefcase where the numerous and different baits were jealously guarded, preparing to be able to fish in peace, without having to listen to all those people who populated his betting shop daily.

He would not have heard the number combinations of horse racing fans, nor the list of results of any sporting event of regular customers; today he would have enjoyed the quiet and silence offered by his sacred place.

He had some difficulty in putting on his rubber boots, his sixty-three years had begun to be felt about a year before, after the removal of a hernia that had made him feel older and weaker than his great-grandfather.

Despite his age and his ailments, Jeremias was in good health, he still had most of his hair and one day of fishing was enough to recharge himself with weeks of work and useless speeches from oppressive customers.

After taking a few steps in the lake, he made his first launch, watching the hook fall into the dark waters, slowly withdrawing the line with the reel.

He hoped to catch a nice fish and to be able to see it in his wife's pot the same evening, but he knew that time and patience would be needed, so he tried to free his mind and began to contemplate the surrounding nature.

After about ten launches, while observing the wake of an airplane in the blue sky above him, he felt the resistance in withdrawing the bait, therefore he started to pull harder helping himself with both arms.

"Wow, this must be pretty big", he said aloud without being heard by a living soul. After a few seconds, his satisfied look froze, when a part of what the hook was caught on emerged.

Jeremias let the rod drop and screamed as loud as he could seeing the hook stuck in the empty cavity of the orbit of what was to be a human body.

"How could it be said, this stone does not exist?"

Katrine Steward had left the police station to buy herself something to eat for lunch, taking advantage of that moment of solitude to update Ivan Varichenko.

"I don`t know how it is possible, believe me, but the only fragment found of the mask worn by Robert Hudson is unknown to our computers. Experts say that the stone is not found anywhere on the planet.

I can't tell you anything more about this topic, I'm sorry".

"And what about my daughter's investigation? How's your job progressing? I haven't received a message, but I paid on time. What should I do Agent Steward? My daughter is all I have of dearest in the world..."

Katrine was out of breath hearing the chocked voice of the Russian on the phone, but could not tell him that she was still on the high seas, completely on the mercy of the decisions made by the killer who was wandering around Summerville.

"Well, here...we are following a track, we only need more time".

She heard the Russian sniffle loudly and waited for him to blow it before receiving an answer.

"Okay, I can give you more time. I will wait, Agent Steward...if I can do something you just have to call me, you know my number".

"I will Mr. Varichenko, now I have to leave you, we will here from each other".

Katrine put her cell phone in the pocket of her military trousers and went in to the supermarket to look for a pack of mixed salad ready to be seasoned in the canteen next to the police station.

After paying at the cashier she headed for the sliding doors of the exit, but once outside she retraced her steps because something had attracted her attention.

Her photo stood out above the copy of the *Sunshine* leaning on the small newsstand counter inside the books and magazines department.

"Can I have a copy?"

The young girl took the coins from the counter while realizing that she had just sold the newspaper to the woman who appeared on the front page of the newspaper she had before her eyes.

Katrine felt her face seething with anger as she read more carefully the title and article of the front page of the *Sunshine*.

In the lines written by the same reporter of the previous articles the escape of *The Mask* was described to the detriment of the "super-policewoman" of Summerville, emphasizing in particular the ineffectiveness of law enforcement in the case of the serial killer who appeared in that quiet town a week earlier. Once again uncomfortable details had been disclosed such as the escape, the mockery of Katrine in the warehouse without electric light and the unsuccessful attempt to rescue Eric Preston two nights before.

She decided that the time had come to end that story, she marked the reporter's name and sent Warren a message, telling him not to wait for her in the office.

She opened the door of the jeep and after throwing the newspaper on the passenger seat, she directed herself to the *Sunshine* office.

Walter Bridge was sitting on the bench in front of the newspaper office for which he worked, while devouring a hamburger from the most famous fast food chain in the world.

After licking his fingers soaked with barbecue sauce, he tried to move the tuft from his forehead using only the back of his hand, experiencing some difficulties.

He decided to get up and enter the nearby park to be able to wash his hands in the fountain immediately next to the entrance and take a walk, after all there was still one hour left for his break.

In those days he had been busy: the manager smiled every time he saw him enter the door of his office in spite of a few weeks before. In the previous months, every time he was called to the director's office, his blood froze, fearing yet another rebuke or presaging a imminent dismissal. Things seemed to be going in the right direction and luck had returned to smile at that almost nineteen year old boy with the device still between his teeth.

He had also fucked more, after his girlfriend had read his name on the front page of the newspaper, being able to prey with her friends about her boyfriend reporter.

When he had finished to wash his hands, he heard a known voice behind him.

"You should be Walter Bridge. I would have a few things to tell you if you have a moment of time".

The boy swallowed conspicuously twice before he could reply:

"W-of course, what do you need?"

"Well I don't know where to start. Maybe I can know how much they pay you to write those bad things about me? Or what authorizes you to criticise my work or that of my colleagues?"

The boy's eyes began to look for a point where he could look, so as not to have to face the authoritarian gaze of the woman with the military trousers in front of him.

"I only communicate the news, my colleagues help me to write an article that can attract people's attention".

The woman removed a hand from her hip to point the index finger towards the yellowish pimple on the young man's nose.

"You and your colleagues should bring more respect to the police force and the people you don't know, but I'm not here to make you a moral business: I would like to know only one thing and see that you are sincere at least this time because I swear that I will find a way to get it paid, Kid".

Walter did not know how to respond to that provocation and since he was only a boy who followed the advice of some colleagues to find a place in the world, he limited himself to uttering an almost imperceptible "tell me" to Kat.

"How do you know all those things and so quickly? Who gives you the information?"

"I'm sorry, this I can't tell you I was told..."

The woman took the boy's jacket and brought her face a few centimetres from her own, making him feel her strong vanilla fragrance and the fresh breath of mint that accompanied her words: "Here me well boy, I am not going to waste precious time with you, as you know many people have died and I am not the type of woman willing to beg someone, especially a half-saw like you, so spit the toad and answer my questions".

"Okay easy easy, there is no need to get excited. I receive information via anonymous phone calls. It all started after the first murder, that of Sarah Phinningham, which allowed me to write my first important article. The following evening a call informed me of your interrogation and subsequently it went on until yesterday evening".

"Have you not thought about the reason for those calls? Was it the voice of a man or a woman?"

"No, I just thought about this possibility, I think it could be one of your colleague that dislikes you or the work of someone who hates you or who you have done wrong in the past. This person was trying to camouflage its voice, but I could swear it was a female voice, I`m 99% sure".

Katrine put her hands in the pockets of her jacket: "Female you said? This may be enough for me, but try to think about what you write next time, brat".

Walter watched the woman turn and climb back into the jeep parked with the four arrows just outside the park.

He never expected such a grooming at his age. That woman definitely had to have more attributes than he did.

CHAPTER 30

Summerville Police Station   *March 28th, 2017*

Katrine's amphibians strode down the corridor leading to her office.

Warren was sitting at his desk, staring at the wall with the faces of the missing people, when the colleague's entrance attracted his attention.

"Where have you been? I tried to call you a little while ago because..."

"Where's Judith?"

"She must have gone to talk to another colleague from the forensics about the fragment found by you after the chase. If you let me talk..."

"Fuck Warren, it's her. The guy who wrote the articles told me about a telephone informant. He confessed that after each murder or step forward in our investigation, he received a call from a woman who updated him on the facts, getting him the scoop of the day every damned time".

Warren crossed his arms as he leaned against the wall opposite Katrine.

"My God, you were right then. I didn't think it would come to this, but why would she do it for?"

Kat handed the newspaper over to her colleague: "I have no idea, I thought she did it for money, but I'm starting to think that my presence is starting to be uncomfortable for someone in here.

Please , put the newspaper away and pretend that nothing happened, I want to solve the question myself".

"Okay. Now try to listen to me Katrine; a little while ago we received a call from a citizen of Summerville, a certain Jeremias Bailey, who found the corpse of a person while fishing at Serenity Lake, about twenty kilometers away north from here".

Katrine sank into the swivel chair feeling her arms and legs tired and heavy as if she had just finished exerting an intense physical effort.

"Do you know anything else? Sex, identity?"

"Actually no, the news came about an hour ago and it was our chief Philip De La Cruix who went to the place indicated by Jeremias. He was nearby to meet with the Rockford police chief when he heard the Radio call. He should be here any minute.

The only thing he wanted me to tell you is that the left hand ring finger is also missing on this body, for the rest he said to wait for him at the police station".

Katrine put her hands on her face, felt her head throbbing and felt a mixture of anger and disappointment: it must have been Victoria Varichenko.

"How can I tell her father? I heard him a little while ago to reassure him and told him that we would have saved her Warren".

The colleague put a hand on Katrine's shoulder and tried to console her: "It's not your fault, you said the same thing about Eric Preston. We try to do everything we can, but times are tight and the killer is very smart Kat, don't give up right now, we will be able to beat him in the cell sooner or later, I'm sure".

Katrine wiped a tear with the sleeve of her sweatshirt: "You're right, sorry, it's just a moment of weakness, I can't forgive myself for letting him run away the other night".

At that moment the office door opened and Judith made her entrance with a package of papers in her hands.

"What's the matter with you Kat? Does Philip's call just have anything to do with it?"

Katrine raised her red eyes to her colleague and was seized by a sudden anger that corroded her stomach.

"Why do you care so much about it Judith? So you can pour another scoop on your new boyfriend and make me sink even deeper into the shit?"

Judith put the papers on the desk and showed a surprised and startled expression.

"What's the problem Kat?"

The policewoman could no longer restrain herself, got up from her chair and pushed her against the wardrobe next to the entrance door.

I'm broke to stay here pretending not to know that you're stabbing me in the back, do you understand?"

Kat clapped her hand against the closet, making a deafening noise as Judith sought Warren's help with her look.

"I don't know what you're talking about. Warren what's going on?"

Warren watched her silently then looked down to the floor, letting Katrine's aggression continue.

"I want you out of here immediately and don't even dare to speak to me again, do we understand each other?"

The eyes hidden behind the frightened woman's lenses began to tear, while no sound escaped from her mouth, despite wanting to strongly respond to that sudden attack. Kat gave another strong blow to the closet, leaving a small dent right next to her colleague's desperate and frightened face.

Warren came over to pull Katrine away under the forensic scientist's pleading eyes when the door next to the three opened suddenly. Philip De La Cruix appeared in the doorway, filling it almost entirely with his imposing figure.

"What's going on in here?"

Katrine moved away from the closet while her colleague sagged on the floor, bursting into tears, covering her face using the shawl around her neck.

"Agent Steward in my office, right away"

Katrine followed quickly her superior slightly shaken: she had never heard him call her by her surname.

She sat in the chair in front of her superior's plate, while Philip closed the door behind him and took a seat on his armchair.

"What came to your mind? I've never seen you act so violently, especially towards a harmless girl like Judith".

Katrine was unable to lean back or even look straight at her superior's eyes.

She stared at her clenched fists trembling with astonished repressed anger, as she had rarely lurked that way.

"Katrine, look at me straight in the eyes and explain what happened in there".

Kat tried to find the best way to present the facts, took a deep breath and looked up to meet that of the man sitting in front of her.

"Judith secretly passes on the information to the press. I found out just this morning, the journalist who deals with the front pages of the *Sunshine* throughout this period confessed it to me".

"Even if that's the case, I can't allow you to act like that in the Summerville police headquarters. It's certainly not the example I intend to give to people or your colleagues. If you really want to know, Katrine, this time I don't believe you".

The woman felt a pang in the stomach as if she had just received an invisible punch from under the desk.

"How do you mean?"

Philip put his hands to his nose, in what was commonly used to end the prayers of believers.

Katrine, I went to inquire about what you told me about Zack. He was working and as soon as he noticed my presence in the carpentry shop yesterday afternoon, I could not see anything different in the behavior of the person I know for over twenty years. Zack is dating a girl and to hear his superior he has always gone to work: punctual and diligent as a model worker.

The morning before he was late because he asked for a permit to accompany his girlfriend to the gynecologist, is it probably this fact that has bothered you so much Katrine? I talked to him and he didn't mention in the least your meeting or any stalking".

Katrine got up from her chair and began to raise her voice, gritting her teeth: "Phil, that bastard is lying, he is very good in hiding things, I can swear you, he followed me on several occasions and…"

"Try to calm down and sit composed and listen to what your superior is saying to you!"

The woman sat down again: her throat burned and her mouth dry and saliva-free after the latter excess of anger.

I have come to make a drastic decision towards you, after the story on Zack and your last attack on Judith I must also add the hasty and incorrect conclusions of the investigation I had entrusted to you. Probably I was wrong to get you started immediately with a case like that of the *Mask,* I should have given you a little more time to be able to readjust to Summerville and integrate with the rest of your colleagues".

Katrine listened motionless to the words spoken by her boss: she felt exactly like when the teacher as a child had made her stand behind the blackboard after a scuffle with her classmate.

This is why I decided that it is better entrust the assignment to Warren and leave you a week or all the time you need to recover and be able to calm down. You have exposed yourself too much and the newspapers will tear you to pieces, I warn you, another body was found this morning, have you already been informed of this?"

Katrine nodded silently as the world collapsed under her feet; had she misunderstood or had she just been released from her duty?

We managed to identify the body found in Serenity lake, I believe it has been underwater for at least two weeks and the bad weather of these last days must have dropped some of the weights used to keep it hidden on the seabed. The cavities of the eyes were devoid of the two eyeballs and the left ring finger was missing, as well as in all the other victims of the *Mask*".

The woman tried to assimilate as much information as possible by waiting for the final verdict, that is, that Philip pronounced the name of the daughter of Ivan Varichenko.

Obviously we made a mistake from the beginning. The body found this morning is male and we managed to ascertain after contacting the mother, that the body found this morning is that of Robert Hudson.

Katrine stared at her boss's mouth saying those words without really looking at him: images of a week of work flowed through her mind, research and hypotheses that turned out to be totally wrong.

PART THREE

Down the Mask

CHAPTER 31

Place not specified   *March 30th, 2017*

Victoria slowly opened her eyes. As soon as she realized she was not in the darkness of her bedroom in Moscow, but in the squalid cell in which she had been chained for days, she began to cry silently.

Despair had led her to imagine her death several times, she would have liked to have a gun or an object with which to end that torture, but her suffering seemed destined to continue for a long time.

Since the previous day's lunch, not only had she no longer received other rations of food, but she had been able to hear her tormentor grappling with drills and other tools, just outside the door in front of her.

She understood what that bastard had in store for her: he was hiding her only possible way out, building a wall so that no one could ever find her remains once she died of hunger and hardship.

She had spent the whole previous day crying and screaming in vain, feeling her neck burn because of the bruises she had made in the fruitless attempts to tear the steel chain from the reinforced concrete wall to which it was attached.

When the noises had ceased, the silence and its blatant death sentence had fallen into that room: the countdown had begun which would have marked the end of Victoria Varichenko.

She felt an insect run over her back and managed to kill him by pressing her spine on where she felt him walk, against the wall of the concrete wall as she screamed in horror.

The survival instinct had blocked her idea of overturning the plastic bottle containing the last reserve of water when she thought of giving up and speeding up her death.

Hope was always the last to die in agreement, but hers had gone out the day before and Victoria had begun to pray to a God she had never believed in, promising a radical change in her lifestyle and interpersonal relationships in case they had managed to help her before the inevitable fate that her jailer had planned for her.

Once again she thought of her father, the way she had treated him the last time they met and the apologies she wanted to make before leaving.

Victoria managed to twist her arm until she collected the insect killed just before and put it in her mouth in an attempt to take on some protein essential for her survival.

She was a Varichenko after all and would not give up until she no longer had a modicum of energy capable of making her body live on.

Katrine woke up on the sofa of her apartment hearing shots.

The noise came from the TV news, tuned to her channel that informed viewers of what was happening in the world 24 hours a day.

The current service was the reply broadcast four hours earlier in the ten o'clock edition and described a gunfight between two factions competing for a large slice of Iraqi territory.

She got up to go and wash her sleepy face: she had spent most of the night observing the ceiling beams completely in a sleepless state, she had been able to rest only a couple of hours in the morning and the half hour in which she had fallen asleep in front of the TV after lunch.

Around eleven she had conversed on the phone with Ivan Varichenko who, despite having learned of her suspension, continued to trust her.

He had to be very desperate to listen to the woman being denigrated by the local channels and the major newspapers of the state.

Just then a journalist behind the screen of her plasma TV quoted her name, reminding her for the umpteenth time, of the oversight about Robert Hudson, of the failure of her pursuit and describing the recovery of the corpse found in Serenitz Park.

"The body found by a citizen while he was fishing, would have caught on the hook of his rod just yesterday morning and seems to be that of Robert Hudson, the main suspect of the chain of murders that occurred in the quiet town of Summerville. We are now asking the police officer, Philip De La Cruix, for further information on the matter".

Phil's serious and furious face appeared on the screen trying to find the right words to calm the citizens and give as little information as possible.

"We are all shocked by what is happening in our city, but at the moment we are analyzing possible evidence, organic materials found on Robert Hudson's body that we are certain will lead to the resolution of the case. We urge citizens to respect the curfew suggested by the numerous warnings displayed in the city, until we have managed to capture the murderer and finally close this case.

"Mr. De La Cruix, we have heard that detective Katrine Steward, also known as *Ghostbuster,* has been suspended from office, can you confirm this or are they just rumors without any basis?"

Philip took a long breath before looking at the camera lens as if he were directly observing Katrine himself.

"Agent Steward has been temporarily suspended, for reasons I am not allowed to tell you right now. I hope she finds the calm and serenity that allowed her to capture the *Ghost* last January, so that we can help ourselves in the future to keep Summerville's criminals out of the way".

Two other reporters addressed questions to the chief of police who walked away with Judith at his side, while the cameraman was framing the woman whispering something in her boss's ear.

Kat turned off the TV thinking about the dispute that had just occurred with Judith the day before.

She pulled out her cell phone and dialed Warren's number, waiting for his answer.

"Hey...are you all right?"

"Hi Warren, not much. I am forced to see Judith take my place alongside Philip during this morning's interview. Were you able to offer my apologies?"

"Not yet Tommy, you will see that I will be able to get your DVD`s back in the next few days, I can't here you very well, wait a moment, I will go out to smoke a cigarette..."

Katrine waited for her colleague to leave the office, she knew he was close to her at that moment.

"Here I am Kat, as you can imagine she was there with me. She doesn't want to talk to you and she is still upset by your behavior, but you will see, she will go over it, time heals every wound".

The woman thought back to that phrase that she had forced herself to remember whenever Zack had come to her mind in her experience in Los Angeles, but which she had hardly managed to apply in real life on other occasions too.

"Okay, it doesn't matter at the moment. I heard the news as I said, are there any news?"

"Judith will analyze Robert Hudson's body only tomorrow evening looking for possible evidence, but Philip lied shamelessly under his advice about what was found, at least as far as I know".

"Damn Warren, what are you saying? You're the person in charge of the investigation and I don't think Judith can manipulate a man of sound principles like Philip De La Cruix, so if you don't want to tell me what you found, just say it, okay?"

In the pause that followed there was the metallic noise of Warren's Zippo, intent on lighting a cigarette.

"Listen Katrine, you know I'm close to you, but in this situation I am not allowed to reveal any details to you, you will have to wait...Are you still there Kat? Hallo?"

Katrine through her cell phone on the sofa after putting it in airplane mode. She then went into the kitchen to prepare a relaxing herbal tea, deciding to abandon any attempt to communicate with her former team and abandon the investigation. If no one wanted Katrine Steward's help, they had managed to make her understand it.

She would do her training run within the next two hours, then call her sister to go out and distract herself and forget the faces of the victims of the case that had been taking away from her and that of all the people seen during her week of service at the Summerville police station.

Observing the boiling water in the cup in front of her change color contact with the sachet containing the herbal tea, she thought of Ivan's call that morning, his voice broken by tears and the money he had paid without receiving any news of his daughters release.

A quarter of an hour later Katrine was sitting on the carpet in the center of the room, surrounded by the files of each victim of the *Mask,* trying to find something useful that had escaped her over the previous week.

"It was her, is that right?"

"Yes, Judith. Deeply sorry for the quarrel with you and furious at the loss of her job".

The woman sitting at the desk adjusted her glasses with the strange frame on her face, massaging the red wrist that Katrine had tightened on her while she had been slammed against the wardrobe, the previous day.

"I'm sorry, I still can't forgive her for that nervous breakdown, it scared me to death and mostly for no good reason".

The colleague raised his eyebrows without Judith been able to notice and preferred to change subject.

"So we will not know until tomorrow evening if Robert's body can give us some useful information to be able to continue the investigation?"

"Exactly, unfortunately, the body won't arrive before then. So how do we continue with the investigation Warren? You are now the boss".

Warren sat down in Katrine's place, but after a few seconds he returned to his own, busy until before the colleague's departure the day before.

"Let's see…Mrs. Andrews contacted us this morning to confirm the death of her husband a few days after the operation by Olivia Harris, so the killer decided to punish her on the basis of this fact found by us last week. As for Robert Hudson, can we say that the murderer may have pulled out his eyes because of his blinding jealousy towards his wife?"

"Mhmm…let's say it could be, all we know about the couple was this overwhelming jealousy of the husband towards his wife and the extra-marital relationship with Tom Hackett on the part of the latter. According to Tom, it was only a matter of brevity and it is unlikely that her husband came to find out".

"Probably the killer used Robert Hudson as the scapegoat, so he could get all the blame down on him and get out of this whole story unscathed once the names came out of his list. The only thing he could not foresee is the wave of bad weather last weekend: the force of the river in flood must have released some of the weights that kept Robert's body anchored to the bottom, so as to allow the current to carry it to the banks of Serenity Lake. At the time of his discovery it was possible to estimate that the corpse had been in the waters of the river for about two weeks, so in just a moment, as the main wanted person, he could be found to be the first victim of someone else's diabolical plan".

Judith nodded with each of her colleague's pronounced sentences;

"The killer was a genius, he managed to organize everything perfectly, if it weren't for the heavy rain, we would have closed the case without ever finding what made us believe he was responsible for all the murders. Unfortunately it doesn't make much difference now, all the missing people have been executed..."

Warren watched as he fiddled with his cell phone, continually spinning in the center of the desk.

"Judith, I would like to ask you a question and I would like you to answer in the most sincere and honest way possible...

How important was it for you to be part of this team, to work with Katrine and dedicate yourself to the first real hunt to a serial killer here in Summerville?"

"A lot. I devoted practically every second of my time to this investigation, to teamwork to help Katrine capture this killer...yesterday I felt very bad when Kat accused me of those lies and let me tell you, even when you did nothing to stop her".

"You're right Judith, but last night I thought about your reaction, you really seemed to fall from the clouds when Kat started accusing you of passing information to the *Sunshine,* so I apologize.

In fact I could not understand why you should have done such a thing, but the information with which they described the articles the day after our discoveries belonged only to the three of us. There must be someone who spies on our work or our conversations..."

"Thank you Warren, but you could have listened to my version instead of banging me on the wall like a cheap thug. As for the spy I agree with you: someone follows our movements and listens to our conversations...yesterday Katrine said something about her ex boyfriend. You think that..."

"No I don't think so, but it's not a hypothesis to be discarded at this point. Okay, now that I know I can count on both, I feel I can involve you in a more complicated affair, of which it is right to let you know, but know one thing: if tomorrow should appear on the *Sunshine*, I will never be able to forgive you and I will report you directly to Philip".

Judith adjusted her glasses with the help of her index finger:

"Warren...you can count on me, what is it about?"

"There is another missing person. It is Victoria Varichenko, the daughter of the Russian mogul owner and founder of the most widespread communication company in Russia."

Judith absorbed the news; it was as if she had received a slap without having the opportunity to reply.

"Don't be offended, Katrine was contacted privately by her father who asked her to keep her disappearance secret for the time being. She wanted to involve me to help her in a parallel investigation, since everything seems to lead to the same author of the murders of last week. There is a ransom note and there is no reason why she was kidnapped, but in order to catch him we have to work on her...Kat needs all the help she can get and if she was here today, I'm sure she would have reflected on her mistakes, asking for your help. I'm sorry, we were fools to doubt you, but that *Sunshine* thing..."

"Shut up Warren! I've had enough of your apologies . I'm an adult woman, not a girl to keep secrets from . I don't care what you choose to tell me or not to tell me, but every second that passes we risk losing the last person involved in this crap, so let's get to work and give me all the details on this case. The life of a girl depends on the three of us and since the killer has always struck in a short time, within two or three days, we have until tomorrow evening at the latest to try to stop him before it's too late".

Warren observed with different eyes what he had thought until a week before the shy little girl marginalized by her colleagues, wacky and lonely. That case had allowed him to get to know each other better when Katrine wanted her in her team. Judith was thus able to show her hidden side, the grit and personality of a woman of the past, the commitment, constancy and dedication to her work, hidden from the nerd world to which it belonged and from the confidentiality of its character.

While telling the details of the story about Victoria, he thought of what his mother used to say to summarize the female universe: appearance sometimes deceives.

The courier who had rang Katrine's doorbell handed her a large box, after having made her sign the receipt.

"But, it's really true. Delivery within one day".

"Sure. We always keep our promises", said the man, pointing to the sentence imprinted under the logo of the uniform.

Kat laughed and left a small tip before saying goodbye and bringing the package inside the room.

Once she extracted the contents from the box and the polystyrene padding, she went to the basement to take her father's toolbox: she would have taken an hour to install the object resting on the floor.

CHAPTER 32

Kat's Apartment, 25 Elm Street   March 31th, 2017

Elizabeth lifted the covers of Kat's bed.

"Wake up, that's not how cases are solved. Whoever sleeps doesn't catch fish!"

Katrine opened her eyes slightly, managing to focus on the outline of the body of her sister standing in front of her, surrounded by the morning light penetrating through the bedroom window.

"Mhmm…Elizabeth! I was up until three in the morning last night, you should also be aware of the fact that I was suspended from office".

Her younger sister sat down next to Katrine and gave her sweet big eyes that she used to do to beg someone.

"Oh poor Kat…since when do you care what people think?

Even if you are no longer in charge of the investigation, you know very well that you are the most qualified agent to solve this story".

"I don't think so, I took a false lead from the beginning as a beginner, I know the case files by heart without understanding who may have dealt with all the victims and I have no idea how to go on without the support of my team or the resources I had at the police station".

The policewoman got out of bed, dragging the black dressing gown to the walk-in closet, in order to choose the clothes to wear during the day.

"I know I've never been able to help you or at least console you in your total blackout periods, but I can only tell you one thing: everyone makes mistakes Kat. You are used to planning everything and never making a mistake, but you have to accept the fact that you are not in an automaton, sooner or later a situation like this had to happen, if not more drastic".

"Ah yes? What's worse than being suspended by Dad's best friend after being treated for years with velvet gloves, or appearing on most local news, while in the subtitle strip is described as an incapable?"

Elizabeth observed her older sister as she put on a gray sweatshirt she had given her when she returned from her honeymoon in Polynesia and an olive green jeans.

"Um, I don't know...think if I didn't have a little sister to let off steam with, for example".

Katrine glared at her as she tucked her hair into the usual ponytail, then moved to the bathroom to freshen up, followed like a shadow by her sister.

"I thought I saw someone at my bedroom window last night..."

"It must have been a nightmare, the only way to reach your window is to climb the tree of your neighbors. Why would anyone spy on you during the night?"

Kathrine wiped her face, meeting Elizabeth's gaze in the mirror above the sink.

"I don't know, it could have been *The Mask* to scare me or to think of a way to...kill me".

"Stop Katrine! It's not funny at all. Don't mess around with these things".

Once out of the bathroom, Katrine took her sister in a friendly grip, squeezing her neck with her right arm.

"But then you love me a little…anyway if I were you, I would make a new haircut, before being mistaken for Katrine Steward, the Ghostbuster, at least until this story is completely over".

"Ah – Ah, very witty…can you offer me a coffee at least?"

"Sure, but first follow me in the living room, I would like to show you how the Kat you knew has not changed a iota. Did you really think I was here doing nothing, waiting to be torn apart by the press and my boss?"

The computer screen came on and Katrine started a fresh installer, double clicking the mouse arrow positioned on its icon.

"What do you mean? What is this stuff?"

The older sister sat in a wheelchair in front of the computer and a triumphant little smile appeared on her face.

"You have to understand Elizabeth, that your big sister is always right…I believed that you knew it after years of living together under the same roof, but apparently you too underestimated me, like everyone else. I ordered an infrared camera, I needed evidence to accuse a stalker who has been chasing me around since I came to Summerville…so look here, around seven this morning".

The images on the screen portrayed a man climbing the tree near her home and positioning himself in front of her bedroom window, to remain motionless staring at her for about ten minutes while she slept.

"But that seems…that`s Zack!"

"Not exactly Elizabeth...I lost Zack five years ago, this is a madman who decided to ruin his life on his own, after trying to ruin mine".

Her younger sister found herself staring at the images with her mouth open while Kat's green eyes seemed to burn with anger beneath her.

Around eleven o'clock in the morning, Judith entered the office, finding Warren annoyed and furious.

"For once, I'm not the latecomer. Is this the time to start work?"

The woman placed two A4 sheets on the desk and took off her scarf, revealing a red spot on her right cheek.

"I can explain everything, I wrote exactly everything on these sheets, just give me a minute to catch my breath".

Warren watched the woman greedily sip her bottle of mineral water, she seemed very hot, she must have rushed to the office or being particularly agitated, just like the first time he had seen her several months before, while exposing her analyzes in front of the classroom full of policemen, to ascertain the arrest of a rapist caught previously.

On that occasion Judith had seemed quite agitated in describing the rape in front of all the staff, probably because it was one of the first times she was found in situations of this type, but now he could not understand the reason why she was so nervous.

"I fucked up, I admit it, but now I've discovered a very important thing Warren".

The policeman approached her trying to calm her down: "Don`t worry Judith, what happened this morning?"

Judith finished drinking and through the bottle into the trash can under the desk, then took a deep breath and started talking.

"This morning I woke up early, assailed by a doubt that had tormented me for some time. The stone found by Kat was found to be a mineral not present in the table of elements as you know, right?"

Warren nodded, then sat down on the chair opposite her.

"I went to the laboratory and did something that a forensic scientist should never do with a possible proof. I wanted to feel the effect of that stone on my skin, to touch that unique and new element with my hand, therefore I locked myself from the inside and placed the fragment on my cheek, after weighing it and touching it with my hands. A few seconds later, as I placed it inside its plastic bag, I felt a slight tingling sensation where my skin had touched the stone. I will hardly be able to describe what I have experienced, but I will try to do it in as much detail as possible.

At the beginning I felt an extraordinary sense of wellbeing, like as after drinking a glass of too much alcohol or taking drugs, you know what I mean?"

Warren observed her colleague trying to imagine her revved up, but he just nodded, unable to match her to any kind of high.

"Instead, later I felt a strong anger towards Katrine, for what she did to me here in the office last time and I started to behave without having full control of my body; I remember taking a scalpel, thinking of killing her and imagining other violent scenes towards other people: an ex classmate of mine, my first boyfriend and my uncle John".

"Judith, what are you saying? Are you going mad?"

"Let me finish. After a few minutes the effect was gone and I found myself wanting to try to touch the stone again. I know it seems absurd, but in contact with the skin, that fragment releases a substance that penetrates the depths of the dermis and it acts on the nervous system, well I`m sure".

"I don`t know what to think of anymore, Judith, but I`ll pretend to believe you".

"You must believe me Warren! I feel ridiculous to expose these facts, but I can swear to you that I really felt different: if a very small fragment was enough to trigger an attack of anger of that magnitude, imagine wearing a mask made of that material for a long time. I noticed some liquid inside the bag after putting the fragment inside, that object is able to produce a substance that acts on our brain, it blocks some actions of the body in order to make it act involuntary. Absurd, totally absurd, but I guarantee you that it is so".

Warren closed his eyes and put a hand on his forehead.

"Okay, I`ll try to believe you. If that were the case , the effect of the whole mask would be explained, a trail of corpses killed in the worst possible way. Katrine has also touched the stone: this could explain her aggressive behavior in recent days, including your aggression in here then".

"At this point I begin to think so too".

Warren got up and took his jacket: "Come on, let`s go".

"Where do you want to go?"

"The only way to fully believe you is to test the stone on me. Come on hurry up".

"No, no, no. Warren I can't make you do it, I've already made a mistake this morning doing the same thing, I don't want to make you feel those feelings too".

Warren tied his jacket and put his hand on the door handle: "Don't worry, you will chain me to something with your handcuffs and then the mark on your cheek will be gone".

Judith touched the soft skin of her cheeks, no longer feeling the burning sensation she had experienced until recently. "All right, Warren. We will do as you say".

CHAPTER 33

Judith's Scientific Laboratory   *March 31th, 2017*

The cuffs around Warren's hands made a loud metallic noise, after being tightened around a pipe by the colleague.

"Courage Judith, do it without hesitation".

His hands wrapped in two green latex gloves were trembling in holding up the small fragment of stone, while Judith was looking for a point in Warren's face to place it on.

"Wait a minute, I'm looking for a beardless spot, you could have shaved this morning".

"I haven't had the time, okay? Come on, rest it on your neck without fear".

Judith put a little pressure on the skin of Warren's neck and after a few seconds put the stone back in the plastic bag.

"Done, let's wait a moment. How are you feeling?"

"As always...are you really sure of what you told me? Isn't it just that you just drank last night and you had a hangover this morning?"

"Don't joke Warren, I went to bed very early last night, after feeding my animals I collapsed with the case files still in my hands".

"Discovered something? I didn't know you were an animal lover".

Judith checked the stopwatch on her wristwatch, looking for any change on her handcuffed colleague: they had decided not to talk to anyone about this initiative because it seemed too ridiculous to be told.

"Yes I live with my dog Sharky and I have a small building behind the house with a donkey, chickens and rabbits.

I have only dug into the past of Dylan Rogers and the numerous processes he has had to face. The bond with the professor, excluding the one between the couple composed by Sarah and Robert himself, it is the only connection between the victims that really catches the eye".

"Well, if only you possessed goats you would be the main suspect at this point. As for the victims, it is now clear why the killer chose them".

"I know this, but to know certain things, the killer had to know his victims very well. I have puzzled in every possible way, the professor, the pupil, the tattoo artist, the doctor and the secretary. What can really connect these people or their faults?"

Warren tried to understand if he was experiencing some strange symptoms, due to the simple contact with the stone, but he felt nothing different than normal.

"You're right. I bet that Katrine is also puzzling to find some connection, it must be the real key to be able to trace the killer and at the moment we have all the pieces. Robert's jealousy, Sarah's betrayal, the murders of Dylan, Olivia and Eric; at this point I would really like to believe this story of the magic mask, believe me. By the way, could you untie me?"

Judith checked the stopwatch: she decided to wait another seven minutes before releasing her colleague. At the end of the set minutes, Judith gave the key to Warren's handcuffs.

She had really experienced everything she had described to her colleague immediately after touching the stone, while the man seemed to show no change on his skin or behavior.

"There must be some other factor that has helped to unleash my repressed anger and that of Katrine, I would like to know which one".

The scientist turned to take the plastic bag containing the stone and managed to notice a small leak of the same strange liquid that she had noticed herself a few hours before.

"Wait Warren, here we go, it should take effect…"

Warren pounced on her, trying to throttle her with the handcuffs, squeezing with superhuman strength until her feet were lifted off the ground.

Judith felt the air needed to breathe as panic began to manifest itself through her movements, causing her to kick in the void; she sank her nails into her colleague's arms to try to free herself from the man in the grip of a murderous instinct.

She felt the vision dim after a few seconds, she was about to surrender to the end that she herself had sought, when she managed to notice the stone resting on the table on her right.

She managed to reach out and pick it up, then raised it as high as possible and knocked it down against Warren's head with all the energy left.

The seconds that followed were experienced by Judith as in slow motion: Warren let go , the stone broke into very small pieces and the woman fell to the floor.

Warren opened his eyes and stared at his colleague: "But what happened Judith?"

The woman observed the small dark spot that was being created on the bleeding man's neck:

"Exactly what I feared".

After medicating the wound to Warren's forehead , Judith was able to analyze what was left of the liquid emitted from the stone.

"Damn Judith, I never believed in magic until now".

"The scientist looked up from the microscope as she jotted something on the notepad next to her.

"I'm afraid I will have to disappoint you again, I finally found out what caused our reactions".

Warren felt the bump that had been created where the stone hat hit his forehead to test its consistency. "What do you mean?"

"Inside the stone there are traces of diethylamide of lysergic acid, more commonly known as LSD. The extraordinary thing is that the small amount of liquid does not easily come out of the envelope in which it is kept: that prehistoric stone is truly phenomenal".

"What? We were drugged?"

"Exactly. LSD was extracted from a fungus that attacks cereals, in particular Rye Cornuta, is usually taken via orally, often in the form of cards soaked in a solution of the substance, but much more rarely by transpiration of the skin as has happened to us.

This powerful drug acts on the central and peripheral nervous system, changing sensory perceptions and the state of consciousness, to the point of causing visual, acoustic and sometimes even tactile or thermal hallucinations.

This causes effects that can vary from heavenly visions to terrifying nightmares or, as in our case, to imaginary dangerous situations".

Warren listened carefully to Judith's ear as he fiddled with the pack of cigarettes as he passed it from hand to hand.

"Are you telling me that more than ten thousand years ago, our ancestors resorted to the use of one of the most powerful drugs in the world to expand and expand their kingdom as Alessandro Zaretti reported to Katrine long ago?"

Judith moved her glasses slightly, then took off her gloves and threw them in the trash.

" I'm not saying it went like this, but it could have happened. Horned Rye attacked plantations especially during the Middle Ages, but no one can tell us if a few thousand years earlier one of our distant ancestors failed to synthesize it in pure form, that is, a transparent crystal".

"Okay, let's pretend that a mask created in the distant past, capable of altering the perception of reality to its owner, ended up in the wrong hands. How can this help us discover the identity behind its owner?"

The laboratory intercom crackled loudly: Robert Hudson's body could finally be analyzed.

"Unfortunately it's useless, but our last card to find out something useful about this whole story, is going to be carried out on this bed".

Elizabeth sipped the glass of red wine that her sister had just refilled.

"So are you going to end this story tomorrow by handing over the video to Philip in the first place?"

Katrine cleared the table, throwing the remains of the turkey into the garbage before putting dishes and cutlery back in the dishwasher.

"Of course to be able to prove him wrong, at least on this. Do you like some fruit? I prepared a fruit salad last night, I must have two portions left".

No thanks, it would be better if I go to prepare dinner for James, he`ll be back in just over half an hour from going out with a friend of his. Thank you for everything big sister, it was a beautiful day…in case you need a day off, you just need to ask me for an exchange of identity: not even your fellow cops would notice the difference, I bet on it".

Katrine accompanied her sister to the entrance: "Thanks to you Elizabeth for your company, we`ll talk tomorrow, I think we could …wait what did you say?"

Her sister put on her elegant coat before turning to Katrine: "James`s dinner, I really have to run to prepare something for him, he`ll be back soon…"

"No, no, I meant about the exchange of identity".

"That? I was kidding Katrine, I just said that not even your police friends, always attentive to detail, would be able to understand my identity, if only I wanted to replace you for a day".

Katrine stood motionless staring at her sister for a few seconds, then spoke again: "Thanks Elizabeth, as always I can count on you, say hallo to James, please".

"I will, relax Katrine and don`t think about it too much, I was just kidding".

Elizabeth closed the door and Kat stood staring at the front door for a moment. Something had gone through her mind, it wasn't clear what it was, but she knew it centered on the case she was working on and not on the image described by her sister. Hoping something would click in rereading the case files for the umpteenth time, she went to the floor of the room on which they were still arranged from the previous evening.

CHAPTER 34

Kat's apartment, 25 Elm Street *March 31ᵗʰ, 2017*

Katrine sat with her knees crossed in the center of the room, staring at the white curtains of the window in front of her. Surrounded by the files, she had fallen into a sort of trance, as had happened when she had managed to solve the *Ghost* case.

She knew she had left out a small, tiny detail in everything that had happened to her lately, but she still couldn't focus on which.

Her current reasoning was based on the fact that the assassin's plan did not foresee the discovery of the corpse of Robert Hudson, the designated scapegoat on which the faults of all the murders could easily fall.

A small misplaced gear that could have compromised the entire mechanism studied in detail by a diabolical and planning mind.

Who was the mysterious individual who used a mask and a vocal distortion to conceal their identity?

Her mind returned to the moment when Kat met the gaze of the *Mask,* unfortunately she could not give a face to the person who had inflicted the crucial stab on Eric Preston.

Katrine found herself reliving her pursuit until the moment she ended up in the dead end. It was there that the missing puzzle piece began to take shape.

During the race the *Mask* had managed to gain several seconds of advantage: she could estimate about twenty; yet when she noticed the hole in the fence, the killer was still climbing over the wall, for which he must have encountered some difficulty in crawling beyond the fence and in the subsequent climbing on the wall.

Katrine raised her thumb and forefinger of her right hand mimicking a gun as she tried to remember the exact moment she had pulled the trigger to detonate the shot, as in a scene from the movie *Matrix*.

The *Mask* was in front of her, staring at her motionless clinging to the wall a moment before releasing her grip, destabilized by the strength of the bullet. It was only then that Katrine managed to remember a very small, but important detail that she had let slip that night: now she could explain why the individual on the run had wasted precious seconds to climb over the wall, although he turned out to be an excellent runner. A shiver ran through her back, now other things were beginning to make sense: the vocal distortion, the need to make the blame fall on Robert, the ease with which the *Mask* had managed to kidnap people and obtain the tools necessary to carry out his plan.

All the victims knew their killer, in one way or another in the past, they had had a face-to-face meeting, even herself several years before, even if several times she had had occasions to observe the photograph in the second part of the week just spent.

She took the keys to the jeep and put on her jacket as fast as she could: it was almost nine when she left the house, it would take an abundant hour to reach the place where she hoped to find Victoria.

Once the engine was started, she opened the glove compartment of the jeep extracting her M1911, put the first gear in and started at full speed, while typing Warrens number on her mobile phone.

After the fifth ring she heard the female voice of his answering machine and began to record a message: "Warren it's me Kat, I know who is hiding behind the *Mask,* I am going to the old refuge in Pine Forest, north of Summerville. Call Philip and join me with reinforcements, Victoria is up there, maybe I can get there in time to save her. Christ, we could have thought about it earlier, call me as soon as you get…"

The line broke off abruptly and Katrine checked the cell phone screen to find out what had happened.

The display of her iPhone remained black even after holding down the power button: the battery was completely discharged due to the numerous searches made in the afternoon.

"Shit!", she said throwing it on the passenger seat and then squeeze the steering wheel with both hands and fully depress the accelerator pedal.

She felt the cold steel of the gun resting on her thighs as she thought of the *Mask:* this time she wouldn't let him run away again.

Warren's cell phone vibrated five times in vain inside the jacket hanging in the laboratory where he and Judith were analyzing Robert Hudson's body.

"Judith, do you think we can find some fiber on his body, maybe some skin or blood residue under his nails?"

The woman lowered the lens to be able to further enlarge the view of the empty orbits of the body lying in front of the two agents, as she lifted the light to illuminate more the affected area.

"Warren, this is not C.S.I., unfortunately we are not so lucky, the water has swept away any organic trace present on his body…the low temperature of the river has contributed to better preserve its body, but I'm unable to tell you precisely how long it was on the seabed. I can estimate a period of between one or two weeks, certainly not more".

"Just as we suspected. He killed him before Sara, he was the number one victim, I'm sure of it".

"Wow…a good job was done with flakes regarding the removal of the eyeballs. A perfect nucleation intervention of the eye, worthy of expert hands".

"Enu what?"

Nucleation is a complicated operation where the globe is removed, including the cornea, sclera and an optic nerve potion. A job of about an hour, but with a high level of difficulty; I thought the killer had pulled Robert's eyes hastily, using some makeshift tools to help himself in the operation.

Unfortunately I don't think the person responsible for this mutilation has used any type of anesthesia…he must have suffered a lot, certain types of operations require the induced state of pharmacological coma, I dare not imagine what this poor man felt".

"Jesus Christ…"

Warren put his hand to his face, covering his mouth, his gaze on the lifeless body lying on the bed.

"Wait a second…look at the upper part of the neck. How come it is so swollen at that point? After death, gases are formed which cause the abdomen and other parts of the body to protrude, well I am aware of it, but give a look at that protuberance".

Judith`s gloves moved to the part of the neck indicated by Warren and felt a solid object inside.

"You`re right , there is something here, I hadn`t noticed before".

The woman took a small instrument to probe the inside of the oral cavity and the images transmitted on the monitor a little further away revealed a gruesome image.

"Shit…"

"What`s happening?"

The man approached to observe the images that appeared on the screen and felt a strong retching, as soon as he understood what he was actually observing.

"The cause of Robert`s death was not by drowning Warren, but the asphyxiation caused by the foreign body introduced into his oral cavity that you see on the images. Smothered by his own eyes…how can you be so evil?"

Robert`s eyes stared at her from behind the screen, set in two round transparent capsules that had been perfectly positioned inside his throat, in order to obstruct the respiratory tract until it causes an insufficiency of oxygen to his brain, causing him to suffocate.

Katrine parked the jeep at the end of the asphalted road on the way to the Pine Forest refuge, leaving it clearly visible in the center of the square reserved for the cars of hikers who embarked on that mountain path.

A brief gust of cold air lifted her hair as she climbed the only path that led to the refuge: she would have reached it in just under twenty minutes if she remembered well the timing of that walk that she covered a couple of times a year.

After a short climb she turned to look at the parking lot occupied only by her car and a small purple van with no writing: it would have been the means used for the last movements of the *Mask,* she could bet on it.

She took the small flashlight she had picked up from the jeep from her jacket pocket and turned it on by pressing the switch, thus illuminating the dirt road in front of her.

The path went up gently and then lost itself in the pine forest: the walk was famous throughout the region and on beautiful summer days it was hard to find parking space.

Katrine's courage began to diminish when a sound of an animal could be heard from inside the pine forest, but the pistol she held in her hands was enough to provide her with the necessary security at the improvised solo ambush only an hour before.

The situation seemed increasingly clear to her as she proceeded towards the refuge; the closer she got to the person responsible for that carnage, the more she could understand how stupid she had been.

If only she had the chance to contact her team she would have apologized to Judith. I wonder if she would have ever forgiven her for her behavior and the violent reaction she had in the office; after all she was right, she had absolutely nothing to do with the disclosure of the facts to the *Sunshine.*

She raised the hood of her jacket to try to warm her icy ears and pointed the torch towards the entrance of the pine forest, making sure there were no animals nearby. After a few steps the pine fronds completely covered the starry sky above her; there were only about ten minutes left to the abandoned refuge in the middle of the pine forest.

"Sorry Judith, I can`t watch".

"Tranquil Warren, don`t worry. I just need a favor. You should try to extract those two capsules.

The man`s pale face took on a surprised expression: "Are you kidding? Why should I do such a thing?"

The woman looked at him behind the thick lenses of her glasses: "Come on, don`t be a sissy. I sincerely need your help now, to be able to come to a conclusion that may surprise you".

Warren put on a glove and tried to insert his hand into Robert`s mouth, but after a few seconds he gave up on the attempt.

"But couldn`t you use some tool to help you extract that stuff? I just can`t."

Judith stood behind him and put her hand on that of the horrified man : "Come on, you don`t have to look.

Warren inserted his hand into Robert`s corpse, but no matter how hard he tried, he couldn`t even get close to the plastic capsules.

"I can`t get there, you have to open his throat with a scalpel".

The woman dodged him and inserted her hand inside the lifeless body, managing to extract the first capsule and placed it on the steel table.

"As I imagined, there will be no need for the scalpel. I just wanted to make sure of one thing...as you may have guessed, the capsules were inserted manually by the murderer, pushed down the oral cavity and positioned exactly in that way. As you may have noticed, a man's hand is too large to carry out such a task, so what can we deduce?"

Warren's eyes widened as Judith pulled the second capsule out of Robert Hudson's body.

"You mean that…"

"Exactly Warren, the killer behind the mask must necessarily be a woman".

When Katrine saw the old refuge in the heart of the pine forest, she felt a mixture of satisfaction and fear; the awareness of being right about the place where the *Mask* was hiding gave way to the terror of being alone again, to face a serial killer for the second time in a few months.

She could see the faint light of the lighting on the ground floor despite the shutters being closed and smoke escaping from the chimney on the roof; this meant that the killer was there and probably Victoria Varichenko too, so she decided to turn off the torch. The position of the refuge was extremely tactical as a little further on it was possible, equipped with good binoculars or telescopes, to observe the entire Summerville.

At that time of the year you could enjoy all the privacy offered by that place surrounded by nature: as the refuge had been abandoned twenty years earlier and almost nobody walked the path to reach it, preferring the one that skirted the panoramic side of the mountain.

Exactly halfway between the refuge and downtown Summerville was Sunset hill, the place where Dylan Rogers had lost his life the previous week.

She heard the flow of the Blurry River a little further downstream: probably Robert Hudson must have been killed nearby. Once the two weights that kept him anchored to the bottom had been stripped, the current must have carried his body along the Serenity Lake inlet, she was sure.

Everything now seemed obvious to her: even the abandoned stable adjacent to the refuge, apparently unused, but a stopping point in case of bad weather for shepherds and animals during the summer.

With a beating heart, Kat went to the refuge to try to detect the position of the two woman inside: with her back to the wall she tried to peek through the cracks in the shutters, but she could not see anyone inside, only the table to be cleared, a toolbox along the corridor and little less: She could hear music: she recognized the verse of the refrain of the song *You`re so Vain* by *Carly Simons* echoing in all the rooms during her patrol of the outer perimeter of the house.

The back door had been closed with a padlock and the cellar windows had been closed with wooden planks: it would have made too much noise to remove them or blow up the padlock. She decided to take advantage of the background music by sneaking in through the main entrance, squeezing the grip of her gun more and more.

She slowly lowered the handle and the door produced a slight creak, however made imperceptible by the music coming from the nearest room.

After a few steps she managed to enter in the kitchen and her attention was captured by the photographs placed on the dilapidated hob: between the faces of the killed people she could also see her own, in a photo that portrayed her on the newspaper article concerning the solved case in Los Angeles.

Suddenly she felt someone behind her and turned abruptly to aim the gun, but the other woman was faster than her: she kicked her hand making it fall and threw herself on Kathrine, pushing her against the wall.

Kat managed to free herself but felt a slight tingling at the base of the neck and a burning sensation at the point where the needle of the syringe had penetrated her skin.

"What`s going on Katrine? Aren`t you feeling well?

The distorted voice of the woman with the mask in front of her echoed in her head with a deafening echo.

Staggering in the middle of the kitchen, she overturned a glass shattering into a thousand pieces, as she tried to drag herself along the corridor under the amused gaze of the woman with the syringe still in her hands.

"The drug that I injected to you is the same one that I used on Eric Preston, you won`t lose consciousness, but soon you will be completely immobile and harmless.

Your head will spin for a few minutes, then the substance will block all your muscles and movements, making you helpless like a puppet".

The woman unplugged the distortion and took off her mask as she watched Katrine slam from one wall to the other and end her desperate escape in the corner of the corridor next to the stairs.

She tried to support herself with the help of the handrail, then slumped on her back, with her glazed paralyzed but conscious gaze turned towards the woman declared dead up to that moment: Olivia Harris.

CHAPTER 35

Judith's Laboratory   *March 31ᵗʰ, 2017*

"Are you really sure?"

Warren threw his gloves in the trash and went to wash his hands at the sink, rubbing them vigorously with soap as if it would help him get the disgusting action taken just before, from his head.

"Listen to me, she was really very smart, I have to admit that she managed to deceive us all, but if we are looking for a woman, with experience in the medical field, with whom all the victims could have had related to her, then I can only think of Olivia Harris".

"But it`s absurd, Olivia died in the industrial oven, remember? Wait…you`re right, in the end we only found her ring finger and some blood, she could have designed everything and simulated her execution creating a false track".

Judith took her gloves off, coat and mask then washed her hands, imitating her colleague. "Nobody would have suspected her, if we hadn`t found Robert`s body, all the charges would have been directed towards him and Olivia could have safely fled without ever being discovered".

"We have to tell Katrine, I want to hear her opinion".

The scientist put on her quilt and pulled out the keys to close the laboratory:

"All right, it seems a great idea. I`ll call Philip to update him on the discovery".

The two exchanged a nod of understanding and both took the mobile phone from the pockets of their jackets to contact Kat and Philip.

Warren realized he had a voicemail message and listened to Katrine's voice recorded over an hour ago; Judith waited to hear their boss's voice before she could update him.

"I'm sure Philip. Olivia Harris is the *Mask,* there is no more doubt, she was able to use medical instruments by taking them from the hospital she worked for: the acid with which she killed Finningham, the scalpel found on the cart in the factory, the drug used to paralyze Eric and other substances with which she managed to seize the victims easily. Furthermore, I believe it was she who informed the young journalist giving him all the details with which she completed the murders…wait a second online…Warren is here?"

"Have reinforcement sent to the old refuge in Pine Forest, Katrine is in trouble".

Olivia dragged Katrine to the old sofa in the common room of the refuge: she was able to seat her without difficulty then she took the toolbox and began a long monologue.

"I know what you're wondering about Katrine Steward…with a little patience I'd like to tell you the whole story, but unfortunately I don't think we have much time left. You friends are probably on their way…"

Katrine managed to move her eyes towards Olivia, following her in every movement and listening to her words.

Compared to the Photo hanging on the wall of her office, the woman appeared changed, had resorted to special changes to not be recognized.

The hair had been shaved on the right side of the head, while the remaining dark locks took on a cut similar to that of Judith, the cut and tint to which she had probably done it herself. Olivia hid the green irises of her eyes with colored contact lenses, so that anyone who had met her gaze in passing , would not have noticed any similarity with the photo of the woman printed in the newspapers.

"You don't know how easy it was to get around the city undisturbed at this time. I am not talking about the changes on my face or the disguises used to move me through the crow; have you ever realized how much people hang on cell phones now a days? Even if I had kept my identity, nobody would have noticed. What do you say, Kat?"

The policewoman tried to move her fingers, one foot, whatever responded to the commands of her brain, but it was like living in a dream where one is forced to listen in silence.

"Too bad you can't speak, but before long the drug will end its effect and you will be able to resume the word, just in time to say goodbye to this world. You know, you're the only one missing to completely realize my work, then I will be able to leave and act undisturbed elsewhere".

What was she talking about? Where was Victoria at the time? She had not heard any noise or noticed traces of her imprisonment and Olivia had never mentioned her until then.

"We are not very different me and you Katrine, we try to bring justice to this false and corrupted world, I hope at least you can understand this. The people I killed were all guilty in one way or another and you also killed a person, is that not so?"

How the hell did she know about the real course of events during the shooting with Alan Wilder?

She was really beginning to believe that the mask had magical powers.

"See, some time ago Sarah Finningham and her husband Robert come to me for a very delicate matter: Sarah had become pregnant and they both didn't want to keep the baby. Despite trying to convince them, I was forced to give her the contacts of a center where Sarah could practice abortion. Isn't it murder Kat? To take a life out of pure selfishness, to deny the greatest gift to an innocent, sinless creature?"

The policewoman listened attentively to that part of the fact completely unknown to her, while Olivia expressed herself gesturing animatedly.

"Well, you must also know that I chose Sinners thanks to the help of this mask, without her I would not even have been able to imagine realizing my path of revenge and purification.

Do you like it? My daughter gave it to me a few days before she died...I discovered its potential by wearing it by chance one day last summer and from there it all came to me automatically: I guarantee you that it can bring out the best in me. But let's go back to that absurd couple; after studying them for a few months I was able to discover Sarah's betrayal and the violent behavior with which her husband let his jealousy vent and a great idea came to my mind: why not blame everything I had in mind to that violent man, possessive and blinded by his mad jealousy?

So I thought I'd leave it on the bottom of the river until the waters had calmed down, but the rain from last weekend messed up my plans. You should have seen how those two killers begged me; yet when it came to taking their baby's life they didn't make a lot of fuss".

Olivia took out the battery-powered electric bone saw with which she had cut Dylan Roger's finger and placed it on the table next to her.

"Then Dylan's turn came, I have to admit it: the whole plan revolved around his death. As you know that junkie took the life of my daughter Lucy, in a car accident where he was surely driving under the influence of drugs, but luckily my lawyers were unable to win the case and get him thrown in jail: so I could revenge her with my own hands: You can't imagine how much I thought about how to make him suffer, kill him in the most atrocious ways…but the mask prevented me from doing it…he wanted him to die that way so it was".

Katrine watched Olivia take off her gloves and could see what had made her understand the identity hidden behind the mask: the stump of her left ring finger had given her some difficulty in climbing the wall on the night of the chase and in the flashback that took place an hour earlier she had managed to remember the strange grip used by Olivia while receiving her bullet.

"What are you looking at? Ah, this? Great isn't it? I Haven't even suffered much, a little sacrifice necessary to make you fall into my trap…you cops are so stupid at times. Don't worry Katrine, in a few seconds you will know exactly what it feels like losing a finger".

The bone saw began to whirl around at the end of that sentence.

Warren traveled up the hill towards Sunset Hill at the maximum speed consented by his pick up, while Judith sat by his side checking the map of the mountain trails in the area on the internet.

"How did Katrine find out about Olivia Harris and the Pine Hill refuge? That morning I told her about her disappearance, she briefly mentioned it, it seems that Olivia's father managed the refuge in the Pine Forest and during one of her summer walks as a young woman she saw her up there. Kat knows these mountains very well and grew up just like you in this city, didn't you know anything about this place?"

Judith turned to look at the two police cars that followed their pick up with the serene full gas: "To tell the truth, I didn't go out very often even when I was young; I have always been a lazy student".

Warren shifted down the gear and faced a sharp bend, pushing the woman against the door due to the centrifugal force.

"Imagine a mind like Olivia's under the influence of that drug...the death of her daughter also helped drive her crazy".

"I was thinking the same thing, she went so far as to cut a finger to make us think she was dead, when in reality she was killing those poor people in peace. To seize the four victims you don't need the strength of a man when you have an entire supply of drugs and substances such as chloroform".

"Yeah, I thought so too. We haven't been very clever, I feel like a fool now that I know the truth".

"You shouldn't feel that way, she was very clever and attentive to detail; the amount of blood found outside the oven was much more than that lost by amputating her finger. She must have taken it by herself previously and then spread it on the floor, making us believe that she was tortured before being locked up in the oven. The symbol and the clues left after each murder, however, do not suggest that a part of her wants to be captured; I'm sure that if she hadn't broken into Eric's hut, she would have left the symbol again...if you were a murderer, would you leave clues deliberately to risk being discovered ?"

"I don`t think...unless I want to brag my work or..."

The two looked at the same instant, then Warren swerved sharply to turn onto the road on the foot of Sunset Hill, halfway from their destination.

Judith concluded the sentence by raising her voice in a few tones: "My God Warren, Olivia wanted to be found by Katrine, she plans to kill her too!"

The pickup overtook a bump by lifting the four wheels off the ground for a few seconds, followed at full speed by the police cars with the sirens on.

Katrine suffered in silence, while tears streamed down her cheeks: she could see her finger on the floor right in front of her. Despite the paralysis, the sharp pain was felt immediately.

Come on , get up, you should be able to walk now, we don`t have much time"

Olivia picked up a shoulder bag containing everything she needed to escape and put it on her shoulder, while Katrine managed to move some muscles, but continued to pretend to be still, hoping to gain precious time.

"Damn, I must have injected more than I expected"

Olivia took out the mask and, after picking up Katrine`s gun and putting it inside the bag, she put it on.

The woman managed to load Katrine`s full weight on her shoulders without difficulty, on the contrary, she seemed to feel almost no effort even wearing that horrible mask.

Now that she could see it better, she could observe the small amber crystals on its entire surface, the part with the missing fragment on its right cheek and the bright blood-red patch that divided the face in two, as if it had just been passed a coat of red paint.

As far as Eric Preston was concerned, it was a pure case to learn of his murder. You must know that I was the first person to help Gary Hoffman and before he died he managed to describe me a tattoo of his attacker. A few days later Eric Preston shows up in my studio to have his arm cast and when I saw the red skull tattooed on his neck, I immediately understood that he was responsible for the robbery that took place on the same day that Gary Hoffman died as a hero. I had to put him on my list too, you understand? I certainly could not wait for you cops to catch the thief, I wanted to keep all the credit, I know, I am damned self-centered sometimes".

The two woman left the refuge leaving the stereo and the lights on, following a treaty of pine forest unknown to Katrine who was trying to regain the sensitivity of her right hand in order to be able to remove the gun from the bag under her.

"End…did…Victoria?"

"What are you babbling Kat?" It`s not about winning or losing in this story, it`s about purifying the city from scum, a task that should be up to you law enforcement, or incompetent lawyers, but I prefer to continue this mission alone, now that the mask managed to give me back a goal".

"Acting…in the…same way as your…victims?"

"Ha ha. But listen to this. I must also listen to the preaching of the woman symbol of justice in this city. I heard a lot of interesting things, thanks to the two-way radios that I installed in your apartment just before your return. Thanks to them I have always been a step ahead of you and I have been able to inform that stupid reporter, making you suspend. Too bad you never talked about what you did…Your worst sin. You know, I was right there when it happened".

Katrine could feel her left foot begin to respond to commands imposed by her brain; soon she would be able to break free, or at least that was the only plan she had in mind.

"What do you know" You couldn`t have been there".

Olivia climbed a small difference in height which brought them to an area without trees, you could hear the flow of the river a little further downstream than where they were at that moment.

"See when you and Elizabeth came out of the room where your mother was, I noticed the small hole on her IV. At that moment it seemed to me a very generous action on your part, put an end to her suffering by giving her a product that would have never been discovered: truly admirable.

Euthanasia is a very difficult choice to take and still illegal in this country fortunately. I knew of the conditions of your mother, fed by machines and reduced to the vegetable state; at the time your choice seemed right to me, but once again the mask managed to show me the right way, for this reason, after you it will also be your sister Elizabeth. I will inject the same acid as Sarah Finningham directly into the main veins. It will be terrible, I`m sure, but she will understand where she went wrong".

Katrine remembered their visit some years earlier to the hospital room where their mother was in critical condition, but this new truth disturbed her slightly because she had left her sister alone to go to the bathroom when they returned to the room on the day of her death.

This could only mean that Elizabeth had carried that heavy burden for all these years and it was she who had put an end to the life and suffering of their beloved mother.

"Elizabeth has nothing to do with it...it was me...leave her alone".

"No, no, no. Katrine, it doesn't work, not with me. I know about your bond and how you make decisions together, I remember in high school how you shared everything: the moped, the clothes, maybe even the guys? Get over it, you will both see your parents very soon".

"You are a monster, we are not at all alike you and I, on the contrary we are the opposite extremes: good and evil. As you well know at the end of each story, only one of us will remain".

"I see that the word has returned to you Katrine, why don't you go down and walk with your legs if you don't mind I'm sick of..."

Katrine tried to grab the gun, but Olivia noticed her desperate attempt and so dropped her down on the cold surface of the ground below them.

Olivia gave her a powerful kick at the base of her stomach and Katrine curled up on herself, finding herself breathless.

"Kat, Kat, you never give up, don't you? Come on, on your feet, we have arrived".

Katrine felt the steel of the gun press against her temple and tried to get up, despite feeling the pain spread all over her body. After a few steps they reached a huge rock overlooking the river, the jump had to be at least ten meters and now that she was on the brink, she could see the white foam of the rapids below her.

By now there was very little at its end.

"Warren, promise me we'll save her. I can't bear to leave her without having spoken to her since that day"

"I promise you. I saw Eric Preston die before my eyes and it was difficult to accept. I wouldn't even be able to look in the mirror if something were to happen to Katrine".

Judith took the man's hand and squeezed it into hers, as tears began to fall on her face.

"Thanks, whatever happens from now on, know you can count on me, have no more doubts".

"I will, I apologize for not believing you the other day and for not having approached you in the past".

The woman sketched a smile, then returned to look at the road, suddenly becoming serious.

"Now press that pedal Warren, there is someone who risks not having time to apologize".

Olivia lifted the mask and pointed the gun on Katrine's back.

"Come on jump, the movements won't be enough for your survival, the Summerville youth swimming champion will die drowned, isn't it fun?"

Katrine whispered something in a low voice, and then turned to her, finding the gun pointed at her forehead.

"What did you say? Come on one more step...you wouldn't want a bullet in the forehead?"

"I said I won't let you harm other people, especially my sister, shoot me if you want: I won't jump without you".

Katrine approached Olivia and took her arm with both hands, dragging her towards her, while the woman pulled the trigger of the gun, without however feeling the shot. During their walk Katrine had managed to move the safety of her gun and had noticed it just a second before, when she pointed it after her fall: she was an expert doctor after all, but she was sure she had never held a fire gun.

Katrine and Olivia fell into the freezing waters of the river below them, while the policewoman managed to take possession of the mask and hold it close to her chest in the impact with the water.

She tried to move her legs to the surface, but the muscles were unable to produce the necessary strength, so she decided to resort to one last desperate move.

Katrine put on her mask as the current dragged her downstream.

CHAPTER 36

Blurry River, near Pine Forest   *March 31th, 2017*

The perception of the outside world suddenly changed for Katrine. She opened her eyes and she seemed to see the bottom of the river below her moving very fast, illuminated by a strong blue light.

She kicked her legs to get back to the surface and get some air, now that she felt she had control of her body.

Her head emerged for a few seconds, just long enough to get some air, then she was pulled again underwater, this time grabbed by the hand of Olivia Harris.

Strangely she managed to react very calmly, despite the panic that such a dangerous situation could provoke. A single thought whirled in her head: to save herself and her sister Elizabeth.

Olivia tried to remove her mask, scratching her neck, but Kat managed to push her away with her legs. A few seconds later she emerged looking around to see her opponent, but she couldn`t see her.

Kat fell from a waterfall a couple of meters high, ending in calmer waters: a huge tree obstructed the course of the river and had created a puddle where you could stand up without problems.

Despite the loss of the finger, the drug assimilated by her body and the bath in the icy waters, she felt full of energy and in perfect condition, it had to be the effect of that magic mask.

She walked on tiptoe to reach the shore the shore and with the help of a couple of strokes she touched a point where she could stand perfectly balanced. After a few steps she stopped, the moon illuminated her reflect image of the body of water in front of her.

The woman in the reflection followed her movements, but she had a different face from what appeared in the mirror of her bathroom every morning; she wore a bow and a quiver, long red hair braided together, long down to her legs.

Katrine could recognize the green irises of her eyes, but a stranger appeared in the image and could not give herself any logical explanation.

Concentrated in that strange vision, she did not feel Olivia approach her shoulders, put her hands around her neck and drag her into the water under her.

Warren went up the slope feeling his breath, while Judith ran at breakneck speed just ahead.

"It must be this way, move Warren!"

The policeman motioned for his colleagues to follow him up the hill, and after catching his breath for about ten seconds, he followed Judith along the pine forest.

All the agents ran without stopping the distance that separated the entrance of the pine forest from the refuge, Then the lights inside attracted the attention of the woman who had first come to vicinity.

"It must be there, there we are! Pay attention, there should also be Katrine and Victoria, do not shoot on sight".

Warren swung his index finger upward and the agents arranged themselves neatly around the perimeter of the building: each guarded an entrance or a window.

At the next signal, the team of policemen entered the refuge, carefully inspecting every corner inside, with weapons ready and aimed at a possible enemy.

"Free. There is no one here".

Warren addressed everyone raising his voice: "Search better, they must be around here. Check the stable. The basement and the surrounding area. They cannot be far and they have not walked the road that we came from".

Judith bit her nails nervously then ran to the investigator and shook him vigorously.

"Damn it, Warren. We arrived too late!"

The policeman's heart was beating quickly inside the chest were Judith had just placed her head to hide other tears. Panic and fear reigned in the room together with the notes of an old song by Frank Sinatra, while the two watched the finger and blood on the floor of the room.

Katrine's life was about to end: trying to free herself from Olivia's grasp seemed impossible, even with the help of that prodigious mask.

She had been able to hold her breath more than she ever had in the past and she knew she would open her mouth in search of oxygen shortly thereafter, marking her end.

She thought of her sister: she hadn't been able to protect her and none of Olivia's next victims.

She shook her head to the side in search of a stone with which to hit the woman above her and realized thanks to the brightness with which the mask allowed her to see from the two narrow slits around the eyes, of her gun deposited on the seabed a few centimeters from her.

With no more breath in her body, she managed to give the kidney stroke necessary to grab it, remove the safety and aim it towards Olivia's head. She prayed that the water would not compromise its functioning and lifting her right hand she pulled the trigger.

"What was that? It sounded like a shot".

Warren ran out and turned to the agent in the doorway: "Did you hear where the shot came from?"

"I thought I heard it over there, along the river bank".

Warren and Judith snapped down the area indicated by the policeman, waving their torches in search of something other than the surrounding conifers.

Gliding along a slope they managed to get to the shore of the Blurry River, without finding anything strange.

"Wait Warren, look over there; the water is red, it could be blood".

The two went up the river until they noticed a huge tree trunk felled that connected the two sides.

Going up a little they managed to see the lifeless body of a woman stuck in one of the places where running water leaked, surrounded by a large patch of water made dark by the liquid normally contained inside the blood vessels.

"Don't tell me…"

Warren sank his boots into the water, feeling the stiff temperature as soon as he entered them, then gently turned the body in front of him to ascertain the identity of the victim.

"Olivia, or at least it seems to be her, does not look at all like the photos in our possession".

Behind them, a little higher they could hear the voice made trembling by the cold shivers of their colleague: "Of course it`s her, who do you think it is, stupid cop?"

"Kat, luckily you are safe and sound, now we will bring you in the warm. Guys, this way!"

Judith threw herself into the policewoman`s arms, kissing her on the cheek and holding her tight.

"Don`t worry, I`ve just seen my whole life running past me and I`m all a bruise"

The two woman stayed like that for a few seconds, while Kat winked at Warren, standing in front of her.

"Great job, foreman".

"Don`t say bullshit Kat…what happened to your finger?"

"Oh, this? A war scar. The important thing is that it`s all over".

Judith moved away to be able to observe the lack of Katrine`s left ring finger.

"Holly shit".

"Judith…a bit of content, please!"

Warren took the thermal blanket from one of the agents and wrapped it around Katrine to warm her up.

"Is there any trace of Victoria or the mask? We need to tell you a few things we discovered".

"Give me time to recover…the mask was dragged along the current, you know I was trying to save my life. As for Victoria, I have some bad news to give you. Olivia has absolutely nothing to do with her disappearance".

The three remained silent while the agents recovered Olivia's body from the river.

"Her kidnapping is the work of someone who wanted to imitate her modus operandi: there is another bastard in freedom to capture".

CHAPTER 37

Summerville Police Station *April 1th, 2017*

Philip De La Cruix looked at the front page article of the *Sunshine:* finally things seemed to go in the right direction.

All the events of the capture of the *Mask* were described in detail in the first five pages and this time the local police were praised thanks to the work of Katrine and her team.

The press conference scheduled for the afternoon would have been decidedly more pleasant than those faced in the previous week.

He heard someone knock on the door of his office, than lowered the newspaper to welcome the person inside.

"Come in"

Katrine came in, taking off her sunglasses and undoing her black leather jacket, carefully observing the expression on her boss: she was having difficulty holding his gaze.

Really strange for a man of his age and with a build able to make his interlocutors uncomfortable, as she herself had noticed on more than one occasion.

"Good morning Kat...I think I owe you an apology. To confess I feel like a perfect idiot right now".

"Agent Steward, please. I came to draw up the report of what happened last night".

The man looked at her for a few seconds, then brought his hand to slightly untie the knot of his tie. "Ah ok. You can put it on the desk, agent Steward".

The woman looked at him seriously for a few seconds, then smiled laughing under her mustache: "Philip, I'm joking. I reflected on your decision the other day, you had every right to suspend me from the investigation. It only bothered me that you didn't believe me about Zack, despite the deep friendship that has bound us for years.

"Fuck Kat, it's really hard for me to turn to you as Agent Steward".

The policewoman raised her eyebrows: "Yes you didn't have much difficulty doing it the other day".

The man took a cigar from the box on the desk in front of him, breaking the seal printed along the edges.

"Know that I never doubted you, if it can help make you feel better, only I was forced to make a drastic decision to ward off my ass when we found Robert Hudson".

"Excellent idea to put the blame on me; on the other hand, it is what happens to those who put their faces on it, even the best coaches are fired badly, despite the trophies won in lucky seasons".

Philip lit his cigar, took a puff towards the policewoman and exhaled slowly.

"You're right, I was wrong, I'm really sorry Katrine. I'm very proud of you and I promise you it won't happen a second time, you can count on it".

Katrine closed the zip of her jacket, looking down on it: "No, it won't happen. I'm going to leave the police force. I don't believe in our work anymore, Olivia made me think about some things".

The smoke from the next puff went sideways, making him cough, then after taking a sip of water, he started talking again.

"But what are you saying? This job is your life! What are you going to do? Think about what your father would say if he saw you right now, after solving a case of this depth, in a remote town like ours, before making hasty decisions…"

Katrine took a case containing a DVD out of her bag and placed it on the open cigar box.

"Trust me Philip, I am not angry with you and I know very well that work has been the center of my entire existence, many have pointed it out to me; I don`t know what I`m going to do, but in life everything changes and you have to adapt to every situation, you told me this years ago, you remember?"

The man nodded and listened to the rest of the words of one of his first pupil, perhaps his favorite.

"I have yet to resolve a matter and I would need free access to my office , the police and my team`s databases for another week, if you will allow me; after that you will have my written resignation, my father would understand, he has always respected my decisions and allowed me a lot of freedom in letting me take them, it was the way he expressed his love, you know that too".

The gaze of both fell on the photograph on the wall: a young Philip De La Cruix was portrayed while delivering an acknowledgment to Katrine`s father, accompanied by the enchanted faces of two very similar girls.

"Okay…I know very well the consequences of those who try to make you change your mind, so I will give up, at least for the moment. As for the office and the team, you are one of ours as long as you want".

The man held out his hand and stood and waited for the firm grip of the woman who had grown up within those walls. Katrine walked around the desk and hugged Philip De La Cruix, feeling a lump in her throat.

"I'd better go, I have a thousand things to do, you know..."

"Of course, I guess after last night...see you soon Katrine Steward".

"One last thing...on the DVD there is a film that portrays Zack near my house and shows how on several occasions he treys to spy inside my house. I hope you will get rid of him once and for all".

"Your sister had already warned me yesterday, we are taking care of it, I assure you he will not bother you anymore: it seems his fiancée has decided to move to San Francisco, and now that he is becoming dad he must absolutely follow her and start taking his responsibilities".

"Thanks Philip, you are a friend".

Kat closed the door and Philip picked up his cigar again, approaching the photo on the wall.

"If only I could see how woman your daughter has become..."

"So guys, we are back and forth. Let's forget about Olivia, the *Mask* and the whole story that happened this week. The celebrations will be postponed until the last missing person is found. I heard Ivan Varichenko this morning, he seemed at least as relieved of the end of the story as we are, but still desperate for the kidnapper's silence since the ransom was paid. Today we will begin to create the basis for a new investigation, any ideas?"

An awkward silence fell in the office.

"Well...exactly as I thought, for this I will illustrate on the blackboard everything we know about Victoria, retracing the events of the evening when she was kidnapped".

Katrine took the chalk, observing the silent faces of her teammates: they were sitting so close despite the large space that had been created by moving the desks.

"Victoria Varichenko is not only famous for her extraordinary and rare beauty, but also for her character and her somewhat questionable ways of doing things; in my research I managed to trace back to an event a few months ago that sees her as protagonist.

It would seem that an individual had filled the Ferrari of the Brazilian model with whom she has carried out a photo shoot in France, with horse dung, only because she has appeared several times more than her in the magazines in which the photos were subsequently published. Of course the author of the gesture declared that he knew nothing, but you know, silence can always be bought even if at a high price".

"But…what a temper, I would never choose to be her friend".

Judith cleaned the lenses of her glasses using the cloth contained in its case.

"You better not know what her last boyfriend found under his sheets then…"

Warren turned to Judith, looking at her as she searched the internet, using her Smartphone, for the details of that story.

"I would say to focus on the reason for her presence here in Summerville and on the day of her disappearance".

"Thanks Warren, I was just getting there. The Russian woman came here up to her father's request: in exchange her billboards would appear for the next advertising campaign of his telephone company. However, the girl hates the monotonous and boring life to which the inhabitants of Summerville are accustomed and has always gone out on her own, dedicating herself to other pastimes such as shopping and the Spa: right there we find her last public appearance, at least until meeting with Warren. Do you want to take over?"

The man cleared his throat and after getting up he took the chalk from Katrine, giving her a seat on the chair attached to Judith`s.

"I would prefer to help myself with the map of our areas; I will hang it right next to the blackboard, so we can realize its...our last move.

You see, I talked and joked with Victoria for the whole evening, she`s not the monster that the newspapers describe at all. She likes to show off her economic power and her charm on men, that's all.

The two woman looked at each other then raised their open palm to invite him to continue the speech.

"Okay, let's forget about these details. After leaving Trevor`s Pub we walked along this street, more or less around midnight, if I remember correctly, the same traveled by Olivia in those moments with the stolen car: you will remember the video in which she is taken wearing the mask, right?"

"Sorry if I interrupt you, but we managed to establish that Olivia went by that road to go and steal the car with which to carry out the subsequent murder, going to Sunset Hill, where Dylan Rogers was waiting for her aboard the purple van. Victoria has nothing to do with this story".

"I know Judith, I just wanted to highlight how bizarre fate is sometimes: Victoria was kidnapped on the same street and on the same night when Olivia was preparing to kill another person, it was this that upset our ideas.

"Anyway, where was I...ah, here. After saying goodbye I waited for her to go up the hill to reach her father's house and, after seeing her walk about halfway, I went home: unfortunately I don't remember the exact time".

"Don't worry, Warren. Did you notice anything strange? A car following you, someone inside the Pub staring at her maybe?"

"You've already asked me Kat, Unfortunately nothing. We spent a lovely evening having a drink together, afterward everyone went back to their own life, or so it seemed. I didn't notice anything of what was happening around us".

"Did you just kiss or did you have sex or some strange effusion in the alleys?"

Katrine and Warren turned to look at their colleague in the eyes.

"What's wrong? I think it's important. If someone had observed you, they might have wished to have her in excitement, a horny voyeur with some disturbance maybe, don't you think?"

"Nothing happened Judith, just a walk to recover us from the alcohol".

The colleague blushed slightly, but Katrine pretended not to have noticed continuing with the reconstruction of the events, without dwelling on that nonsense. Incredible: Judith had a crush on Warren and had a jealousy reaction before her eyes just then.

"We don't have the videos of the street surveillance of that area. The intersection where Olivia was filmed is more than three blocks away, we were lucky to get a copy because the camera is pointed at the entrance to a bank, unfortunately, video surveillance is mostly present in the most developed cities and in places of public interest or at risk of robbery".

"Do you know if her father or she herself had enemies here in Summerville or someone they could give bothers to?"

"No Warren, despite having asked Mr. Varichenko several times, they don't appear to have any enemies nearby".

The blush on Judith's cheeks seemed to fade when the discussion resumed.

"We have to focus on a person in need of money, so desperate to formulate in blackmail to one of the most powerful men in the Russian scenario. There is no other explanation then".

"You are right. I'd like you to analyze every criminal or offender in our database. Someone tried to get there by using the same modus operandi of the mask; after the first ramom, I remind you, we only received her first left ring finger and no other messages, so let's get ready for the worst. The perpetrator does not have to be an ordinary junkie, a common street criminal, but a person willing to kill in order to get the money requested".

"Well, now he got it, he should stick to the agreements if at least he felt a bit of compassion for her father.

Katrine got up and removed the chalk from Warren's hand with which he wrote the dates and time of the events concerning Victoria.

"Unfortunately, not all people are human enough to be defined as such: Olivia Harris is an example of how a human being can have no scruples in torturing or killing his fellow man".

After an afternoon of inconclusive investigations, Katrine returned home, took a short run and then took a hot shower before receiving her sister.

With the capture of Olivia, spring seemed to have returned: the temperature had slightly increased and the cold winter seemed to have greeted the city, setting a new appointment for the following November.

During the evening run she had been able to meet more people than usual on her journey travelled by the most avid and constant joggers and had not had the need to wear her ear muffs for the first time since she returned home.

The doorbell rang in the hallway and Katrine hurried down the stairs as she finished buttoning her red linen blouse and adjusting the straps of her bra.

"Good evening, do I have the pleasure of meeting the city's new ironies?"

"Come on Elizabeth, come and sit in the dining room, I opened a bottle of a new renowned red wine from central Italy".

"Mhmm....I would say you want to celebrate last night's capture. By the way, you were a bit of a fool to go to that place completely alone: you could have had a bad end".

Katrine closed the door and crossed the corridor, taking her sister under her protective wing.

"Yeah, too bad...it seems that you will have to put up with me for a little while more sister, even if I risked a lot, I admit it".

Katrine exhibited the stump on her left hand: it had not been possible to try to stitch it up.

"But are you kidding? Katrine you know how hard everyday life is, let alone if you look for it more. Does it hurt you? Do you want me to medicate it, change your bandages or…"

"Don't worry Elizabeth, it's just a finger, I can cope it on my own, don't worry about me. Sit down, we have to talk".

The younger sister poured the wine and handed Katrine a glass tasting the reddish liquid slowly, savoring it while studying the label on the bottle.

"Good taste. What do you have to talk to me about?"

"First of all I have to thank you for encouraging me to continue the investigation and helping me to take the right path".

Elizabeth winked at her: "Come on, you want to make me blush? The credit is yours, you know it very well".

Katrine crossed her legs after lowering her skirt slightly before sitting down.

"There are two reasons why I called you: the first is to announce my imminent withdrawal from the police force".

"Yes, sure. I bet you will start selling vacuum cleaners door to door. Don`t fool your little sister".

Katrine reached out to take her sisters hand and to be able to look at her closely: "I`m not kidding, I finally decided to listen to you. Last night`s clash made me reflect on the most important things in life and this morning I communicated my decision to Philip, I have the feeling that he took it well".

"You are serious…but this is fantastic news! You know it disappoints me a bit that you made this decision after the nice squeeze last night, and not thanks to the currents of thoughts expressed by your intelligent, magnificent sister throughout the years".

Katrine observed the manifestation of joy of her younger sister, her bright eyes perfectly described her state of mind.

The happiness in hearing those words, after trying to make her reason for a long time, was comparable to the signature of an armistice after a long period of war.

"Pull the brake Elizabeth, I have not yet communicated the second reason, which is the most important: Last night Olivia revealed the truth about our mother's death".

Elizabeth lowered her glass and visibly swallowed, but did not dare to reply to those words, so Katrine continued the conversation.

"I don't want to criticize your decision, on the contrary, I support what you did, in that situation you showed more courage than I. I just can't explain myself why you didn't tell me: we have always trusted each other since we were little, we supported and helped each other during the most difficult moments, we have overcome many challenges together. Why did you keep me in the dark about this?"

Elizabeth watched her seriously, sitting on her sofa in which she had shared the quarrels with her husband, the discussions with the hateful neighbor, but she had not been able to confess the choice to let their mother die.

"I'm sorry Katrine I....she asked me several years ago. She knew about your vision of justice, your strong sense of duty and your strong personality: if we ever get to such conditions, I would have had to act against your will. You would never have helped her die Katrine, we both know this".

Katrine dropped her glass on the floor, sprinkling it with glass fragments immersed in a pool of red wine.

"Damn...leave it. I'll take care of it. You don't know anything about me. I could have endured such a burden and not leave such a difficult task for my younger sister".

"Stop Kat! You don't have to see it like that, for once Mum had chosen to turn to me, you have to accept it! I am also her daughter, just like you!"

Katrine took the broom and began to collect the glass splinters, the tones of their voices were increasing more and more.

"The doctors said there were possibilities regarding her recovery, we should have made the decision together!"

"Together? I can perfectly imagine how things would have been if only I had confessed to you Mums speech, for once don't preach to me, so she stopped suffering and letting us live with false hopes".

"She stopped living because you decided it, without questioning me, you are no different from a serial killer that I dealt with last night!"

The sisters looked at each other in silence, then Elizabeth reached for her jacket and walked down the corridor.

"Wait Eli, I exaggerated, I'm a fool, I didn't mean what I said..."

Elizabeth turned before going out, showing her face in tears: "Yeah but you did. Do you think it's easy to live with all this? I relive that scene every day, asking myself if I was wrong in paying attention to our mother's will; she always described euthanasia as an act of immense generosity and I knew you would have not agreed, so for once in my life I made a decision and my responsibilities alone and now I suffer in silence the consequences of that action. Sorry if I'm not perfect like you, *Ghostbuster*".

Elizabeth slammed the door violently, leaving behind only a sad silence that made Katrine feel even more lonely inside the house.

She did not want to chase her sister, she would have passed it in a few days, but she knew that in the end she was right in everything she said: Katrine loved life, but she herself had managed to take two people's life already, believing that they deserved it. It wasn't up to her to decide what was right or what was wrong, this was also why she decided to withdraw from the police. Contrary to what she would have done in the past, she opened the door and ran to her sister's car hugging her before she managed to get in the car.

"What do you want? Leave me alone!"

Katrine kissed her and said a phrase in her ear that she had rarely uttered in her lifetime.

"Thank you, I love you".

CHAPTER 38

Suvarnabhumi Airport, Bangkok *April 2th, 2017*

The man unfastened his seat belt and folded the sheatshelf in front of him.

After following the mass of people who, like him, had taken one of the 4000 international flights to reach the capital of Thailand, he queued up waiting for his luggage to come out of the conveyor belt.

Once he recovered the heavy bag and loaded it on the trolley together with the travel trolley, he walked the distance that separated it from the exit of the second largest terminal in the world.

In Summerville it must have been morning at this time and he was able to confirm it by checking the clocks hanging at the entrance where you could find out the time of any part of the world.

He checked his pocket making sure he had his passport and especially his wallet full of cash, then went outside to try to communicate in English with one of the local taxi drivers at the airport.

After having pronounced the place written on the note he was holding, he adjusted his wristwatch on seven o`clock in the evening, then he looked out the window and enjoying the panorama of the city he would live in for the coming years.

The 132 meters height of the tallest control tower in the world seemed to touch the clear sky above them as they entered the lane following another taxi.

After a few kilometers in which he tried to avoid any talking with the toothless Thai driver, he remembered the wonderful image of the Russian girl lying under his body, the screams muffled by the gag he put in her mouth and the moment he enjoyed while he was raping her from behind.

Unfortunately Victoria was able to see his face, because he had lost his headdress while dressing and had been forced to change his original plans, continuing to keep her in prisoner.

He tried to get rid of those thoughts and, when he later reached the hotel, booked under a false name, he prepared to extract his new passport, observing the excellent work done for a great price: on the other hand now that he had 15 million dollars it was certainly no problem.

He stared at the photo imprinted next to Arthur Douglas's name, he had found it in the family album and it was about ten years ago, when he still wore his hair very short.

After leaving the taxi driver a sumptuous tip, Arthur tested his new identity with the woman sitting behind the reception desk, even though he knew there would be no problem.

"Room 101, the suite was prepared just this afternoon for you, Mr. Douglas".

"Thank you miss, how far is the Pat pong area from here?"

The woman looked at him slightly disgusted, another American tourist looking for sexual entertainment in the most famous red light district of the city, but tried to remain as neutral as possible while informing him of the route to take in order to reach the area.

"Thanks, these are for you. In case you want to keep me company tonight I will offer you ten times as much, you know I'm very tired from travelling and the jet lag, tonight I'm not going to move".

The woman watched him as he climbed the stairs and checked if the banknote he had left her was real: she had never had the opportunity to receive a banknote of that denomination as a tip before then.

She got up and checked her makeup in the hall mirror. She would have settled down better at the end of her shift so that she could think of the well-paid overtime that awaited her upstairs.

After throwing his bag at the bottom of the bed, Arthur dashed into the bathroom to shower, change and shave. Looking at himself in the mirror he wondered what kind of person he had become. He had always thought about money, but he had never realized how far he could go to obtain such a sum.

He restarted the electric razor and decided to do one last splurge to celebrate the beginning of his new life: locks of dark hair fell on the tiles of the first floor suite as Arthur Douglas repeated aloud the story of his new identity.

As soon as he finished he passed his hand over his head. He felt even freer after that haircut, his wife had always forced him to keep a suitable hairstyle to look neat and tidy towards work colleagues.

Fuck the wife. Fuck Summerville.

On the other side of the world, an unknown cell phone alarm rang and Warren opened his eyes and tried to remember where he was.

The animal lying on his feet helped him to refresh his memory and once the sheets were lifted, he went over to kiss the woman with whom he had spent the night.

"Is it already half past seven?"

"To tell the truth it is half past nine in the morning and I think you are the only woman who sets the alarm on her Sunday off".

"Who knows what other oddities will make you run away from me... I`m used to it, you know?"

Warren got out of bed, wandering around the room completely naked.

"Where the heck did my underwear go?"

"I have no idea. You drugged me and raped me last night, I have proof".

"Oh yeah? I thought you couldn`t resist my charm".

He approached to kiss her, but the dog`s muzzle prevented him; wagging his tail he showed off his new trophy, depositing it on the pillow.

"Sharky? No! You don`t do this!"

The animal`s sweet eyes, stared first at the owner and then at Warren, begging for forgiveness.

"Ha ha, good puppy, you found my underwear for me. You are a really good dog, you know?"

Judith took her glasses from the bedside table and observed the man carefully as he stroke the dog: it was the first time she hadn`t been forced to leave him in his kennel outside, despite having a guest in her bedroom.

"He must really like you. Almost as much as his mistress does".

The woman regretted having said that sentence, because she blushed instantly, feeling like a fifteen-year-old, so she tried to divert the subject by jumping up to start dressing.

"What do you want coffee, milk... if you want I have some fresh oranges, I could make you a juice".

"Thank you, you are very kind, but it won't be necessary. I'll go downstairs to prepare a coffee for both of us, ok?"

Judith watched the man leave the room and heard him go down the stairs, enter the kitchen and rummage through the cans in search of coffee.

In her previous relationships she had been used to serving her partners and no one had ever offered to prepare breakfast for her; she took the dog's muzzle and met his gaze.

"You see Sharky? I told you that sooner or later the right one would come".

The dog seemed to understand her words, because he started to wag his tail and slightly revealed the sharp canines that had given him that name.

Katrine woke up very early, around six in the morning, had breakfast at the bar not far from her apartment and then took her jeep to go to the woods where the clash with Olivia Harris took place.

Her trekking shoes quickly travelled the path that led to the refuge, but once she reached the entrance to the pine forest, she swerved downstream to cut on the path that would take her to the place where they had rescued her.

She had spent the whole Saturday evening with her sister, they had cleared up and both felt more united when they left each other; that brief bickering had helped to strengthen their relationship, even if for a moment she had thought it might mark the breakdown of their splendid relationship.

The newly risen sun would have melted in a short time the frost that was deposited on the grass under her feet and Katrine was sure that it would raise the temperature by at least five degrees.

During the night she had thought for a long time whether to decide to put into practice what she had in mind or to let go of that crazy idea by blocking it in the bud, then had managed to sleep after opting for the first choice.

After dreaming of finding herself in that place, she decided to interpret that chance as a message from heaven, so an hour before she had changed her mind.

She jumped off a rock, managing to stop not far from the river bank, then she managed to see the trunk of the felled tree where the showdown had taken place exactly two nights before.

Back where they had rescued her, she returned to the right and walked a few meters until she reached the base of a huge pine tree. She lifted the flat stone she had placed two days earlier in order to conceal the hidden object under it.

Katrine picked up the mask and walked towards the viewpoint where most people went to be able to wear it again.

She could not explain why she had kept it hidden from the rest of the group, perhaps because she considered it a dangerous weapon in the wrong hands, perhaps because the rumors she had heard that night had suggested it to her several times or perhaps for the simple desire to wear it one last time.

The visions of the different perception of reality led her to think that that mask could help her in other investigations, so she went back to the place to be able to recover it.

Once she climbed the gentle slope she put it on and surveyed the whole city below her. She tried to think about Victoria, about her father, but nothing strange happened; she was a fool to think that she had used a magical object, so she took it off and put it in the backpack.

When she turned to leave, she found herself face to face with Olivia, the woman staring at her with a hole in the middle of her forehead.

"We are not very different you and I Katrine, aren`t we?"

Katrine started running to the sound of the laughter of that dead woman who died two days ago and returned as quickly as possible to the jeep.

Every time she turned to check if she was following her, she could see her ever closer; by now she was almost close to her when she tripped over a stone and began to roll towards the valley, dragging the backpack containing the mask.

After the fall Katrine lay unconscious on her back on the ground covered with coniferous needles.

CHAPTER 39

Blurry River, near Pine Forest *May 16th, 1994*

o.

Katrine opened her eyes again: she did not recognize that place as the forest in which she was just before, the trees that surrounded her were different.

Chesnutt and walnut trees extended far beyond her view and the ground was no longer strewn with conifers, but with tall, thick grass.

She heard noises behind her so she hurried to reach the base of a tree, big enough to hide her tall and slender body.

The rustle of branches and twigs revealed a familiar face to the policewoman, even if she struggled to remember it by now, too many years had passed since she last saw him.

Vincent Steward emerged from the woods, revealing the tag on his uniform a little tight around his biceps intent on moving annoying twigs and brambles in front of his path.

He was exactly as she remembered him: tall, handsome and strong, like the superhero she had drawn as a child on the greeting envelope on his 50th birthday.

"Father! Father!". Katrine tried to run towards him, but found herself anchored to the ground, as she had roots that prevented any movement.

The man seemed not to hear her voice and concentrated to continue along the bush, without noticing the presence of his daughter a little further on.

"It must be a dream, it can't be real". Katrine remembered the fall in Pine Forest and realized she was in the middle of a vision produced by the mask.

Her father stopped in the middle of the woods and took a turn on himself; he seemed to be looking for something and someone, but only at his next words, Katrine understood exactly where and when they were.

"Come on Billy, stop. You will only get away with a couple of years in prison, if you keep running away you will only make the situation worse.

Katrine began to sweat and found herself silently observing the scenario of the saddest day of her life.

Next to her, an armed man in his thirties materialized: the clothing and facial signs would have made even a boy understand his passion for drugs.

"Stop following me Vincent, this time it is as I say".

The agent saw the gun in the boy's hand and instinctively looked down at his holster, finding it empty.

"Exactly, now we play guard and thieves in reverse roles. Start running towards the car without ever turning around otherwise I swear I'll kill you, shit cop!"

Katrine watched the slow movement of her father's footsteps as he tried to get closer to Billy, regardless of the weapon he was holding in his hands.

"Put the gun down, I know you're a good lad, but you made a mistake. I won't tell anyone about this stunt of yours, I promise you, nor about your escape attempt, you have my word of honor".

"Stop or I'll kill you, don't move! Now turn around and go, I'm not going back inside! Wait a minute... if I shoot you, no one will know about the drug you found on me and I will be able to be free, no one will ever find out".

Katrine yelled at Billy trying to reason with him, but as she well knew, all of this had already happened and events could not be changed; the mask was making her relive that nightmare in first person.

"Don't bullshit Billy, you're going to be wanted for murder, you're aiming my service gun at an unarmed man with wife and children, are you insane?" They will be able to trace back to you, the gun, the bullets, the witnesses who saw you in my car a while ago, I'll tell you one last time, lower your gun and don't bullshit".

Billy's trembling hand kept pointing the gun at the cop as he watched him approach him.

"I can't go back to prison, I just can't...I'm sorry Vincent".

Katrine could see the terror in her father's eyes just before hearing the shot that lifted all the birds in the woods to a new destination.

Vincent Steward fell to his knees, putting a hand on the stomach where the uniform had started to turn red, while Billy turned to run away.

"Father! No! Father..."

Vincent managed to get up to reach the shade of the tree in which Katrine was, then he collapsed with his back towards the tree, until he sat down right in front of her.

"Daddy, they got him, he then committed suicide a year later in his cell...I'm sorry, I'm very sorry, I can't do anything even if I'm here..."

Vincent looked around, his gaze passed through Katrine's body and studied the surrounding ambience: "Katrine, is it you? Why are you crying?"

The woman approached her father, she tried to touch him but found herself unable to do so: it was the mask that prevented her, she was sure, but now the man seemed to be able to at least hear her.

"Yes daddy I'm here, I'm Katrine".

"I'm dying, isn't it? I didn't expect such a reaction from Billy, I'm getting old it's time for me to retire, your mother always tells me…you will think about it anyway Kat, I know. You will become better than me, Philip promised me that he will help you if you want to follow your dream".

Katrine smiled: despite that terrible memory she was pleased to hear again the voice and the presence of her father after so long.

"No dad, I'll never be like you. I'm big now and I've become a policewoman, just like I told you; but I let four people lose their lives and I can't find a young woman. I think that sooner or later I'll lose her too".

The man managed to raise his hand to indicate his identification plate: "Don't worry, you are Katrine Steward, you will see that you will succeed in your exploits, I remind you, you have my same blood running through your veins; you just have to concentrate and work hard on the investigation, the rest comes by itself".

"I know, I've always followed your advice, but I'm not like you, in fact I've decided to retire".

Vincent spat a trickle of blood and winced briefly before resuming speaking: "For God's sake, Katrine? Do you want me to die twice? I was just going to tell you how proud I am, but don't worry, whatever you decide, I'll be with you. Forever".

Katrine's father stretched out a little finger as he used to when she was small, so she imitated him and managed to twist it around his, just as life left his body.

"Forever Dad".

A small cone of light penetrated from the trees, which managed to annoy Katrine's eyes, until it forced her to wake up. So she found herself in Pine Forest again, no trace of Olivia around, so she realized that the effects of using the mask had vanished.

She opened her backpack and checked the mask: the red spot seemed to pulsate on the surface. She checked her wristwatch and marveled when she realized she had been passed out for so long: It was nearly three in the afternoon. She took her mobile phone out from her backpack pocket after feeling the vibration and noticed Judith's call coming in that instant.

"Katrine, what happened to you? Warren and I have been trying to contact you all day, where are you? I want to remember you for the interview scheduled in half an hour for that TV show, what was it called…ah yes, that's it: "Crimes and homicide". Are you ready?"

The woman rolled her eyes, she had not forgotten about the interview, but she had not been able to predict such a trance: two days earlier the effect had vanished immediately.

"Just give me an hour and I'll meet you at the police station, or rather…call Samantha and give her my address, I'll certainly be more at ease in my kingdom".

"Okay, but be sure to be there: the population is waiting for all the details of the case. I'm sending you the entire video surveillance film by email, the moment Olivia appears is exactly halfway, the clock indicates the one and forty-two minutes".

"Thank you Judith, I'll try to hurry".

Katrine ended the call and walked towards her jeep: she would have arrived late, but she certainly couldn't say that she had gone to retrieve the mask without the knowledge of her colleagues and without giving any explanation.

Samantha Hillmore was waiting leaning against the white van containing the television equipment along with the plump cameraman who accompanied her.

"So Jerry, are you really sure this is the address Judith Law gave us?"

The man replied chewing a croissant in a disgusting way, licking his sugary fingers without taking into account the judgment of the red-haired colleague.

"Yes, but she doesn't seem to be home. On the doorbell is written Steward, too bad she punched us".

A black jeep pulled up beside their van and turned the engine off: "Sorry I'm late, I was staying with my sister and I didn't pay attention to the clock".

The reporter looked at her with her blue eyes, lingering on the trekking shoes still dirty with dirt and assumed a disgusted expression that immediately jumped to Katrine's eye.

"Let's go in, just a minute and I'll be ready. You can start setting up the instruments".

The woman with the red hair nodded to her assistant and they both began to take the tools to take to the interview room.

Katrine ran upstairs for a quick change of clothes, leaving the two struggling with tripods, cameras, and papers containing questions to ask at the interview.

She opened the wardrobe and put on the suit prepared two days before for the occasion: an elegant gray suit and a pair of pumps of the same color, she transformed herself in a few seconds.

Once back on the ground floor, she noticed how Samantha's gaze studied the family photographs positioned above the fireplace, perhaps trying to find out if she had a boyfriend or a partner to hide from the public.

"Are you looking for something?"

The woman's straight hair twirled up to reveal a small tattoo hidden just below her left ear. "Nothing, I was just looking at the family photos. You and your sister look a lot alike".

"Yes, when we were little we hated this thing, but now we don't notice it anymore".

"You seem very close and united...Jerry are we ready?"

The cameraman raised the camera over his shoulder and showed the thumb raised, so Kat and Samantha settled respectively on the lounge chair and black leather sofa.

Samantha waited for the end of the countdown from the fingers of the man next to them and began to speak towards the camera, starting the interview.

"Good evening friends viewers. Today we meet with Agent Katrine Steward, of the Summerville police, who will show us her recent enterprise live and answer some of your questions taken directly from our site".

"Good evening everyone".

Katrine stared at the camera embarrassed and tried to smile, she didn't know how to behave even if it was not the first time she was in a such a situation.

She was grateful to have told Judith to move the interview to her home: by doing so she would not have felt the curious faces of her police colleagues on her , at least.

"Katrine will show us how she and her team managed to stop the homicidal doctor who terrorized the city last week. How did you manage to find her? The people at home would also like to know if they could see the Mask used by Olivia Harris for the murders; we didn't get to see it on the photos in the newspapers".

The policewoman looked for a moment at the backpack hanging in the kitchen across the room; then answered the thousands of people who were watching the live interview sitting on their sofa.

"We did not recover the Mask used by Olivia, it was lost in the waters of the Blurry River; if anyone finds it , please give it to us. Regarding the other question, you are all aware of our clamorous mistake since the beginning of our investigations: in fact we believed that one of the victims was the responsible behind the Mask, but later I will tell you how me and the members of my team were able to reveal the true killer. If I may, I would like to start showing you the video with which we started the investigation: unfortunately the face is covered as you well know by the masking used also during the murders, you have to apologize for the quality of the video, as it is the original copy, it was not possible to change the format".

Katrine got up and took her laptop, then started the video contained in her mailbox and turned the screen towards the camera.

"Thanks Katrine, we were able to contact Alessandro Zarretti to let us know the story of this Mask. Have you ever thought of believing in its magic?"

Katrine went back to what had happened during the clash with Olivia and during the morning: "No, I can only confirm its horrible aspect and that I turned to Alessandro to try to understand something more, but unfortunately it did not prove very useful to learn about its ancient history".

Katrine put the laptop down in front of her, the images on the screen continued to show the deserted street of the stretch taken the night Victoria disappeared.

"I would like to turn back for a moment and ask you some more details about your colleagues if possible: people would like to know who they can thank besides you of course".

Citizens can count on the work of all members of the police force, in addition to that of Judith Law and Warren Valentine; without them I would not have been able to get the complete picture of the situation.

The interview continued retracing each significant stage: the murders of Sarah and Dylan, the rescue attempt and the chase of Eric Preston`s shed until the discovery of Robert Hudson`s body.

Katrine was answering Samantha`s questions when she noticed a detail that appeared on her computer screen.

"...so after my suspension the command past to Warren and...sorry, just a moment".

Samantha watched Katrine bend over her computer and lose her speech, then turned her gaze to Jerry to try to understand what the policewoman was doing.

The man shrugged at Samantha, feeling uneasy, he turned to the viewers with the best of his smiles: "Friends from home, excuse us for a moment we have to give the line to advertising, but don't change channel, soon Katrine will tell us about her meeting with Dr. Olivia Harris and how she managed to win. See you later!".

Jerry lowered the camera and Samantha took her bottle of water to drink before clearing her throat: "You've been doing great so far, what did you think of doing, playing with that contraption on live TV?"

The reporter's reproach seemed to slip on Katrine who continued to carefully observe the surveillance video reproduced on her computer screen.

"I'm sorry, but we will finish the interview another time. I have to reunite with my team, I must apologize".

Samantha stared at Katrine, then Jerry and finally at Katrine again: "What are you saying? You can't leave the interview right now, you'll ruin the service!"

The policewoman closed the computer screen, picked it up and pulled out her cell phone to send a message to Warren and Judith: "Of course I can, it's a matter of the utmost importance, tell the viewers. If you want we can continue later, please leave the equipment, I have to close the door, it will be safe".

Katrine put her jacket on, then looked for the keys in her pocket and headed for the door, waiting for the two journalists to come out.

"Come on Jerry, we'll continue later".

The woman managed not to get noticed as she winked at her colleague, greeted Kat and boarded the van.

295

The man followed her and got into the passenger seat, placing the camera in the free place in the center: "Why didn't you insist on letting her stay? The boss won't be very happy".

Samantha started the van, reversed, getting onto the carriageway and waited for Katrine's jeep to exit: "You idiot, turn on the camera. She must have discovered something important so we will follow her in order to be the first to reveal it to the public".

Jerry took a chocolate bar from under the seat and began to unwrap it: "Do you know Samantha? Even if you have a breathtaking body, it is you're brilliant mind that makes men lose their heads, I'm sure".

Samantha waited a few seconds and began the chase with a smirk on her face: that fat man was not entirely wrong and she knew it very well.

CHAPTER 40

Summerville Mall

Warren and Judith stared in amazement at the cartoon on the big screen that had replaced the live broadcast of Kat's interview.

"But what are they doing? Can they cut the interview, just like that?" Warren finished his cappuccino with a last sip then looked away from the screen and turned to her colleague: "Typical of Kat, she has the opportunity to make up for it thanks to this interview, and she decides to ruin it, leaving the audience with a dry mouth that will continue to speak ill of her, I'm sure".

Judith took out a banknote from her wallet and placed it on the receipt left earlier by the waiter: "Too bad, people seemed to hang on her lips until recently".

Warren returned the money to her colleague and noticed the cell phone screen light up giving life to the ringtone linked to Katrine's calls: "Speak of the devil and the horns pop up. Forget it , you will pay next time Jud".

The woman carefully watched him answer Kat's call, happy with the sound produced by the voice of what seemed to be her boyfriend in all respects.

"Kat, Judith and I were watching your interview in the mall, you were doing great, what happened?"

Warren's brows furrowed and Judith realized something serious had happened.

"We arrive immediately, we'll meet at the police station so you can explain better...what do you mean there is no time? Okay, we are leaving, see you on the street, I'll tell Judith".

Warren put his cell phone in his pocket and got up from the table as Judith picked up her bag and asked him what had happened.

"She's coming to pick us up. She's reviewed the video and now she thinks she knows who kidnapped Victoria.

Katrine reached for the glove box holding the steering wheel with one hand as she made her way down the street to the mall. She opened it and took out the car documents in search of the only sheet that interested her at that moment.

During the interview, the playback of the surveillance video had continued uninterrupted for about fifteen minutes, when a familiar car appeared on the screen. Exactly seventeen minutes later, the vehicle was speeding along the same road as Olivia's stolen car, and when she managed to connect who owned the yellow Hummer whizzing in the images, her hand began to shake.

She picked up the insurance sheet and put it in her mouth for the time it took to pass a moped then copied the emergency number to her cell phone.

"Hallo Grey Insurance Assistance, I'm Samuel, how can I help you?"

"I need to speak to Tom Hackett, it's an emergency and I can't reach him on his mobile number, I'm Katrine Steward".

"I'm sorry, but I can't help you, I only deal with accidents and friendly findings to facilitate..."

"Look you have to get me in touch with him right away if you want to avoid an accident and an unfriendly encounter with me in the next few days. A woman's life is in serious danger, do you want to be responsible for her death by accident Samuel?"

A dead silence followed, then the operator spoke again: "I'm sorry Miss Steward, but believe me I also wish I could talk to him. He suddenly left without paying us our salary immediately after his wife left to be able to return to her mother in Canada with their two children, at least these are the rumors that are circulating, I am only an employee of Grey Insurance, I cannot tell you anything else that can help you".

"Okay, thank you, have a good day work Samuel".

"To you, Miss Steward".

As she turned into the parking lot of the shopping center, she felt more and more convinced of her intuition after that phone call.

Warren and Judith opened the doors and took their places in the jeep, Warren sat next to Kat and, without saying hallo, asked her about the phone call received shortly before.

"Can you tell us why all this rush? The interview did not seem to go so badly, apart from your tight smiles and the too gory details of Sarah's murder; I was sik again to hear you say "liquefied remains" and I also believe most of the people who followed the program".

Katrine exited the mall's large parking lot avoiding a truck as she pulled onto the freeway a little too hastily.

"I didn't notice and in any case I was asked to be as detailed as possible, so no one should complain. During the shooting I let the video surveillance of the night in which Olivia went to Sunset Hill to be able to kill Dylan Rogers".

Judith leaned forward from the rear seats to be able to hear better and participate in the conversation: "Can you tell me where we are headed? Add the fact that I would really like to arrive in one piece, you are driving like mad Kat".

Katrine swerved to overtake a car with a canoe loaded on the roof: "I'm getting there, don't worry I care about my self-preservation, but I'd like to be wrong about what I'm about to tell you. Continuing with the playback of the video I noticed a car speeding in the same direction as Olivia only a quarter of an hour later, this made me remember where I had seen that yellow Hummer before. Warren, does this say anything to you?"

The man squeezed the handle above the window much more vigorously after noticing the speed stamped on the speedometer increase dramatically: No, should it?"

"Warren, always pay attention to details! The solution can come thanks to details, not by chance linked to the investigation. Tom Hackett had a photograph in his office showing himself next to the same vehicle that appeared in the video: we are heading straight to his home".

The two passengers looked at each other to utter the same sentence in unison: "What does Tom Hackett have to do with all this?"

"Believe me, that's the same thing I thought, but then I remembered trying to contact him one day last week, after the interrogation that helped unearth his connection with Sarah Finningham. He had seemed desperate, in the throes of a fit of anger. Sure, we know it was Olivia who broke the news, but Tom couldn't have known it at the time, so he held me responsible for the disclosure and subsequent abandonment by his wife, who then decided to leave home and also take his children with her".

Judith took advantage of that pause to express her opinion: "I perfectly remember your entry into the office that day, you went on a rampage when the blame was attributed to you. I find it hard to believe that Tom Hackett lost his mind to the point of kidnapping a woman by pretending to be the killer who rocked the town last week".

"Judith, desperate people act on instinct, without thinking about the consequences of their actions. My father's death could be a clear example of how fear can lead to making mistakes or pulling a trigger against the common sense that mankind should have. Unfortunately a person's wickedness emerges in similar situations. Despair, revenge, anger and other negative feelings often appear to us as the only solutions, clouding our rationality and sometimes our actions. I don't know exactly what clicked in Tom Hackett's mind, but once his marriage, his career and his public image collapsed, he decided to raise as much money as possible and change his life. Ivan Varichenko recently bought a car here in Summerville and I think he decided to bet on him, kidnapping his daughter and extorting large sums from him through the ransom later requested".

"Now that you mention it, I think I noticed the Hummer outside Trevor's pub, he must have followed us, waiting for the moment I parted from her; if only I had your observational spirit…"

"It could just be a big misunderstanding, but I am increasingly convinced that there is Tom's hand behind Victoria's kidnapping. From our interview he seemed to be a person capable of anything to get what he wants and money has always been his main goal. His wife is the daughter of a well known director, the world must have collapsed on him being abandoned immediately after the scandal".

Judith turned then turned again to Katrine trying not to turn again so as not to arouse suspicion in the driver of the white van behind them: "I wouldn't want to interrupt you, but we are followed by a white van since we got into the parking lot at the mall".

Katrine glanced in the rearview mirror, managing to catch the eye of the red-haired woman driving the van behind them: "I know Judith, but thanks for reminding me; it`s nice to know that from now on Warren will be able to count on a woman who is awake even outside the police station".

Warren looked in the side mirror, then turned to the woman intent on putting the arrow in order to turn into a side street: "Did you notice? But when did you manage to…"

"Please Warren, I am a police officer, I can understand the look of a man in love since eighth grade, there is no need to give further explanation, I am very happy for both of you, but now we have something more important to talk about. As I was saying, Tom Hackett was very clever in taking advantage of the chaos generated by Olivia's murders, so he cut off Victoria's finger and made us think of another target by the killer behind the mask. Unfortunately I realized the differences between my cut and that of the other victims too late, I should have understood that it was carried out by an inexperienced person with this type of operation".

The jeep went up a steep and bumpy road, always followed by the van behind them.

When he found out about the chase with Olivia, he must have gotten the shits and so decided to cut and run, in case we arrested Olivia and found out she was innocent, at least with regards to this story, so he decided not to free Victoria and stopped texting to her father. His only mistake was to act using such a flashy means, otherwise we would never have been able to unmask him. Hold on tight and fasten your seat belts, I'm about to leave the van behind".

Kat engaged the 4x4 and swerved towards the woods, entering a dirt road and raising a big fuss immediately behind her car.

"Fuck, they must have noticed us. Hold on Jerry, I'll try to keep up with her".

The van took the same road as the Jeep, sweeping away the cloud of dust left earlier.

"Film everything, people will have to know why our Katrine Steward decided to take a trip in the forest with her friends, abandoning the interview right in the middle of the direct she reserved".

The man tried to keep a correct shot, despite the continuous ups and downs caused by the old shock absorbers of the van used for the chase.

"Turned left, cut behind that tree".

The woman swerved abruptly, trying to shorten the distance from the policewoman who until recently seemed willing to cooperate.

The jeep went down a slope and prepared to face a steep and dangerous climb; after about ten seconds and a short skid in the middle of the climb, they saw its summit.

"We won't make it Samantha, she definitely has a 4x4 we shouldn't ..."

"Do you want to become famous Jerry or do you prefer to continue to gorge yourself with crap with the meager pay of our regional broadcaster? Shut up and keep shooting".

The van descended at full speed, traveling down the slope trying to use all the thrust possible to reach the jeep in front of them.

The van seemed to be able to do it, but a couple of meters from the top the tires started spinning without finding grip on the ground, the engine lost power and reversed towards the valley, ending up stuck at the point where the two hills met.

Jerry got out of the van which had turned off and made no sign to restart, hearing the jeep`s horn about twenty meters above them, before seeing it disappear behind the summit of the slope not reached by the two journalists.

He raised the camera to point it at the red-haired colleague who was hitting the steering wheel repeatedly: "A beautiful smile from the woman who was just fucked by Katrine Steward".

CHAPTER 41

Hotel Phangan, Bangkok

Arthur Douglas, alias Tom Hackett, was getting dressed while the girl from the reception was taking advantage of the spacious shower offered by the suite.

That would be the first of a long line of woman paid to satisfy all his desires, Arthur`s life had begun in the best way. He sat on the edge of the bed and waited for the young Thai girl to come out, immersed in his thoughts.

He couldn`t get out of his head the image of Victoria Varichenko chained and forced to wait for her death, immersed in darkness and completely alone.

The day before his departure he had taken a spade from the tool shed and had gone to the place where he kept her hidden in order to kill her, thus avoiding a prolonged and painful agony until the moment in which she would have died of hunger and hardship.

Right after placing his hand on the handle of her cell, he had pulled back, he did not have enough courage to look into the eyes of a young woman dying beheaded or, worse still, see her agonize for an imprecise blow.

After all he was not a monster, he kept repeating it: he had simply abandoned her as his wife had done to him and with a bit of luck her body would not be found for a year.

He realized he was still wearing the wedding ring. It was the last thing that kept him tied to the name of Tom Hackett, so he took it off, toyed with it for a few moments and read the sentence pronounced by his wife on their wedding day: until death do us part.

He knew he had big faults about their separation, but which couple had never had a period of crisis or was hiding a little secret? If she had truly loved him, she would have been able to overcome what had happened and would have kept the promise engraved inside the ring.

He heard the flow of water stop suddenly, so he got up, opened the window and threw the ring towards the hedge that separated the swimming pool from the hotel's outer courtyard and stared at the chaos of street traffic through the open gate a little further away.

"You will see, you will like the city. First time here in Bangkok?" Said the receptionist without veils and in perfect English.

"Not really, I was here with my ex-wife on our honeymoon, but I'd rather not talk about it, it's an old story".

The girl approached him between the legs and looking at him in the eyes, then began to whisper something in his ear: "If you like we can do it again for the same price, this time I add a little extra that will make you forget your ex-wife".

The man grabbed her by the shoulders and threw her on the bed with the back to him : "Let's make a deal: you stop naming my ex-wife and I'll give you triple the money, do we agree?"

The young woman spread her thighs with a wink: she would be able to pay for the university studies that she had been forced to abandon.

Katrine parked the jeep on the gravel of the yard outside Tom Hackett's house.

"Are you sure it's the 27th? It looks like a billionaire's mansion".

Katrine picked up her 1911 and locked the jeep and put the keys in the pockets of her gray dress pants used for the interview.

"Yes, it's his home. Amazing how some people are able to ruin a family and a life like that for the thrill of an extramarital experience".

Warren observed her colleague as she walked with difficulty, digging the heels of her décolleté into the gravel ground: "Pretty…they seem like the shoes suitable for a new chase. Ok I understand, Warren fasten your laces, this time it's your turn".

Judith went to the intercom undecided about what to do and checked the presence of the surname Hackett on it: "So you want to announce yourself Kat or we pretend to be representatives?"

"I'll try and talk to him, there shouldn't be any problems".

The policewoman hit the switch and waited for an answer that didn't even come in the next three attempts.

There is no one. We have to enter anyway".

Warren observed the spikes on the upper ends of the rods that made up the tall gate in front of them and studied the smooth, hard-to-scale walls of the perimeter walls: "Are you really sure? If only you were wrong we would be guiltz of at least three counts including…"

"Cut it short Warren, you can stay out here to guard if you like, I will not stand idle doing nothing".

Judith approached a tree on the sidewalk outside the house and managed to climb the lowest branch; reaching the top would have been child's play.

"Hey come here, I think we will be able to get in without any problems with the help of the guest tree. Warren stop whining and help Kat up, don't think I should give up right now and if Katrine was wrong this time, the whole team would have been the ones to have made mistakes and take the responsibility".

Katrine and Warren looked at her in that strange position, hanging by one arm from a branch with her feet crossed in order to be able to stand in the confined space where the trunk of the tree split into two parts.

"All right. Katrine come, I`ll help you get in".

Once the trio set foot in the beautiful garden inside the villa, they were able to admire the exterior of the main façade of Tom Hackett`s mansion.

The terraces and windows were surrounded by white frames that detached the blue chosen for the paint used for the load-bearing walls. The roof was perfectly intact. One could make out the end of a scaffold on one side of it; maybe some workers were carrying out maintenance work or finished replacing what appeared to be brand new tiles.

The garden was well cared for and, despite the winter being over, the pool was still covered by a well-stamped tarpaulin.

Once they climbed the three steps that led to the luxurious front door, Katrine wasted no time trying to use the swing in the center of the blue door, but peered inside the windows in search of unusual movements: her lightness and haste to act had cost her a finger just two days ago.

"It seems deserted, be careful I will break one of the window panes".

The woman took off her right shoe and used the heel as if it were the emergency hammer that is usually seen on the sides of buses, trains and coaches.

The glass shattered and Katrine managed to insert her hand to open the handle of the door.

"Unbelievable: three cops behaving like thieves; I just hope this won't turn out to be a hole in the water. Your reasoning ranks Kat, I hope to find Victoria as much as you do, but I hope there are will not be negative repercussions".

Judith stepped over the window and turned to the man left outside who had just finished saying those words: "Now that's enough Warren, it seems to me that there is clear evidence that can indict Tom Hackett, so let's hurry up and carry out this inspection and let's leave hoping to find something useful".

Warren looked towards the gate one last time, then stepped inside the mansion without saying a word.

The interior furnished with class and good taste, reflected the same style of Tom's office, order and police seemed to have been respected following appropriate criteria: perhaps he had hired a maid to eliminate every trace of dust on the furniture in the corridor and in the main room.

Judith and Warren decided to start inspecting the upstairs rooms, leaving Katrine to probe the ground floor premises.

After about ten minutes Katrine was on the verge of surrendering to the evidence, she must have caught a crab: Tom had simply come home very late last night, maybe after getting a good hangover at Trevor's pub and decided to change his life, simply counting on his savings, after being abandoned by his family.

She leaned against the wall of the room intended for recreation by Tom's children, immersed in her thoughts as she looked from the large screen on the wall to the football-table in the back corner of the room.

She was on the point to call her colleague s to leave when she heard a faint noise behind her. She leaned her ear to the wall and was able to hear imperceptible knocks until a short while before, when the sound of her own footsteps had given way to total silence.

The door opened and the newly formed couple walked in: "We looked everywhere, there is nothing strange about…"

"Silence! Come and hear…what does this noise sound like?"

The two imitated Katrine and leaning their ears against the wall they could not perceive anything.

"I swear to you I thought I heard a knock, a moment before you entered that door".

"I don`t hear anything Kat, I wouldn`t want to fight you again, but you must have imagined it; the house is completely deserted, but if you want we can take a further look".

The woman ran out of the room and began to lift the carpets in search of a trap door leading to the basement; it was impossible to believe that a man with refined tastes like Tom Hackett did not hide a small cellar of wines inside his home.

"Bingo, look here".

She managed to find it under the kitchen carpet: a singular entrance, she had never heard anyone guard so jealously the entrance to a simple cellar.

"Wait, I`ll help you".

Warren managed to lift the hatch, revealing a narrow spiral staircase and a switch that illuminated the huge room beneath their feet.

"Come on, follow me".

Katrine went down the ladder, helping herself to move by leaning on the handrail and once her heels rang on the floor, she was able to see an exaggerated amount of wine embedded neatly in place on the bottle shelves on the wall in front of her.

When Judith and Warren were also at her side, they could admire the walnut table with an ancient manual flywheel slicer on top, a wall where various forms of cheese were neatly stored and sausages hung and another hidden by two large barrels of wine.

"Well...not bad, I would have never thought he would be a fan of this kind. Kat, Judith...look here".

The two woman approached the spot on the floor indicated by Warren: a huge dark circle had remained imprinted, although several attempts had been made to try to clean it up. The three looked at the two huge barrels leaning against the wall, then Katrine got up to walk towards one of them: "Warren, Judith, help me move it: it is evident that one of these two barrels had been moved towards this wall recently, perhaps to hide something".

After a few attempts and a lot of effort they managed to move one of the two barrels to the space necessary to shed light from Judith`s Smartphone.

"Nothing. These barrels are overflowing with wine, they may have been here a long time". Katrine pointed to the two plastic crates full of empty bottles: "I say, that after moving he moved one , he filled it up to prevent anyone from moving it. Come on, help me with the other".

The three strove to move the other barrel as well and after a minute of intense effort, they managed to illuminate a point on the wall that caught their attention.

"Here the concrete has a different color, someone must have sealed a passage…come on Warren, go and find something to tear this down, I have a bad feeling".

The man went upstairs and, once out of the window, went to the nearby tool shed to look for a tool that could open a gap in the wall.

In the corner next to the entrance door he saw a pickaxe and took it, brandishing it in his right hand; then after leaving, he could see a large hammer with a long wooden handle and so picked it up with his free hand.

Once back in the cellar, he handed the pickaxe to Katrine and so prepared to break through the wall.

"Get away Judith. Kat, try to alternate with mine , it will take a while to create even a small gap".

Judith backed away slightly leaving the field free for the blows inflicted by the two police-officers who immediately went to work.

After a couple of minutes they managed to create a hole the size of a hand from which a nauseating odors came out.

Katrine coughed, inhaling that stinking air, then pulled out her cell phone to light up the inside of that secret room: "Don`t tell me that…"

Her heart leapt into her throat as she saw what appeared to be Victoria Varichenko`s hair, chained to the wall with her head facing forward, unconscious.

"No, no, no! Come on, let`s free her! Judith call an ambulance, quick!"

The two began to shoot harder and harder until they managed to create the necessary passage to enter the room, then Kat dropped the pickaxe and, putting a sleeve of her jacket over her nose to try to mitigate the stench coming from Victoria`s body, entered the cell where she had been held captive for more than a week.

The beautiful woman who appeared in the main high fashion magazines was in an unrecognizable state: who knows how long she hadn`t been washed, fed and forced to stay in that position.

She approached Victoria preparing herself for the worst, as she had not mentioned any reaction of her at the moment of the small breach, either to that of her entry into the small room without light.

Yet she had heard a noise in the room above, it must have been her. The ceiling allowed the entry of that little air necessary for her survival even if it had to be almost completely soundproofed.

Katrine squeezed her wrist, as a steel collar did not allow her to place her two fingers on her neck to check the pulse, then turned to her colleagues: "Even if it`s very weak, she is still alive!"

CHAPTER 42

Summerville Hospital , room 304   *April 3th, 2017*

The nurse outside room 304 carefully looked at the identification card of the woman who had been in the waiting room for almost one hour , waiting for the permission to ask Victoria questions outside of visiting hours.

With a nod and a smile she moved to allow access to the policewoman, then walked down the hospital corridor to be able to deliver the medical records of the young Russian hospitalized the day before.

When she entered the room she found her father holding her hand, as if afraid of losing her again and it was he who spoke first.

"Agent Steward, I knew I could count on you. Victoria, this woman made it to bring you back into my arms".

The girl turned and looked sadly at the woman who had just entered the door: she had seen her a month earlier on TV, after the capture of a serial killer in Los Angeles.

Victoria said nothing, she was still under shock after the terrible experience that Tom Hackett had put her through.

"Don't worry Agent Steward, my daughter understands your language better than I and so she will be able to answer your questions shortly. I'll leave you both alone, I'm already aware of the facts, I'll go out and take some fresh air with Dimitri and Boris.

The Russian stood up giving way to Victoria's bed and went to the entrance, forcing Katrine to move from the threshold to let him pass.

The woman started to approach Victoria, but then turned to address her father, as he was walking towards the hospital terrace followed by the two bodyguards.

"Mr. Varichenko, I almost forgot. Thank you for listening to me, continuing to keep this terrible story a secret. My boss is aware of this and has promised not to let anything leak out, so as not to alarm Tom Hackett.

It will be much easier to catch him by making him think he got away with it".

In response Ivan raised his hand in a military sign and, once he retraced his steps, he began to whisper something in the ear of one of his gorillas.

Katrine closed the door, isolating the room occupied only by her and Victoria from any external noise or contact.

The girl had been medicated, cleaned and fed following the practices dictated by the doctors who had taken care of her: her conditions had improved a lot, she would surely recover and overcome what had happened; on the other hand she had shown that she had enough strength, courage and tenacity to overcome a week of imprisonment and torture.

Katrine sat down and looked into the sad eyes of the young Russian, then raised her left hand to show her stump.

"It seems that we have something in common you and I, it must be the fashion of the moment; you know, on the one hand it reassures me to know that I will never wear a wedding ring, Weddings have always made me very nervous.

The Russian continued to stare at her: it seemed that that joke had not had the desired effect, but after a few seconds she laughed out loud, followed by the policewoman sitting next to her.

"You are strong. I am not telling you this just because you saved my life, but I immediately understood it from your way of doing things and from how you answered the awkward questions of those reporters in Los Angeles; you have a new admirer Katrine Steward".

"Those vultures...always try to make you pass for what you are not reallz, without thinking about your private life or your feelings; don't worry, you won't be forced to give any interview or statement.

Your kidnapping will only be made public once Tom Hackett is caught".

The woman bit her lower lip and tried to hold back her tears as she heard the name of the man who had sentenced her to certain death, so Katrine waited a moment before she could ask any questions.

"The heels".

"What did you say Victoria? I didn't understand you".

"Your heels. Yesterday I managed to throw a couple of hits on the wall to try to make myself heard with the last strength left. If you hadn't worn those heels I wouldn't have been able to cling to that last hope".

Katrine wiped a tear from her, stroking her cheek with her index finger: "I hope that sooner or later we women will be able to demonstrate our intellectual superiority".

Victoria laughed again; that woman was doing everything to make her feel better and seemed to succeed.

"I know you are still shaken and in shock, so if you don't feel like telling me how it went I can perfectly understand".

"No, no. I can manage, just give me a moment to blow my nose and sit up on the pillow".

Katrine helped Victoria carry out her requests then waited for her to begin.

"The night I was kidnapped I met a man: it will seem strange to you, but he spent almost two hours talking to me about you, it must be your colleague, Warren Valentine, do you know him?"

Katrine seemed amazed to hear that statement, but did not get upset in the slightest: "Sure, he's part of my team and it's also thanks to him that we managed to free you from that hiding place in time yesterday afternoon".

"He seems to care a lot about you, not just as a colleague I mean, anyway…as I was telling you, I had a good time with him, I had a nice evening listening to his talks and enjoying his company until he accompanied me home.

After saying goodbye, I walked towards my father's house, but once in front of the entrance I recognizes the individual driving the yellow Hummer: the same man who made my father sign an insurance for his new car, bought days before.

He asked me if I could give my father's mobile number, as he had lost it in order to contact him the next day. At the time I did not think about his bad intentions, I was slightly drunk, but no one has ever dared to hurt me even for fear of a reaction from my father: he would be beaten to death by Dimitri and Boris the following day if only someone had tried to twist a hair out of me".

Unfortunately, facts have emerged that in a short time upset Tom's life: his wife abandoned him, leaving for Canada with their two children, the company he worked for would soon have fired him and his mistress was killed, dissolved with a very powerful acid.

Some people think of suicide when even one of these unpleasant situations happens, but not Tom Hackett. He must have seen in you the hope of a new life: with the money of your ransom he could have run away undisturbed, but he couldn`t free you because you saw his face and you would have turned to your father or the police. I know from experience that a part of the human soul has to crack in order to commit murder, and Tom Hackett must have lost his mind after the events of last week, but he did not manage to give you the coup de grace, leaving you to rot in the cellar hidden under the floor of his home, however, allowing us to find you and rescue you".

Victoria nodded to Katrine`s reasoning, but was keen to add all the details of her imprisonment: by doing so, perhaps she would help to capture her tormentor.

"After I approached the car, he put a gun to my head and forced me to get in. I tried to free myself but hit me with the butt of the gun, making me pass out".

"You risked a lot fighting while you had a gun aimed at your head".

"Yes, but you must know that my greatest fear has always been that of finding myself helpless in a similar situation: I would have preferred to die rather than be raped by a stranger".

Katrine put her hand in front of her mouth: "You mean Tom Hackett abused you?"

Victoria replied without being able to look into her eyes: "Yes, my father knows about it too, I was raped the same night he kidnapped me, he put that steel collar on me and it was easy to take advantage of my body after making me ingest something as soon as I woke up".

Katrine tried to comfort her, but she knew that this would be a difficult wound to heal.

"But it's terrible, I never expected such a revelation".

"Judging by the preparations in my cell, it must not have been the first time a woman was imprisoned without the knowledge of his wife or family. The day I signed the contract he looked at me in a strange way, I can recognize perverted simply by the way he looks at me. I was a fool that night, I shouldn't have gone near his car. At this time…"

"You couldn't have imagined such a torture Victoria. Now that you mention it, he looked at me with the same look on the day of his interrogation; that man is used to having control over everything, woman with a strong character like ours annoys him but also it attracts him at the same time: he wanted to take revenge on you, but I could have been in your place if only I had your father's bank account".

Yeah, I think so too. He boasted that he nearly killed a prostitute once, one of those dominatrix's".

"Unbelievable, then yours may not be an isolated case! Tom Hackett did not act out of desperation: he's always been a lousy, slimy liar. We will try to investigate his past in depth, maybe his wife noticed something, but did not want to make the facts public, so as not to ruin the family or her image, while Olivia Harris helped unearth one of her husband's betrayals. Once the matter was made public, she ran away just like him: she will have to answer several questions, it's hard for me to think she didn't know anything about the cell in their cellar".

Victoria turned to the window to be able to admire the splendid sun she hadn't seen for days: "The devil shows up in a suit and tie. At first glance, a man of his caliber and a family like his may seem perfect, but no one can know what really happens behind the walls of a house. My father and I have had a lot of arguments lately, I know I was not the best daughter in the world, but I am going to make up for it and raise for good. During my captivity I had a lot of time to reflect on my character and my life in general; I'm sure I can become a better person in the future and all this thanks to you".

Katrine shook her hand around that of the woman: her release had brought her joy and relief, sweeping away the negative feelings she had lived with since she returned to her hometown.

"It is I who must thank you, Victoria. I could not bear to lose you too, you are alive only thanks to your strength and your great attachment to life; we are very similar in this".

Victoria freed her hand from Katrine's grip and undid the necklace she wore around her neck: "I wish you'd keep it to remind you of saving the person who wore it for eighteen years. I'll be grateful to you forever, luckily I took it off before going to the Spa".

Katrine admired the precious stone set in the center of the pendant that was offered to her, it must have been a very precious diamond: the symmetrical cut, the purity and color, confirmed the generosity of that gesture.

"I can't accept, it must be worth a lot".

"Maybe, but it's nothing compared to the gift you gave to me: a second chance".

The bedroom door opened slowly and Ivan Varichenko made his entrance again: "I'd like to let you stay a while longer, but the nurse has to visit Victoria. If you want you can continue in the afternoon with your questions, Miss Steward".

"Sure, see you soon Victoria".

Katrine kissed the girl's forehead and went out with her father, heading to the vending machines for a hot drink.

"How did the interrogation go?"

"It was not an interrogation, but to get to know your daughter a little better. You are a very lucky man Mr. Varichenko, Victoria is a very sweet and generous girl".

"Did she mention about her…suffered violence?"

"Yes she was very courageous to talk to me about it. We also made other considerations about the man guilty of her kidnapping".

"In the past, the testicles were cut off and glass powder was inserted into the rectum for rapists and individuals like him. I must ask one last favor Miss Steward, I would sleep well knowing that Victoria is safe".

Katrine inserted a coin into the slot of the machine and pressed the button to select a hot tea.

"What is it about? My colleagues have already tried to track down Tom Hackett, we will soon know his movements".

"You have to find him and tell me where he is hiding. Ivan Varichenko will take care of the rest".

Katrine stared at the dark liquid coming down to fill the plastic cup: Mr. Varichenko, what you are asking me is illegal: I know you want to Track Tom down to torture him, believe me, acting like him won't make you feel better".

"Maybe it will avoid more suffering to young and innocent woman, people don't change: you know this well, don't you Katrine? Her ex boyfriend has been following her for days".

Kathrine took the cup out of the machine, it was hot, but it gladly warmed her hands: "Have you been following me these days by chance, Mr. Varichenko?"

"Not me, but Dimitri and Boris, they saw your fight in front of your house. Try to think of your sister , your colleagues or some of your friends being kidnapped by such a bastard".

Kat sipped her tea, thought briefly about the moment she shot Alan Wilder in Los Angeles, the fight with Olivia Harris and the looks of Zack Ebbott and Tom Hackett.

"I have to think about it, also because you are asking me to act without the knowledge of my colleagues and my boss".

"I ask you to act as a woman, not as a policewoman; I asked for your help because you are different from other cops, you are more human, am I right?"

"It`s not about humanity, but about offering you the position of Hackett in order to take your revenge on the criminal who kidnapped and raped your daughter".

Katrine remained silent and finished sipping her hot drink: probably Tom Hackett would have continued to act undisturbed, kidnapping other woman without any hindrance, now that he had the large sum obtained by Varichenko.

"When I managed to find out the last place he was spotted or used his credit card, I`ll try to let you know, but for now I promise you nothing else".

"All right, you have my phone number. Thanks also on behalf of Victoria and other woman, victims of Hackett. Goodbye Agent Steward".

The man watched the policewoman put on her jacket and leave the hospital: she would return to see Victoria on the following days and with a bit of luck she would show her the place where Tom Hackett was hiding. After all a Varichenko always gets what he wants.

CHAPTER 43

Summerville Police Station   *April 4th, 2017*

"You should get an email shortly with Tom Hackett's latest moves, as you asked me yesterday afternoon. How is Victoria? I heard she will be discharged in the evening".

Judith took an apple and began to remove the peel with a small knife also used as a key ring.

"Perfect. Victoria is fine, she is deeply grateful to all of us for being alive and I think she will turn her life around once she gets back to Moscow. By the way. Has anything been leaked about her case?"

"No, all the people who rescued her, kept the matter away from the reporters and the chase by that couple who interviewed you did not air: probably because they didn't know where we were headed and the way which we left them behind, must not have been particularly liked by their financier".

Warren checked the clock on the wall above their office door: "Girls, I'm going out to smoke a cigarette, with your permission…"

"Wait Warren, I'm coming with you. I have to get something from the car, I'll take this opportunity to stretch my legs".

Katrine and Warren went outside, feeling the heat of the sun's rays on the skin of their faces: since Olivia had been unmasked, the city had enjoyed a beautiful climate and a clear cloudless sky, as if to sign the calm after the storm.

"Look Warren, I wanted to talk to you about something, but I wish you won't say anything to Judith".

The man lit his cigarette and inspired a puff of smoke: "What is it? In the meantime I`ll walk you to the car".

"I don`t have to take anything, I needed to be privately with you, Victoria told me the details of your meeting, how you spent the evening, what you talked about…during dinner at Sergio`s I had confirmation that you liked me and I`m sorry I was too direct with you.

You are a very interesting man, but above all it is not the right time to start a relationship, I hope you understand".

Warren blushed slightly but let the woman continue her speech.

"I`m just trying to tell you, that I hope your relationship with Judith is not some kind of nail, she`s a good woman and would suffer a lot in your abandonment, she cares a lot about you, you can read it in her face".

"Katrine, this speech of yours is not needed. You`re right, I like you since the first day I saw you open the box containing Finningham`s finger, you are a beautiful, intelligent and smart woman…"

Kat rolled her eyes, his flattery embarrassed her…" but believe me, thanks to you I got to know Judith better and I have no intention of letting her get away. Don`t be offended, but you`re not the kind of woman a man would want to be with. You are too authoritarian and the only thing you really care about is being able to catch the criminals you follow with so much interest. For me it`s just about work, yours is a real obsession and luckily you are! Thanks to you the city can sleep peacefully and by this I mean to tell you that you are better than me, better than all of us here; I love you Kat, but only as a colleague".

Katrine remained serious trying to assimilate every single word of that speech; Warren took another puff and after getting no reaction from her, he stared at her without meeting her gaze, as she seemed to point to the building behind him as if it were transparent.

"Are you offended? I exaggerated, sorry…"

"Offended? I am relieved! My God it was embarrassing enough to have to live with that doubt. Now I feel stupid for having confessed to you, what a shame".

"What are you saying? You've done very well, you must have lifted a burden. Listen, about the sentence a while ago, I exaggerated a little, I didn't really mean that you don't arouse the interest of any man, I'd be a hypocrite, I must admit".

"You sound like my sister, you are both so damned right. I should take a cooking class, go out with my friends and once out of work, stop thinking about all the evil that surrounds us".

Warren through the butt on the ground and stepped on it with his shoe: "Don't be too hard on yourself, you'll see that you will gradually become more malleable".

The woman stared at him as if she wanted to stab him.

"Well…very slowly, I would say, I add being touchy among the particular signs of my character".

Katrine laughed then slapped Warren on the shoulder, causing him to stagger. "Let's get back in before you say any more bullshit. Can you explain me how Judith can handle you? She must be completely blinded by the broad. See, when I saw you both…"

They both went inside, happy to have doted their beautiful relationship.

After work, Judith immediately went to the kitchen, while Warren took advantage of the shower in her apartment.

Once he came out of the shower he put on his bathrobe, went downstairs and lay down on the sofa next to Sharky.

"You know Warren, I was wondering how much you spend on rent in that flat on Roxy Avenue".

The man started stroking the dog on the hairy belly, until he was forced to move his paw in a sort of nervous tic due to tickling: "Too much. I had to ask for a loan last month, because the mechanic asked me an exaggerated price for repairs on the pickup. I should change area, why are you asking me?"

"So...I was thinking".

Suddenly Warren realized where the woman in the kitchen was headed and looked for a way to get her to go through with her real question: "I heard that in this area , rents are very low and there are lots of cute women with which to spend the evenings…"

The woman continued to speak without turning, even though a smile suddenly appeared on her face: "You must have heard badly then, in this area there are only me and a dozen other spinsters who looks after stray cats and rummage in the garbage for something for dinner".

"Ah ah, even? Then it will mean that I`ll give it a little thought, quiet areas have always attracted me, and I really like animals".

Judith turned to see the concentrated man in front of the TV screen, completely crushed by the weight of the dog who had decided to take a nap right on his stomach.

She was going to call her mother that evening so to tell her the good news: she would pass out, she could bet it.

"Warren...did you notice something strange about Katrine? When she got the email from our colleague who dealt with the matter, she left disappointed barely saying goodbye".

"You know Katrine, there must not have been anything useful written on the list of movements and she wanted to continue the research at home. She didn't say hallo only because at the moment she is whirling something in her head, not because she has something against us, I guarantee it".

That must be it. When you fixate on an investigation, the world around her seems to change, have you noticed?"

Warren did a quick zapping, not finding any interesting quiz at that time of the day: it was still too early.

"Yes, that's the way she is, luckily for us. You too, when you commit yourself, you get lost in the world of clouds: last night I had to turn off the bathroom tap after you received your mother's call, you didn't remember to turn it off. The tub was about to overflow, luckily I went in to brush my teeth".

Judith left the kitchen utensils and came over to give him a kiss on the cheek: "Oh, my hero, what would I do without you...I have one last question. You and Kat...have you ever thought about going to bed? She has a stunning body and whatever she wears makes her pretty damn sexy".

"Someone here is jealous...No, I've never fantasized on her".

Judith looked at him in the eyes then returned to the kitchen after giving him a pinch: "This evening minestrone, I had in mind to prepare you a plate of lasagna, but as you well know, I hate liars".

Katrine was sitting in the armchair in the living room of her apartment and holding her cell phone in her hands with Ivan Varichenko's contact prominently on the screen.

She was very undecided on what to do since she had that conversation in the hospital the day before.

A few moments ago she had checked the latest purchase by Tom Hackett, on a plane ticket to Bangkok and instinctively she had chosen to keep it hidden from her colleagues.

Only the last step was missing and she would have condemned Tom Hackett to a certain end. The Russian tycoon would have done everything to take revenge for what had been done to his only daughter, but she didn't feel like calling him, she didn't want to be involved in that shady business.

Her job was to stop the killers, not to help them, so she decided to lock her cell phone screen and start preparing dinner. She filled a pot of water and added salt to it, then lit the fire on the larger stove and opened the fridge to look for a tomato sauce and onions to prepare the sauce for her spaghetti.

She heard a noise in the hall, despite the loud music coming from her screen, almost as if they were banging on the door, or rather, drumming.

Once she had approached the sofa, she lowered herself and took out the box from which that sound came from and picked up the mask hidden inside, holding it in her hands.

Maybe it would help her make the right decision, after all it was thanks to that mask if she survived Olivia Harris and could communicate with her father again.

Katrine decided to wear the mask for one last time, vowing to destroy it after the vision showed her what to do with the information on Tom Hackett.

The world around her began to spin, and she managed to turn off the gas before sitting down on the sofa, falling into a deep sleep and experiencing firsthand what would happen only two weeks later.

CHAPTER 44

Yaowarat Discrit, Bangkok   *April 8th, 2017*

Arthur Douglas was located in Bangkok's Chinatown, famous for its markets and numerous retail and wholesale shops.

He had bought clothes at the Sampeng market, fed up with Western dressing and wearing the clothes he wore in his previous life; it was time to change style and so decided to follow the advice of the girl from the stall who had made him try on a pair of trousers typical of Thai fishermen, very wide, comfortable and colorful.

If only his wife could have seen him dressed like a yoga teacher, she would have laughed at him, but the greatness of his new life was, to be able to do whatever came to his mind without taking into account crazy expenses and people's opinion: he would have been an anonymous resident of the city who enjoys his life by drawing on an almost inexhaustible source of money for the rest of his days.

After a quick lunch he would go to the beach to enjoy complete relaxation and the wonderful panorama offered by that exotic paradise.

The change of identity, the enormous distance that separated him from Summerville and his new life as a tourist in Bangkok had not served to calm him completely: every two hours he checked the sites with the news from the world, fearing for the discovery of Varichenko's daughter.

Till now, no one had discovered anything, indeed the disappearance had been reported only the previous day; that

Russian had hoped for her release until then, then he had turned to the police.

Who knows what Katrine Steward's face would look like, if she had known that behind the kidnapping there was the familiar face of the person questioned by her a couple of weeks earlier.

He decided to turn his cell phone off and go back to his occupations, but before browning in the sun he decided to take advantage of being near the Buddhist temple of Wat Traimit to admire the imposing solid gold statue weighing 5,5 tons, saved from the sacking by the Burmese.

Unfortunately, no one would ever be able to change his two great passions: gold and women.

For the first he had always moved seas and mountains, his dream of wealth had come true the day he had married his ex-wife, combining his wealth, already substantial enough, with hers, thus becoming one of the city's most wealthy family.

As for his passion for woman, he had been able to notice the evolution and change of his sexual tastes and desires right after his marriage: the young babysitter had ended up in his bed first, then the more mature history teacher of his children.

However, only with his tennis teacher could he discover the pleasure of really subduing a woman. In the following years he had to start kidnapping street whores in order to satisfy the increasingly strange sexual desires.

The blood and the beating did not particularly excite him, but once he felt his hands around his prey's neck he felt extremely powerful; or when they were forced to do exactly what he asked when he put that steel collar around their neck that he had it made by a friend with the same perversion.

The degree of pleasure he felt was directly proportional to the screams with which woman asked for mercy: The stronger they were, the greater was the sense of power that allowed him to reach orgasm.

He hadn't had sex with his wife for three years now: he had agreed to keep his erotic games and his affairs secret (even though she didn't know of his recent kidnappings) to keep his family and the financial imperial gold together, but after all the newspapers had revealed the relationship with one of the victims of Summerville's serial killer, he had seen fit to slip away also because his partners at Greyteck would have excluded him from the company to try to remedy the financial collapse of publicly traded shares after the scandal.

He hoped he could continue to exercise his quirks, maybe now that he was in Bangkok he could try younger girls. A friend of his had told him how easily a thirteen-year-old virgin or beautiful girls with an extremely low age range could be bought.

The future would have been bright and carefree now that he was Arthur Douglas.

Once he cleaned his hands with the special lemon-scented towel from lobster residues, he asked for the bill at the table, checking the clock: a quarter past eleven.

His skin burned as he had fallen asleep in the scorching sun most of the afternoon without the use of a sunscreen. The skin in his short hair was very red, as were that of his arms and face; he had got a really bad sunburn.

What was needed after a fish-based binge was a slap-up fuck, so he set off through the streets packed with what he knew were sex tourists. Probably most of those men from all over the globe were still married, given the rings on the fingers with which they would have groped numerous breasts and buttocks during their stay in Bangkok.

He decided to go back to the same room the previous evening to be able to retire again with the splendid sixteen year old who, only after screaming for a whole hour, had revealed her real name, or Yada.

Pushed an old drunkard to be able to enter the door of the club packed with people prey to the effect of the magical mix of drugs, alcohol, loud music and young girls with easy virtues.

He looked around for Yada, but his gaze met that of a beautiful woman who appeared to be originally from South America.

Approaching as if he hadn't paid much attention to her, he was able to admire the dark skin of her thighs and back, put on display by an exaggeratedly short dress, while she conversed with what appeared to be a German.

A perfect body, the sexual movements and her serious attitude made him forget the young Yada, forcing himself to stop in a corner waiting for a new exchange of glances.

The woman dismissed the man with the blond crew cut when he tried to grab her buttocks, moving away quickly to be able to reach the other girls at the bar, without failing to catch the eye again of the elegant American leaning against the wall right next to her.

Arthur stopped her, putting himself in front to prevent her from continuing her walkway under the curious eyes of the other customers of the bar: "That asshole doesn't seem to know the good manners".

The woman replied showing her awake and seductive gaze in a strange English accent: "Yes, I hate it when they do this. We are still women, not animals for sale".

At those words Arthur felt an immediate erection growing in his pants, it would have been wonderful to tame that proud creature, so he asked her what her price was: "Listen you are wonderful, I would like to spend the night with you. I can get you a nice gift, you just need to tell me what you prefer and how you would like to be treated and I will respect it".

Sometimes he felt obliged to check if his nose was growing by a few centimeters, as it happened to Pinocchio after telling a lie.

"We can discuss it privately if you want; I have a room just around the corner and you seem to be a real gentleman".

The woman took his hand and accompanied him outside the club, then they both walked towards the newly built building in the immediate vicinity of the night club.

She smiled at his every glance, while her earrings bounced to the rhythm of her footsteps, just like the firm and prosperous breasts highlighted by her risqué outfit.

She opened her bedroom door and took off her heels, before turning on a red light right above their heads.

Arthur lowered his pants then threw himself on the bed starting to unbutton his shirt, revealing the redness of his chest; he would have made her make the first move to make her believe she had the reins of the game, but once forced into doggy style he would have vented, revealing his true nature.

"I'd like to know your name, the real one if possible".

The woman took off her dress, remaining dressed only in white thong and lace bra: I'll tell you if you can really make me enjoy, but first we still have to set the price".

Arthur saw her straddle the point of greatest interest and heard her whisper something in his ear as he opened the drawer to probably look for a condom.

"Any amount you want beauty...I could not understand your words, you spoke too softly".

The woman bit his ear and slowly repeated the figure pronounced just before: "Let's make fifteen million dollars".

Arthur widened his eyes and tried to get up as soon as he heard the same amount deposited two weeks earlier in his bank account in the Virgin Islands, but the woman managed to block him with one hand and inject him with the syringe needle into his neck with the other.

"*Pozdravleniya ot Ivan Varichenko*", she whispered to him to greet him from the man who had hired her that morning.

Arthur Douglas saw the room spin around and dark spots began to blur his sight, but before losing his senses he managed to notice the two thugs who hurried to enter the room to be to pick him up. When he woke up, he knew he would have to play Tom Hackett again, probably for the last time.

CHAPTER 45

Red Square, Moscow *April 12th, 2017*

Two elegantly dressed men strolled in the main square of Moscow as the sun set behind them, partially obscuring the domes of the Kremlin`s cathedrals.

"So Sergej, will we see you tonight, in the luxurious restaurant to celebrate Varichenko`s birthday, like every year?"

"But how Aleksey? Haven`t you heard the news? This year he decided to give up his celebrations. It seems that he will have dinner in private with his daughter, she must have convinced him to give up the annual dinner with his members".

"That spoiled little bitch; when will he understand that he is being manipulated by that perfidious viper?"

Sergej straightened the collar of his coat, as if it served to protect him more from the cold air behind them.

"You're wrong Aleksey, after her return from America she seems to have changed radically: you know, she even gave her car to the maid as a gift".

"She must have lost her mind during those modeling parties, trust me…that girl will be the bane of her farther and also all of us. Imagine if one day she were to take Ivan`s place…brrr, I think I`d rather shoot myself in the head".

Yeah…so what do we do? Katrina works tonight and Lokomotiv Moskva plays against Rubin Kazan, we could watch it together, what do you think?"

"Okay, I'm in. As long as you come and see it at my place, I would like to show you my new 60 inch screen and let you taste the vodka that Lyudmila bought just yesterday".

The two shook hands as if they were stipulating one of the many contracts of the most widespread telephone company on Russian territory.

Victoria went through the sliding doors at the entrance to the skyscraper where her father worked: this time she would not go to the upper floors, but would have to go down a few floors with one of the four elevators located at the end of the long corridor on the ground floor.

"Hallo Svetlana, how is your husband? He seemed in great shape to me the last time I saw him".

The woman with the exaggerated make-up who answered to this name blushed embarrassed, as it was the second time in her life that this girl had asked her a question.

"M-very well thank you Miss Varichenko…yourself? I mean, how silly, she is always beautiful, but how did her stay abroad go?"

The woman looked at her in fear, thinking back to the time when the cup of too bitter coffee was thrown at her by the girl standing in front of her.

"I mean, I lost a bounty after my vacation in America; you know, dad made me walk to the end of my strength".

Svetlana noticed the smile on the young Russian`s face: something had changed during that experience, she had never gotten to see her so happy and kind, she must have met a boy or something.

"You`re father often trains himself on trips of this kind, he shouldn`t push his princess so hard".

"Ha ha, tell him next time. By the way, do you remember that dress I asked you to repair before I left?"

"Well, it seemed too good to be true: yes, of course. I left it in her office, right in the closet".

"I know, I got to see it just yesterday. Do me a big favor, go and get it and give it to your daughter. I know she is more or less wearing my size and is about to come of age, I would also like to give her a gift as a token of thanks for the numerous services offered by her mother during these eight years for the Varichenko`s family".

Svetlana couldn`t believe her ears, that dress must have been worth at least two years of her salary.

"Are you really sure? I think it would make her very happy, one day I would like to present my daughter in person to you".

"I think we could make this happen…I`m sorry I have to leave you, my father is calling me on the phone".

"Of course, don`t make him attend too long. I thank you Victoria and as soon as you see him, please give him my greetings".

The young woman winked at her then walked down the corridor entering then to the first free elevator.

Svetlana watched her figure disappear behind the sliding doors of the elevator, then pinched her arm to make sure she wasn`t in the middle of a wonderful dream.

Victoria Varichenko got out of the elevator and entered the room with the "Do not disturb" sign written in Russian as indicated by her father about an hour before.

The owner of the skyscraper and the telephone company had made sure to give the keys to access that basement only for his daughter and her bodyguards, to maintain absolute confidentiality of his intentions regarding an alleged new secret project by his company`s technicians.

When Victoria opened the door, she could tell with her own eyes that in that room there would be no presentations regarding future innovations in telephony or the discovery of how to speed up HiRuski`s mobile network.

In the center of the huge bare room a small brick room had been set up with a large mirror that allowed you to see the person chained inside it, but not vice versa, like those used in interrogation barracks.

Ivan welcomed his daughter holding her tightly and lifting her weight high up: "Moy dorogoi...Do you like it? I had this one-way mirror mounted. We will see everything that happens inside, but he will know nothing of the place he is in, he thinks he is in the basement of Bangkok".

Victoria looked at the imprisoned man the same way she had found herself just two weeks ago: he had shaved his hair, but she could never forget that look of him even after a hundred years. "What are you going to do to him dad?"

"You are not forced to stay, it is a teaching, a life lesson to the man who tried to kill you: perhaps he will understand that he acted wrong and so he will be welcomed into the kingdom of heaven, but before then he will have to serve his sentence, undergoing the same torture he inflicted on you, but I`ll try to make some small changes".

Victoria felt a shiver run down her spine: seeing him again brought back the memory of his terrible actions.

She felt deeply changed and really intended to dedicate her life for others, but first she had to close that matter and would not oppose her father's wishes; after all that lousy one had sought it out by challenging one of the most powerful families in the Soviet Union.

"I would like to watch, if I can…"

Ivan put a hand on her shoulder and gave her a smile: "Victoria, you are a lioness, just like your mother. You can leave at any time, Dimitri and Boris will accompany you out whenever you want".

The two men remained motionless as statues, guarding the entrance to the room in its immediate vicinity.

"I think I can stay till the end".

The Russian laughed amused, then turned back to his daughter: "I don't think you want to wait for the moment when he dies of hunger: it could take weeks. Do you remember? He had chosen this end for you…I will force him to eat and feed even against his will; I will make him suffer for a long time before I will permit him to leave this world".

Ivan nodded to one of the two guards. Dimitri moved to bring him a box that had hitherto been hidden under his leather jacket; after removing the lid, he was able to put on the horrible mask that Katrine Steward had given him, along with the paper on which Hackett's last destination was written.

In exchange he had promised to destroy it after its use and would have undertaken to keep the whole affair secret.

Varichenko slowly exhaled until he reached a state of apparent calm then, after having a last look at his beautiful daughter, he entered the small torture chamber built during the week.

Tom started to fidget with convulsive and frantic movements of the body, he could not scream for help because of the gag tight around his mouth.

"Good morning Tom, I think you know who I am. My name is Ivan Varichenko and Victoria`s father, I am here to pay homage on her part. You see, I believe that nothing goes unpunished: you knew in your heart that sooner or later this day would have come, but you chose to continue acting like an animal. How did Esperanza look to you? She was very happy to be able to help me in the capture of a violent man who nearly killed her friend".

Tom Hackett gazed at the hideous headdress worn by what was most likely the man responsible for his death.

"Forgive my English, but from your eyes I can understand that you understand my words and your situation very well. You should have released her when you had the chance Tom".

Ivan Varichenko turned to brandish the long shears leaning against the wall: where he knew Victoria was standing, managed to look at himself, seeing an image totally different from his.

He could not have known that he was looking at the ancient ruler of the Akkrasa tribe, as he held the spear with which he had managed to avenge the death of his son by eliminating his enemy several years earlier.

"Unfortunately I`m not the type to cut fingers off, Tom, but fear not, I will take extremities that you consider fundamental in your useless life".

On the other side of the mirror Victoria managed not to look away from the expression of terror of the chained man, as her father was preparing to use the tool in his hands.

Two weeks later a team would take care of the removal and cleaning of the small room in which Tom Hackett had suffered numerous and brutal tortures: the bloodstains on the floor would never be completely removed, as well as the memory of that time in the Varichenko`s mind.

EPILOGUE

Public Parking, Mellow Park   *May 2th, 2017*

Elizabeth Steward got out of the jeep and put on a pair of glasses with red lenses, like the color of the tips of her long dark hair.

"Do you really mean to tell me that Mrs. Hackett knew about cheating, but she never wanted to go down to the cellar so as not to get involved in her husband's dirty tricks? I would have killed him..."

"I believe her Elizabeth, I don't think she did it for her children, often denying the existence of problems is the only way to manage them and then she seemed very sincere".

Katrine locked the car and put her bag on her shoulders.

"The truth is rarely pure and never simple, who said that?"

"Oscar Wilde. Listen Elizabeth, how did Florence seem to you? Warren and Judith took a week off to visit the city".

"Magnificent, I would say that you too could enjoy a vacation. By the way are you really sure you want to do it? I mean…I can't believe I'm actually accompanying you to deliver the gun and badge".

Katrine remained silent, continuing to walk along the park lane that would have led her right in front of the entrance to the police station.

"I'm so happy that you finally decided to quit that dangerous job, sometimes you really made me worry; do you remember that shooting at the supermarket?"

"Yes, good times. We managed to catch that madman thanks to the reaction of the manager of the supermarket: he knocked him out with a baseball bat, I can still feel the blow".

Elizabeth looked at her sister, she seemed to be slightly melancholy.

Spring seemed to have finally arrived: couples of young boys were frolicking in the park and numerous birds flew over the bright blue sky.

Katrine's cell phone vibrated and so read the words contained in the text message from an unknown number:

"HiRuski thanks you for your cooperation. We wish you a good day and a peaceful future".

Elizabeth watched her sister put her cell phone in her purse; she didn't understand why she looked so sad.

"Hey Kat, would you like to go for a pizza this weekend? You choose the place, but I pay, what do you think?"

Katrine continued her walk with her head held high, waving to a fellow policeman who crossed the path: "This weekend I can't, I'm busy".

"Wow, what sort? Sentimental?"

"Mhmm...work".

Elizabeth mulled to herself, then resumed the conversation, insisting on that subject; "What is it about? I thought you would take a break, I didn't know you had interviewed".

"I didn't do it".

Elizabeth watched her sister silently as they passed the outer gate of Mellow park; who knows what thoughts troubled her mind at the simple sight of the external walls of the police station.

She seemed to be very distant and focused, as if she could see something different in this concrete complex.

"Um, could I know my sister's plans for the future or do you have to be begged?"

Katrine took off her glasses as she rummaged inside her bag for the badge: "Ok Elizabeth, although I know you won't like it at all".

"What do you mean? Aren't you handling in the badge?"

"Yes, I'm doing it don't worry, I always keep my promises, but I'm going to start my own business; I will open a private investigation agency. I'll be able to work alone, enjoy the support of Philip and the others in the central office and continue to do the job I like with more flexible hours and a higher pay, aren't you happy?"

Elizabeth was on the verge of fainting as a smirk appeared on Katrine's lips: "But nothing will change, you will continue to overwhelm yourself with work, chase criminals and risk getting a bullet".

Kat climbed the steps at the entrance to the police station, then turned to her sister: "Exactly, just what I wanted".

Elizabeth snorted and followed her sister into the building in silence, very irritated by her decision.

"Elizabeth, you must understand that some people are born with a particular talent: a good craftsman, a great cook, a brilliant manager or a very good elementary teacher. Sooner or later you will have to accept your sister's role; evil will never cease to exist and to stop it or guarantee short periods of peace between one crime and another, the intervention of people like me is necessary. I do not pay attention to the necessary sacrifices, the nightmares, the dangers that all this entails: for me the important thing is the result. People must be able to enjoy their free time in peace, without having to worry about thieves, murderers or rapists. We have to take care of this".

Katrine started to open the door of Philip De La Cruix's office, but her sister stopped her, pulling her by the sleeve.

"You are a big, great stubborn and irresponsible…but I'll try to be happy for you, you really deserve it".

Katrine smiled at those words then lowered the handle and walked into the office.

Dimitri swerved towards a deserted alley, parking his car near the personal belongings of a homeless man. He got out of the car clutching the black leather suitcase he had taken from the HiRuski skyscraper, walking towards the place agreed with the man he had heard on the phone long ago.

He saw him get out of the dark van parked on the other side of the alley, with its nose facing the road and the tailgate wide open.

"Did anyone see you Dimitri? I sent that clochard to get himself something to eat at the shop down the road".

Dimitri stopped a few steps from the man with the scar clearly visible on his face: "No, nobody knows I'm here, did you bring the money?"

"Sure, but show me the mask first".

Dimitri opened the briefcase revealing the object he had promised to destroy a week earlier, but the drumbeat coming from his own head had forced him to act differently.

"Perfect Dimitri, my boss will be happy. As promised here is your reward...Do svidaniya".

The man quickly pulled a silenced pistol from inside his jacket and pulled the trigger.

The muffled sound of the blow was the last sound that Dimitri heard, now that a small bleeding hole had formed in the center of the head: finally the drums had stopped playing.

The body of the Russian was quickly loaded aboard the vehicle, as well as the suitcase and the mask scattered on the ground.

When the clochard returned to the alley to be able to warm himself in the flames of his own fire, he did not notice the small dark spot that had created near the manhole.

The mask had been placed next to the gun used to kill Dimitri; the driver of the van swerved towards the center of Moscow in order to deliver that strange object to his client, whistling Casatchok`s tune.

Despite the attempts and promises to get rid of the mask by every man or woman who had worn it at least once, there was always a new owner ready to take possession of it and enjoy its benefits.

From the moment it was discovered at the dawn of time, evil had never stopped spreading, sneaking into the hearts of every member of the Akkrasa tribe and every inhabitant of the planet thereafter. Those pure of heart, in the priests or in those who should have tried to put a stop to them: policemen, lawyers, magistrates...no one was excluded from that evil feeling.

When he arrived at his destination, the man with the scar pulled on the handbrake and picked up the mask. He must have gone too far with the heroin injection: a drum roll never stopped ringing in his head.

AUTHOR'S NOTES

Any reference to facts, places or people is purely coincidental, as this work is totally the fruit of my imagination.

I have always had a passion for stories: books, video games, films , personal experiences of friends or acquaintances, no matter where they come from, a good story is enough to arouse my interest.

This is the reason why I decided to create my own book, and within two years I was finally able to complete it.

I started writing this novel during my first winter season in the Engadine, in the small and remote village of Sils Maria. The story evolved following me in the two following summers in Lugano, more precisely in Paradiso, and then stopped for a couple of months until my period as an eremite at Villa Chiavenna. I managed to finish it last December in my apartment in Gravedona and it was like a childbirth, since several times I found myself blocked and forced to modify some of its parts.

This story has grown with me throughout this period and has come to an end, thanks to my perseverance and the support of people very close to me.

I would like to receive an opinion, comments or suggestions on this book and on the protagonist to perhaps follow up on her stories.

I would be very grateful if you choose to take the time to write to the following email, to give me the opportunity to know your points of view, positive or negative of course:

katrinesteward@gmail.com

Sincere thanks for having chosen to read this book, I hope you have been able to appreciate the characters, the setting and in particular the evolution of its history (novel).

Galante Riccardo

Translated from the original book by:

Ivano Ambrosini 6900 Lugano

INDEX

PART ONE 6
PART TWO 109
PART THREE 212
AUTHOR'S NOTE 350

Printed by Amazon Italia Logistica S.r.l.
Torrazza Piemonte (TO), Italy